# TALES FROM CENTRALIA
## CLOAK OF SHADOWS

C.L Gill

This novel is entirely a work of fiction. The names, characters and incidents portrayed in it are the work of the author's imagination. Any resemblance to actual persons, living or dead, events or localities is entirely coincidental.

Edited by Genevieve Ekweozor
Cover art by Duy Phan

First edition

SILVER PINES
PRESS

# Dedication

For my mom, dad, and brother.
Thank you for believing in me even when I didn't. Your love,
patience, and encouragement have been the foundation
beneath every word I write.
To the local businesses and kind souls who supported me and
my first book.
Your belief in a dream that started small means more than
you'll ever know.
And to everyone who helped in any way, shape, or form
Thank you. Whether you gave time, advice, feedback, or simply
shared your excitement, you've left your mark on this story.
This book wouldn't exist without you.

-C.L Gill

# CONTENTS

CHAPTER 1 . . . . . . . . . . . . . . . . . . . . . . . . . . . . . . . . . . . . 1

CHAPTER 2 . . . . . . . . . . . . . . . . . . . . . . . . . . . . . . . . . . 8

CHAPTER 3 . . . . . . . . . . . . . . . . . . . . . . . . . . . . . . . . 12

CHAPTER 4 . . . . . . . . . . . . . . . . . . . . . . . . . . . . . . . 20

CHAPTER 5 . . . . . . . . . . . . . . . . . . . . . . . . . . . . . . . 27

CHAPTER 6 . . . . . . . . . . . . . . . . . . . . . . . . . . . . . . . 35

CHAPTER 7 . . . . . . . . . . . . . . . . . . . . . . . . . . . . . . . 42

CHAPTER 8 . . . . . . . . . . . . . . . . . . . . . . . . . . . . . . . 50

CHAPTER 9 . . . . . . . . . . . . . . . . . . . . . . . . . . . . . . . 59

CHAPTER 10 . . . . . . . . . . . . . . . . . . . . . . . . . . . . . . 67

CHAPTER 11 . . . . . . . . . . . . . . . . . . . . . . . . . . . . . . 75

CHAPTER 12 . . . . . . . . . . . . . . . . . . . . . . . . . . . . . . 83

CHAPTER 13 . . . . . . . . . . . . . . . . . . . . . . . . . . . . . . 89

CHAPTER 14 . . . . . . . . . . . . . . . . . . . . . . . . . . . . . . 95

CHAPTER 15 . . . . . . . . . . . . . . . . . . . . . . . . . . . . . 100

CHAPTER 16 . . . . . . . . . . . . . . . . . . . . . . . . . . . . . 105

CHAPTER 17 . . . . . . . . . . . . . . . . . . . . . . . . . . . . . 111

CHAPTER 18 . . . . . . . . . . . . . . . . . . . . . . . . . . . . . 120

CHAPTER 19 . . . . . . . . . . . . . . . . . . . . . . . . . . . . . 128

CHAPTER 20 . . . . . . . . . . . . . . . . . . . . . . . . . . . . . 138

CHAPTER 21 . . . . . . . . . . . . . . . . . . . . . . . . . . . . . 142

CHAPTER 22 . . . . . . . . . . . . . . . . . . . . . . . . . . . . . 149

CHAPTER 23 . . . . . . . . . . . . . . . . . . . . . . . . . . . . . 156

CHAPTER 24 . . . . . . . . . . . . . . . . . . . . . . . . . . . . . 165

CHAPTER 25 . . . . . . . . . . . . . . . . . . . . . . . . . . . . . 174

CHAPTER 26 . . . . . . . . . . . . . . . . . . . . . . . . . . . . . 179

CHAPTER 27 . . . . . . . . . . . . . . . . . . . . . . . . . . . . . 185

CHAPTER 28 . . . . . . . . . . . . . . . . . . . . . . . . . . . . . 191

CHAPTER 29 . . . . . . . . . . . . . . . . . . . . . . . . . . . . . 195

CHAPTER 30 . . . . . . . . . . . . . . . . . . . . . . . . . . . . . 198

CHAPTER 31 . . . . . . . . . . . . . . . . . . . . . . . . . . . . . 202

CHAPTER 32 . . . . . . . . . . . . . . . . . . . . . . . . . . . . . 209

CHAPTER 33 . . . . . . . . . . . . . . . . . . . . . . . . . . . . . 212

CHAPTER 34 . . . . . . . . . . . . . . . . . . . . . . . . . . . . . 217

CHAPTER 35 . . . . . . . . . . . . . . . . . . . . . . . . . . . . . 224

CHAPTER 36 . . . . . . . . . . . . . . . . . . . . . . . . . . . . . 228

CHAPTER 37 . . . . . . . . . . . . . . . . . . . . . . . . . . . . . 233

CHAPTER 38 . . . . . . . . . . . . . . . . . . . . . . . . . . . . . 236

CHAPTER 39 . . . . . . . . . . . . . . . . . . . . . . . . . . . . . 244

CHAPTER 40 . . . . . . . . . . . . . . . . . . . . . . . . . . . . . 248

CHAPTER 41 . . . . . . . . . . . . . . . . . . . . . . . . . . . . . 253

CHAPTER 42 . . . . . . . . . . . . . . . . . . . . . . . . . . . . . 260

CHAPTER 43 . . . . . . . . . . . . . . . . . . . . . . . . . . . . . 264

CHAPTER 44 . . . . . . . . . . . . . . . . . . . . . . . . . . . . . 268

CHAPTER 45 . . . . . . . . . . . . . . . . . . . . . . . . . . . . . 277

CHAPTER 46 . . . . . . . . . . . . . . . . . . . . . . . . . . . . . 284
CHAPTER 47 . . . . . . . . . . . . . . . . . . . . . . . . . . . . . 288
CHAPTER 48 . . . . . . . . . . . . . . . . . . . . . . . . . . . . . 299
CHAPTER 49 . . . . . . . . . . . . . . . . . . . . . . . . . . . . . 305
CHAPTER 50 . . . . . . . . . . . . . . . . . . . . . . . . . . . . . 310
CHAPTER 51 . . . . . . . . . . . . . . . . . . . . . . . . . . . . . 318
CHAPTER 52 . . . . . . . . . . . . . . . . . . . . . . . . . . . . . 322

# CHAPTER
## 1

The cawing of crows overhead…

And a sharp pain with every intake of breath.

That was how I knew I was alive.

Jagged edges of now-blighted memories—Pa's booming laugh, Ma's gentle touch, Eamon's wild grin—all entangled with the faces of my brothers; Jarin. Cedric. Edric. Memories that could not surface in my mind now without causing physical pain.

'You failed,' a voice whispered in my head, my own thoughts turning against me. A shudder ran through me.

They say our best moments flash like lightning before our eyes when death is near. But all I saw were my failures. My pains. The ones I lost. The ones that followed me to their death. And I found myself drifting, falling…

Falling into the dark void of pain. Of despair. Of guilt.

I fell—faster, deeper—into the blackness, consumed by the echoes of my failures.

\*\*\*

I stirred, my eyes fluttering open as a dull ache radiated through my body. My senses slowly returned, disoriented and foggy. Smoke and ash clung to the air, sharp and acrid in my lungs. I tried to move, but my body was pinned; the weight of something heavy pressed me into the cold unforgiving ground.

Panic stirred. Darkness enveloped me, interrupted only by the occasional flicker of embers glowing through the cracks in the debris above me. Pain lanced through my chest, forcing a groan from my lips. A glint of light caught my eye, drawing my gaze downward: a twisted shard of metal poked from my chest, pinning me beneath its weight.

For one terrifying moment, I thought it had pierced my heart, trapping me here with a mortal wound. Panic bubbled up inside me. Slowly, I reached down. My hand fumbled over the jagged edge, biting into my glove and skin beneath. I winced as I shifted it slightly, fingers trembling as they brushed against something solid lodged beneath the shard.

The amulet!

My amulet!

The old man's voice echoed in my mind.

This is the Heartguard. It will protect you from harm when courage alone is not enough.

It had indeed. It withstood the impact and stopped the metal from driving through my chest. My life would have ended beneath the burning rubble of Brackenridge. A shaky sigh of relief escaped me and a surge of gratitude welled within me for the strange old man who had given me this charm. Was the prophecy fulfilled? Or had it merely delayed the inevitable? Either way, it had saved my life. It had followed me on my journey all these years and grounded me in my purpose, but now, there was a jagged dent in the middle. I gritted my teeth and pushed against the shard. A jolt of agony tore through me, but I shoved harder, screaming as I did. My voice echoed, bouncing off in the silence.

Slowly, inch by inch, I pulled until, finally, I rolled free, collapsing onto my back. The cold air bit into my skin as I gulped it greedily, each breath sharp with lingering smoke. My chest heaved, sending fresh waves of pain through me.

My brother's face rose in my mind's eye: wild-eyed and defiant—the way he looked the last time I saw him in Elsenburg.

"Eamon," I croaked, the name tearing from my throat like a desperate plea.

Never did I foresee that our lives would become the twisted wreck they were right now. On that sunlit morning when I departed Elsenburg in search of him, I could not have imagined the trials fate would lay upon my path.

I sat up with effort, the ruins of Brackenridge stretching around me like the skeletal remains of a beast. The fires had smothered to embers, and the town was eerily silent, thick with death. The morning light, faint and weak, cast a pale glow over the destruction. Shadows stretched across the cobblestone streets, broken by the jagged outlines of collapsed buildings and shattered walls. Bodies lay strewn across the streets.

Desperation drove me to the fallen. I searched for familiar faces; men with whom I had fought, my friends, my commander, I stumbled and staggered, searching for what I knew could shatter my heart more than it had already broken. Searching through the wreckage, I called out hoarsely, "Edric! Sir Gareth!" My voice, raw and strangled, barely rose above the ruin. The air was thick with ash, and debris lay heavy upon the ground, corpses covered in soot.

I had lost everyone, it seemed. Jarin was the first of my brothers to die, felled by fever even before we reached the battle. Then, Cedric had died in my arms. And was now buried beneath this wreckage. There are others whom I could not mention. And others whose fates I did not know.

I moved cautiously, stepping over broken beams and fragments of stone. The remnants of the skirmish lay scattered across the ground, silent witnesses to the violence that had unfolded. Every so often, I caught sight of something familiar—a discarded weapon, a piece of armor—left behind in the Centralians' hasty retreat. The square was unrecognizable. The once-proud central fountain stood dry, its ornate stonework blackened by soot. Nearby, a toppled statue lay on its side, its features barely visible beneath a layer of ash.

I paused and looked around. It felt like I was standing in the aftermath of a nightmare. I had survived. I lived. But what was the point? My men and those I held dear were gone. Had I been brash? Had I been foolhardy? Had my incompetence destroyed our cause? Guilt twisted my insides and I gasped with pain.

Brackenridge was a graveyard now, its empty streets and burned-out buildings jutting out like broken teeth. I trudged on, one foot after another, each step echoing in the silence, my boots crunching against the debris. It was hard not to think about the people who had lived here, their homes reduced to rubble, their lives torn apart. The weight of it all settled heavily on my shoulders.

I reached the edge of the town, where the wall had collapsed in places, leaving gaps that opened onto the snow-covered plains beyond. I took a deep breath, feeling the cold air fill my lungs. The open landscape seemed almost inviting compared to the suffocating stillness of Brackenridge.

Nobody was coming to save me. I had to try and save myself. I would find the rest of my comrades, rejoin the fight, and honor the sacrifices made here. With a final glance at the silent streets, I stepped through the broken wall, one painful step after another, and began my journey away from Brackenridge, leaving the ghost town behind.

***

I trudged up the hill, the path winding through the brittle grass and patches of melting snow. Each step was hard, my legs aching from the strain and my mind racing with thoughts of my regiment. The hill offered a vantage point over the landscape, and I could make out the faint outlines of the Centralian encampment just ahead. My heart quickened at the thought of reuniting with the remnants of my battered companions, finding some semblance of normalcy after the chaos of Brackenridge.

But a sinking feeling took hold as I crested the hill and the camp came into full view. It was in ruins. Tents lay collapsed, their torn fabric flapping weakly in the wind. The makeshift walls and barriers that had once fortified the position were nothing more than splintered wood and scattered stone. A chilling silence filled the air, broken only by the faint rustling of the wind.

I fell to my knees and groaned into the emptiness, but only the wind answered. A cold certainty gripped me—I was truly alone, stranded in enemy territory with nothing but my sword and the amulet in my pocket.

The forest was no safer than the ashes I had left behind. Yet, in the chaos of my mind, it was the only place I had to go. The tangled underbrush clawed at my legs as if the earth itself sought to hold me there, but I pressed forward, my thoughts a jumbled mess of loss, guilt, and a relentless search for meaning in all this ruin. The further I went, the more I understood: Brackenridge was gone, the battle lost, and I was on my own.

The underbrush was thick, branches and brambles reaching out like skeletal fingers to snag my clothes and scratch my face. The air was cold and damp, carrying with it the earthy scent of moss and decaying leaves. My steps were slow and cautious, my senses heightened as I navigated the unfamiliar terrain. The silence was oppressive, broken only by the occasional rustle of leaves or the distant call of a bird. I kept my hand close to my sword, knowing full well I was too weak to use it if the need arose.

My mind returned to the amulet around my neck.

It will protect you from harm when courage alone is not enough.

I didn't feel courageous, but perhaps courage wasn't about feeling. It was about surviving. And I had to survive.

For Eamon. For Cedric. For everyone we'd lost.

The forest swallowed me whole, its shadows stretching long and foreboding. Ahead, the path was uncertain. Shadows danced around me, shifting and merging with the movement of the branches in the breeze. Now and then, I paused, listening for any sign of life—friend or foe—but found only the stillness of the wilderness. The snow beneath me had begun to melt, creating small puddles that reflected the muted light filtering through the trees.

I did not know how many days I wandered, seeking any sign of life, any hand to offer aid, any fleeting comfort from another. My legs burned with weariness, my strength faltered, and hunger gnawed at me, while my wounds worsened with each passing moment.

I decided to take a brief respite, finding a relatively clear spot beneath the shelter of a large oak. As I loosened my breeches and peeled them away to inspect the damage, my eyes fell upon the mottled skin of my legs. At first glance, they seemed like superficial scrapes—mere scratches from thorny underbrush and bruises from treacherous roots. But as I examined them more closely, a deeper concern settled in my stomach, they revealed themselves to be graver wounds. The flesh around the cuts were inflamed, skin stretched taut and glistening with an unnatural sheen. Tiny beads of yellow pus were forming in some areas, and a faint, foul odor wafted up, hinting at the first sign of corruption. A chill crept into my chest. These wounds carried not just pain but the grim whisper of decay, a danger I could ill afford to ignore.

# CHAPTER
# 2

I knew I was going to die.

The thought hit me like a blade, and a heavy dread coiled in my chest as my fingers brushed one of the deeper wounds. Even in the biting chill, a troubling warmth radiated from the gash, a harbinger of worse to come. My thoughts churned, recalling the grim lessons from my training: fever, shivers like winter's breath, and the searing pain that heralded corruption. I bore them all—and more.

The air around me was sharp and cold, biting through the tatters of my cloak. I leaned back against the sturdy trunk of the oak and watched as blood seeped through the fabric of my breeches staining the snow in dark streaks. My limbs trembled. I exhaled slowly, watching my breath mist in the air. Panic wouldn't help me. I needed to focus. I knew I needed to address my wounds, but the forest offered no easy solutions. The truth struck like a lance: the wound was tainted, the flesh succumbing to foul humors. A cold fear mingled with the heat coursing through my veins. Without the aid of salves or the skill of a healer, the blight would spread, and my strength would fail. My path, already fraught with peril, now seemed an impossible trial, shadowed by the specter of my own decay.

The stream nearby gurgled faintly, its surface glittering in the pale light. Dragging myself toward it was agony, but I managed, gritting my teeth against the pain. I cupped my hands in the icy water, letting its sting sharpen my senses before using it to clean the gashes on my legs. The freezing touch sent sharp waves of clarity through my fevered haze. Each splash of water burned like fire, and I had to press my fist to my mouth to keep from crying out. My ears strained for any hint of movement in the unnervingly quiet forest. Every sound felt amplified—the gurgle of the stream, the snap of a distant branch, the shallow rasp of my breath.

As I finished tending to my wounds, I forced myself to stand, leaning heavily against the tree for support. I tore strips from my cloak to fashion makeshift bandages. They were rough and inadequate, but they staunched the worst of the bleeding from my side. Tending the wound sapped what little strength I had left; by the time I had tied the final knot, my breath came in shallow gasps, and dark motes danced before my eyes. The infection showed no signs of abating. If anything, it was spreading, devouring what life I had left.

I leaned back against the bark of a tree, forcing myself to take measure of my plight. Supplies, gone. Strength, waning. The forest loomed vast and unyielding, its shadows towering and mocking in their endless sprawl. My throat was dry as parched earth, each breath a painful rasp. The cold gnawed at me, turning my fingers into unfeeling stumps as I struggled to move. My strength was failing me, a bitter herald of my body's slow betrayal. Yet I couldn't stop. To rest would mean surrender. My hand pressed against my chest, feeling the steady thud

of my heart. As long as it beat within me, I had to
keep moving.

Night began to fall, the once fragmented patches of light
now dwindling into darkness. The temperature plummeted and
the cold seeped into my bones. It soon became eerily silent,
save for the occasional snap of a twig or the distant hoot of
an owl. My mind played tricks on me, conjuring images of
enemy rangers or prowling predators, each worse than the last.
"Focus," I muttered under my breath, "Focus. Live."

My wet hands trembled, and I knew I couldn't endure the
night without warmth. A fire—it was my only hope of staving
off the cold and keeping the shadows at bay. But as I fumbled
for the flint, my stiff, numb fingers betrayed me at every turn,
each failed attempt gnawing at my dwindling resolve.

I leaned back against the trunk of the fallen tree, closing my eyes for a moment but the faces of my fallen brothers
haunted me, the night crawled with shadows, and felt as if it
was closing in on me. My vision blurred, the infection taking
its toll on my strength and clarity. The world around me tilted,
the trees blurring together in a haze of black and white. It was a
slow inevitable decline. Pain radiated from every wound, throbbing in time with my racing heart.

I willed myself to sit up; to make a plan. But my body
failed me, and my mind crawled sluggishly as though moving
through quicksand. Hours passed in the tense vigil. My back
pressed against the ground, as I gazed into the dark night
unable to move my body anymore. I felt cold leeching into
every crevice of my body.

Snowflakes drifted lazily from the gray sky above, melting
as they touched my flushed skin, The snow clung to my lashes
and cheeks, its chill biting against my skin, but even that sensa-

tion began to dull, fading beneath the fog that slowly overtook my mind. The world blurred, the stark lines of the trees above twisting and fading into shadows. My thoughts splintered, fragments of urgency and fear slipping away as my body surrendered to the overwhelming fatigue.

I lay there. Quiet. The stars blurred, their sharp pinpricks of light fading into the same fog that claimed my thoughts. The last thing I saw was the sky above, vast and indifferent, as consciousness fled, leaving me adrift in darkness.

# CHAPTER
# 3

I blinked, my mind foggy and my body aching as if a herd of oxen had trampled me. The first thing I noticed was the warmth—not the biting chill of snow, but the comforting heat of a fire. Then the sound of someone humming, a light, lilting melody that was unfamiliar yet soothing. The sound drew me back, coaxing my mind to awareness. When my eyes fluttered open, it wasn't the melody that greeted me, but a face. She was leaning over me, peering down, her features soft and illuminated by the glow of a nearby fire. For a moment, I thought I was still dreaming. Her alburn wavy curls framed her face, and her lips were slightly pursed in concentration as she adjusted a poultice on my neck, my face furrowed in a frown.

"Hello, soldier."

I blinked.

The familiarity of her voice hit me before her words were fully processed. "Lilah?"

The recognition struck like a slap. How had I ended up here? More pressing still—how had she ended up here? The last I remembered, we'd parted ways in Briarwick during the search for my brother—she and that old thief, Jareth had robbed me blind. And with the mischievous glint that danced in her eyes, I knew she recognized me too.

"What are you doing here?" My throat was dry and raw and my voice came out as a croak. I wasn't sure where 'here' was. "This is my house, Kaelan," she replied with wry amusement, her voice light. "Though it seems you'd have rather perished in the snow, making a fine, tragic tale for the bards."

Only then did I glance around and realize I was within a house. It was cozy, with a stone fireplace crackling warmly at one end. The rich scent of herbs filled the air and modest furnishings were arranged with care. There was a table in the center, a few plates and cups scattered across it.

I looked back at her, confusion wrinkling my brow. "What...How did you...bring me here?"

"Oh, it was no trouble at all," she said with a faint smirk. "You were as light as a feather—slung you over my back like a sack of grain, I did."

I felt heat creep into my face, but I was too weak to retort. She wasn't waiting for any response either, for she turned away, a jar of herbs in her hands, and went outside. She was clean now unlike when we met in Briarwick, and smelt faintly of lavender. I craned my neck to see which way she had gone. But I could only hear the distant call of owls. And the chirping of insects in the dark.

After a long, quiet moment, I realized I was waiting for her return. Her absence, oddly, left me restless. At last, a faint humming reached my ears, and the door creaked open again. Lilah entered, carrying baskets brimming with dry, brittle herbs. She set to work with practiced hands, grinding the leaves in a small mortar before adding a glistening oil to form a thick, aromatic paste.

"How long have I been here?" I asked, my voice weak.

"You've been out for nine days," she quipped, voice cheery and unforced, "I was starting to think you'd decided to hibernate."

"Nine…" I tried to sit up, but a firm hand pressed me back down.

"Oh, no. None of that," she said, wagging a finger at me. "You're not ready for those grand heroic gestures just yet. You're lucky I found you when I did. You'd have been a nice icicle by now."

My head spun as I tried to understand. "You… found me?"

Her smile was quick and easy like she wasn't burdened by any of the weight I carried. "Of course. Just a little further into the forest than you think, but I found you. The rest was easy."

I glanced at my body, now bandaged and clean, the infection subdued by her care. And then my eyes dropped to the cloak around me—it wasn't mine. It was long enough to cover my feet but short of my ankle.

"I didn't keep the tattered clothes. I gave you my cloak instead. You're welcome."

My face flushed again as I pulled the blanket tighter around me, a sudden wave of embarrassment washing over me. "I… see."

She laughed. "Oh, don't be bashful. You've got nothing I haven't seen before. I'm a healer, after all—or I was before this war ruined everything. My grandmother taught me the trade. Herbs, poultices, stitching up wounds. Not that you were much of a patient. Feverish, thrashing in your sleep…foul smell… honestly, I deserve a token of honor for not just letting you keel over."

Her words came in fast bursts, and with such unrelenting cheer, that I struggled to keep up. "Your grandmother?" I managed to ask.

Her expression softened, just a notch, and she nodded. "Gone now. It's just me. Has been for a while. But don't look so gloomy about it—it's not like you knew her."

I fell silent, unsure how to respond, but Lilah didn't seem to need my input to keep talking. She busied herself with a bowl, hovering over the pot, the aroma of stew filling the room and making my stomach rumble embarrassingly loud.

"Oh, good, you're hungry," she said with a smirk. "You'd better be after all the work I've done. Feeding you, changing your bandages, keeping you alive… By the gods, I ought to charge you for this, maybe I will charge you." A mischievous smirk spreading across her face.

"I didn't ask you to—"

"No, you didn't," she interrupted, handing me a bowl of steaming stew. I took a tentative sip of the stew, my pride bristling even as I couldn't deny the warmth and comfort it brought. It tasted great.

I couldn't help but laugh softly, despite the pain in my ribs.

"You're awfully free with your opinions," I muttered.

Her grin widened. "And you're awfully easy to fluster. Don't worry, soldier boy, you'll toughen up again soon enough. For now, eat your stew and rest. I've got more herbs to crush and wounds to check, thanks to you."

I turned my focus to the food, willing the heat in my cheeks to subside. Lilah's fast tongue and relentless taunting disconcerted me, but I couldn't deny the care in her actions— or the growing suspicion that, despite her barbs, she might just be the reason I was alive.

\*\*\*

I woke before the sun crept over the horizon, the room dim and filled with the faint scent of herbs and woodsmoke. I turned my head to find Lilah. She was curled up on a makeshift bed near the fire. She looked peaceful, with her hand peeking from the quilt. And for the first time since we'd met, her sharpness was replaced with an unguarded innocence. Her lips, often quick with a biting retort, were soft and parted as she breathed evenly. I wanted to reach out and cover her properly. But I knew I would not do that.

For a moment, I watched her. In sleep, she seemed smaller, more fragile, and yet she had carried me through the snow to safety, nursed my wounds, and guarded me with the strength of someone twice her size.

I slowly got up, gingerly placing one leg on the floor, and then the other. The sharp, disorienting pain was now replaced by a dull ache that wasn't as bad but still made me wince. Not wanting to disturb her, I slipped out of the house. The morning air was crisp, the kind that bit at the skin and made one feel alive. I sat on a rickety chair outside the house and got lost in my thoughts.

I didn't know how long I sat there, but the creak of the door pulled me from my reverie. Lilah stepped out, her hair tumbling loosely around her shoulders. Her eyes were alert— and in her hand, she clutched a familiar dagger.

"Lilah?"

She blinked, then scowled. "You ought to have said something," she grumbled, lowering the dagger to her side. "I thought you were…"

Her words trailed off.

My lips twitched in amusement. "That's mine, isn't it?" I said pointing at the dagger.

She glanced at the blade, then back at me, and shrugged. "You weren't using it."

I laughed softly, shaking my head. "I suppose it suits you more."

She leaned against the doorframe, watching me for a moment. The teasing light in her eyes dimmed as her thoughts seemed to wander elsewhere. "So what happened to you?" she said quietly.

I sighed, the memories of battle and loss weighing heavily on me. The images of Brackenridge, the screams of brothers, and the chaos of that fateful night flashed through my mind. "I was in Brackenridge." I heard her breath catch. She came closer and sat beside me.

"The battle went south. I lost my friends and men. And I got separated from others."

She nodded thoughtfully, her eyes reflecting a deep-seated weariness. "Brackenridge..." she murmured. "I saw. You are lucky. The war has taken a heavy toll on everyone."

The war, she said so lightly, as if it were a distant matter. But for me, the memories were fresh, raw, and far too painful to bear. The faces of comrades lost in Brackenridge—so many, so sudden—flashed through my mind like shadows in a nightmare. I clenched my jaw, forcing the lump in his throat down, but the sorrow lingered, gnawing at me. We sat in companionable silence watching as the day broke, the light tearing through the clouds, creating a kaleidoscope of colors.

"When I saw you, I thought you were dead," she said quietly. I turned and looked at her. "You were almost rigid with cold and there were a lot of sores. I used that…" she nodded toward a cart leaning by the wall, "… to bring you here."

I looked at the cart and imagined her getting me on the wooden slab and dragging me all the way here. "It must have been very tedious. Why did you do it?"

"I'd like to think saving your life was the decent thing to do. Even if you're one of them."

"One of them?" I echoed, narrowing my eyes as I cast her a quick glance.

She shrugged, settling herself cross-legged on the stool. "A soldier, then. Just another pawn in the endless, senseless grind of war. Don't look so offended—I've seen plenty like you. Bold, headstrong, and utterly blind to the havoc you leave in your wake. But fret not; I've no intention of debating the virtue—or folly—of your cause. You're hardly in a state to argue, after all."

Her words stung, but her tone was oddly devoid of malice. She spoke like someone who had resigned herself to the unyielding ways of the world's grim realities.

"I'm a Wintmorian. I fight, but only to protect myself, and my own. But why do you fight? Why do you kill us?"

The question took me aback. "To protect…" The words were hollow, and they trailed off like an echo of something that once mattered but now had no meaning.

She scoffed.

"The Winmorians killed our crown prince…" I said in a flurry, "They caused this chaos. We have to protect our empire…"

"They did not. That was your excuse to plunder us. But you… Your people interfered in our battle during the Civil War, and our country was left devastated. Look around. See what you people have done here."

I swallowed hard, suddenly overwhelmed with a sense of despair. She didn't know that Wintmore had caused us so much. Yet. And she did not know this, but I carried the weight of every death; ours and theirs. "I lost many good men there," I admitted, my voice cracking slightly. It was rare for me to share my burdens, and I wasn't sure why I had done so now.

Lilah didn't respond right away. Instead, she busied herself with the dagger, chipping at a piece of wood. The silence stretched out, thick and uncomfortable.

"We lost many good men too", she said at last, putting the dagger back in its sheath. "I even dared to love a boy. But the world swallowed him." I turned to look at her. Her face was impassive.

"I'm sorry Lilah."

"Don't be."

She cracked her fingers and rose to her feet. I felt suddenly bereft, and overcome with a need to say something. But no words came to me. I watched her silently as she entered the house and shut the door with a firm hand.

# CHAPTER
# 4

Throughout that morning, the air between us remained frosty. Lilah moved about the house with a purposeful silence, her lips pressed into a thin line as she busied herself with something in the corner. She moved with practiced ease, gathering supplies from a nearby shelf. I watched her as she worked, her movements deliberate and unhurried. When she was done, she brought a bowl of water to my side. "Let's tend to those wounds," she said, her eyes expressionless. I settled back onto the cot and yielded to her deft hands as she applied her concoctions, the faint scent of herbs and balm filling the air.

Afterward, I kept my distance. I sat by the fire, my eyes fixed on the flickering flames, until she brought me a bowl of stew where I sat. It smelled delicious.

"You made this?"

"I stole it," she replied, her face deadpan.

My brows lifted quizzically.

"Of course, I cooked it," she added rolling her eyes.

A grin tugged at my lips despite myself. "It's good," I said after a bite.

She looked at me skeptically. "You've barely tasted it."

"Still good," I said, and her lips twitched like she was fighting a smile.

The frost between us began to melt. We were at ease once more, and later that morning, I spoke of Eamon and my childhood in Elsenburg. He was the reason I found myself embroiled in this war, I said. It has brought me here to Wintmore, in search of him. There was a pause before she spoke again, her tone softer. "You will. If you're half as stubborn as you seem, you'll find him."

Lilah's teasing pulled me back from the brink of my brooding, like a sudden gust of wind scattering dark clouds. I chuckled lightly. "Stubborn? That's the nicest thing you've called me."

She smirked. "Don't get used to it."

For the first time in what felt like forever, I relaxed. The weight on my shoulders felt just a little lighter, and the banter between us grew easier.

Lilah jabbed her spoon toward me. "You have that look about you. The one that says you're not taking me seriously."

"What look?" I asked, feigning innocence, though the grin tugging at my lips betrayed me.

"That one!" she declared, her spoon aimed squarely at my face. "The 'I-know-better-than-you' look."

I laughed then—proper, deep belly laughter that echoed through the small house. It startled me, the sound of it unfamiliar after weeks of silence and sorrow. Lilah watched me, her lips quirking upward as though she were proud to have been the cause of it.

"Well, at least you're not completely humorless," she said dryly, but her eyes sparkled.

"Thanks for noticing," I replied, still grinning.

The tension between us eased, replaced by an unexpected warmth. It was the first time in months I felt the weight of my grief ease, if only for a little while. And as the morning sun spilled through the windows, casting golden light over the room, I allowed myself to hope that maybe, just maybe, brighter days lay ahead.

\*\*\*

Later, Lilah was seated by the fire, her sharp tongue subdued for once. She was staring into the flames, the flickering light softening the hard edges of her face. She didn't notice me at first. I hesitated at the edge of her line of sight.

But then she spoke, her voice quieter than I'd ever heard it. "Do you ever wonder what all this amounts to? The fighting, the fleeing, the struggle—only to find yourself no better off, or worse?"

I moved closer, lowering myself onto the stool across from her. "Sometimes."

She glanced at me, her expression unreadable. Then, as if a dam had finally broken, she began to speak. "My grandmother and I wandered from city to city when Wintmore began to crumble. She always said we'd find a safe place someday, but the war…" She shook her head, her lips tightening into a bitter line. "The war doesn't care about safe places. It swallows us all."

Her fingers toyed with the edge of a blanket draped over her lap, her usual confidence nowhere to be seen. "When she passed, it felt as though the last shard of goodness in the world had vanished with her. I was left with nothing but the clothes upon my back and the gnawing hunger in my belly. I took to stealing again—food, coin, whatever I could lay my hands upon. It was that, or..." She didn't finish the thought, but the weight of her words hung in the air.

I said nothing, letting her speak at her own pace. I wasn't sure what had loosened her tongue, but I let her speak.

She exhaled sharply, running her hands through her tangled curls. Her voice, usually laced with sarcasm, was quieter now—threadbare.

She glanced away for a moment, as if trying to gather herself, before finally meeting my gaze.

"Old Jareth found me when I was nothing but a half-starved brat with more bruises than coin. Sure, he was a thief, but he was also the closest thing to a father I ever had... He taught me how to survive, how to read people, how to disappear when I needed to. And in return, I stole for us. Bread, meat, coin, anything to keep us from freezing or starving."

She pressed her palm against her knee, and looked into the distance "Then you showed up at our doorstep, asking about your brother. You remember that? Jareth always knew things, had his ear to the ground. But none of it was true, I don't think he actually knew." She paused, voice thickening. "But none of it mattered after the fortress fell. Briarwick became a graveyard overnight. We ran like rats from a burning barn."

Her eyes flickered, distant, lost somewhere in the past. "The road was cruel. We thought we'd made it, but robbers found us before dawn. They didn't even want much—just everything. And Jareth…" She sucked in a breath. "He tried to fight back. One of them ran him through like he was nothing.'

She blinked rapidly, but her voice stayed even, like she'd wrung the grief out of it long ago. "I held him, Kaelan. Held him while the light left his eyes, while his hands went cold. I did everything I could." Her lips twisted into something between a smile and a grimace. "But I could not mend it, could I?"

She shook her head. "So that's what happened. Burying the only family I had left. That's how I found myself in this sleepy town. War takes and takes until there's nothing left. She sighed.

"It was hard, Kaelan."

For a fleeting moment, she seemed no more than a girl lost in the shadows of her own life. And in that moment, I saw a tiny crack in the armor she wore so well. I regarded her; the tilt of her head, the downward cast of her gaze. Without thinking, I reached over and brushed a strand of hair that had fallen across her face behind her ear.

She froze at the contact, her wide eyes meeting mine. For a moment, I was acutely aware of how close we were, how the firelight highlighted the flawless curve of her cheek and the unguarded vulnerability in her gaze.

Clearing my throat, I pulled my hand back and leaned against the stool

"You have done well to make this your own," I said, nodding toward their surroundings. The structure was modest, built from sturdy timber, with a thatched roof that looked weathered but intact.

"Your life...This house—It's more than most people have."

She laughed, a hollow sound that didn't reach her eyes. "This house is nothing. Just some timber I found and took for myself. Paid two drunks from the tavern up the hill to fix the roof for me. Im here it because I needed a place to sleep, not because I wanted to stay."

"Why not?" I asked, genuinely curious.

Her gaze hardened, the vulnerability retreating behind her usual armor. "Because putting down roots is dangerous. The Centralian soldiers could come through here any day and raze it to the ground. I'll never again let myself grow attached to something or someone that can be taken away so swiftly."

My chest tightened at the pain in her voice. I wanted to argue, to tell her that not everything had to be so bleak, but the words wouldn't come.

Instead, I let the silence stretch between us, the crackle of the fire the only sound between us. Whatever Lilah had endured, it had shaped her into someone fierce and resourceful, but it had also left scars I couldn't begin to understand.

"You're stronger than you think," I whispered finally, my voice thin.

She scoffed, but there was no real bite to it. "You don't know me."

"Maybe not." I held her gaze. "But I know enough."

For once, Lilah didn't have a retort. She looked away, her expression unreadable, and I decided not to push any further. Whatever battles she was fighting, they were hers to face—but I couldn't help but feel a strange sense of fondness for the young woman who had rescued me from the snow and built a life for herself in the ashes of war. She was a fortress of her own making—strong, scarred, and built for survival. And for the first time, I wondered what it would take to break through her walls.

# CHAPTER
# 5

Days blurred into one another in the small house tucked at the edge of the woods. I stayed in Lilah's house even though I had stopped limping. The pain that raced up my spine whenever I breathed had loosened its teeth and I could breathe more freely. I told myself it was for the woodpile that needed cutting or the game we occasionally caught that needed roasting. But deep down, I knew better. It was easier to lose all sense of time here than to face the uncertainty of what lay beyond.

Still, I knew I couldn't stay forever.

"Is there anywhere nearby where I might find more help? Somewhere neutral, perhaps?" I asked one day as I loaded wood into the hearth. I needed direction, a place where I could find my strength again and maybe, just maybe, reunite with my brother.

Lilah didn't look up immediately. She was focused on cleaning the edge of her knife though a flicker of thought danced behind her eyes.

"Eldermist."

"Eldermist?" I echoed, anchoring the name in my mind like a lifeline.

She sighed, set the knife down, and stood to rummage through a chest in the corner. She pulled out a battered map. "It's a neutral settlement if you can call it that. Wintmorian territory, but no one really cares about the politics there. It's mostly merchants, travelers, and a whole lot of people pretending they don't see the war on their doorstep."

She spread the map on the table, tapping her finger on a spot nestled between forest and hill. "They've got a guild tavern run by the Crimson Merchant Alliance. If anyone's going to help you, it's them. They don't ask questions as long as you can pay or pull your weight."

"Thank you."

The name Crimson Merchant Alliance lifted my hopes. My brother had traveled with them before he was lost. I hoped someone there could tell me something about him.

"You can thank me later," she said, her tone brisk, yet teasing. "It's a few days' journey. The woods are mostly safe, but 'mostly' doesn't mean much these days. If you're planning to go, you'll need to keep your wits about you."

"I will," I said, taking the map. My hands lingered on the parchment as I studied the marked route. "Thank you, Lilah. Really."

Her lips quirked into something between a smirk and a smile. "Don't get sappy on me, soldier. You'll ruin my reputation."

That night, I surrendered to sleep, the warmth of the hearth and the gentle breathing of the healer-girl offering a fragile sense of comfort.

\*\*\*

The next morning, I awoke to the sound of rustling and the faint scrape of boots against the wooden floor. The soft dawn light had begun creeping into the room. Lilah stood by the door, her arms crossed, a faint shadow of impatience flickering across her face.

"Get ready soldier," she said sharply, though her tone held a thread of humor. "Unless you're planning to grow roots and become part of the furniture."

I sat up, wincing at the stiffness in my body. The room was bathed in the soft light of early morning. The fire had burned down to glowing embers, and the room was quiet except for the faint sounds of the forest awakening outside. I blinked groggily, struggling to piece together my surroundings.

"It's time to get moving. We need to cover as much ground as possible before I must turn back."

A small bundle sat on the table—a bag packed with bread, dried meat, and a flask of water.

"Lilah, you didn't have to—"

"Don't flatter yourself," she interrupted, cutting me off with a wave of her hand. "I just don't want you dropping dead halfway to Eldermist. Not after all the effort to save your life."

Despite her words, I felt a rush of gratitude.

As we stepped outside, the chill of the early morning nipped at my skin. The forest stirred with life, birds calling to one another in the canopy above. I turned to Lilah, who adjusted the dagger at her side.

We walked in silence for a time, the crunch of frost underfoot the only sound. Our breaths formed pale wisps in the cold air. I leaned on the walking stick she had provided even though I didn't need it anymore. The forest felt vast and endless, but having her lead the way brought a measure of reassurance. I wanted to ask if she would journey to Eldermist with me. The words hovered beneath my tongue, heavy with unspoken fears. Perhaps it was because I couldn't be certain how long her little cottage would remain safe. Or perhaps, the thought of leaving her tightened something deep within me. Yet, I held my silence. I did not know what perils awaited me there nor could I bear to risk her life. She deserved more than the shadow of danger I carried with me. She was safer without me, though the thought of it felt like a blade twisting in my chest.

The shadows of the towering trees loomed around us. Hours passed, and the dense woods slowly gave way to more open terrain. The sound of rustling leaves and the occasional birdsong accompanied our journey. Lilah spoke swiftly as we walked, unaware of my turmoil, offering advice on the path ahead, warning me of what to look out for. Her voice was a comforting presence. Eventually, the sun began its descent, the light softening as we reached a small clearing.

Lilah turned to me.

"Eldermist is straight ahead." She gestured to the winding trail that continued through the hills ahead. "You've got your map, your food, and, I assume, at least half a brain to get you there." She paused, her expression softening just enough to catch me off guard. "Good luck, soldier. Don't let them get you."

I looked down the path, then back at her, feeling suddenly overcome. "You've done more for me than I could ever repay. I'll never forget your kindness."

We stood there as I gazed at her, unable to move.

"Don't do what you are thinking of doing, soldier. Because I am nobody's lass."

I coughed out a burst of laughter. "Maybe. But if Fate brings us together again…"

"I'm sure she wouldn't…"

I attempted to speak, but I thought better of it. "Thank you."

She smiled and patted my back like a comrade would before turning back toward the forest, her figure soon disappearing into the trees with a wave. As I set off, I glanced back once. Lilah was well on her way, her posture as sharp and defiant as ever. With the promise of Eldermist and the thought of my brother spurring me forward, I stepped into the unknown, leaving behind the little house and the woman who lived in it.

\*\*\*

The winding path led deeper into the wilderness, and I continued onward, my steps careful and determined. The chill of the forest air bit at me, but it wasn't enough to deter my progress. I gripped the walking stick tightly, using it to steady myself as the day stretched onward. The path grew narrower, surrounded by towering pines. The trees stood like silent sentinels, their branches forming a thick canopy that cast long shadows across the ground. Rocks and uneven terrain made progress slower, forcing me to focus on every step to avoid further injury. I kept my senses sharp, listening for any unusual sounds that could hint at danger lurking in the forest. But all I heard was the wind rustling through the branches and the distant call of birds.

By late afternoon, the sun dipped low in the sky, and the forest began to take on a darker, almost eerie quality. The cold seemed to settle deeper as the light faded, and I knew I needed to find a suitable spot to set up camp for the night. I searched along the trail until I came upon a small clearing, where the trees offered some semblance of shelter from the wind.

As the fire burned down to glowing embers, I lay back on the cold ground, using my pack as a pillow. I gazed up at the sky through the breaks in the canopy, the stars shimmering faintly above. The night was vast, and I felt small beneath its expanse. I closed my eyes, breathing deeply as I tried to let go of the worry that weighed on me.

Sleep did not come easily. The forest seemed alive with sounds—the distant rustle of animals, the groan of branches swaying in the wind. Every noise set my nerves on edge, my hand instinctively reaching for the hilt of my sword. But I forced myself to relax, knowing that I needed rest if I was to make it to Eldermist by tomorrow. Slowly, exhaustion overcame my restless thoughts, and I drifted into an uneasy sleep, my dreams filled with fleeting glimpses of Eamon's face and the promise of answers that lay just beyond my reach.

I awoke to the chill of early dawn, my body aching from the hard forest ground, and my first thought was of Lilah. Perhaps, she was bent over a steaming broth or grinding her herbal concoctions. I sat up, rubbing the sleep from my eyes. The embers of last night's fire were little more than glowing ash. My stomach growled, reminding me that the bread and dried meat I had brought with me wouldn't last much longer. I needed to find food.

The forest around me was still and quiet, a light mist hanging in the air as the sun began to rise beyond the tree-tops. I hastily fashioned a spear from a sturdy branch, testing its weight before creeping forward. My eyes swept over the underbrush until I caught sight of a rabbit, its nose twitching as it foraged. Holding my breath, I let the spear fly. It spun through the air in a deadly arc, striking true. The rabbit collapsed without a sound. I exhaled slowly, grateful for the small success.

As I waited for the meat to cook, my thoughts wandered back to Eldermist. The town seemed like a beacon of hope, even though I knew so little about it. The Crimson Merchant Alliance held the promise of answers, news about my brother, and perhaps even some refuge from the harsh realities of war.

I ate quickly, packed my few belongings back into my small pack, and continued my journey. The further I walked, the more the landscape began to shift, and I noticed the subtle signs that I was entering deeper into Wintmore territory. The trees here were different, the tall, ancient pines slowly giving way to twisted, knotted oaks whose branches reached out like skeletal arms. Moss covered the forest floor, creeping up the trunks of the trees and hanging from branches like long beards. The air had a sense of age, a weight that only centuries of untold stories could create. The forest bore other reminders of the world's brokenness. Further down the path, there was a stretch of forest that bore the scars of recent conflict—a stretch of churned earth, splintered trees, and the unmistakable signs of conflict. I could almost hear the echoes of the clash: steel on steel, desperate cries of dying men. My stomach knotted at the sight. This war had touched everything, even the ancient silence of the forest.

By the time the sun began its descent, the forest began to thin. My heart leapt at the sight of rooftops emerging beyond the trees, their chimneys sending wisps of smoke into the cool evening air.

Eldermist.

I quickened my pace, my pulse thrumming with relief and trepidation. The cobbled paths led me to the outskirts of the town. Eldermist appeared, untouched by the chaos beyond its borders —an enclave of peace nestled in a land scarred by war.

Modest houses of timber and stone stood surrounded by small gardens and workshops. The murmur of voices and the faint clang of metal reached my ears—a hum of life that felt almost foreign after days of solitude. Villagers moved quietly, their eyes shadowed by weariness but their hands busied with life's small tasks—patching roofs, mending nets, tending to gardens. Eldermist was a fragile bubble of peace in a fractured world, its resilience both humbling and heartening.

I stood at the threshold of the town taking it all in. I had made it. After all the hardship, the pain, and the loneliness, I had reached Eldermist.

I paused at the threshold of the village, the weight of the journey falling away.

Somewhere out there, Eamon was waiting for me. I just had to find him.

# CHAPTER 6

I was immediately struck by the bustle of activity around me. The town seemed alive, a stark contrast to the somber silence of the forest I had left behind. Vendors crowded the cobbled streets, carts brimming with vibrant fabrics, ruby-red apples, and bundles of lavender. Voices melded into a lively symphony of commerce.

I moved carefully through the crowd, my gaze flitting over the vibrant wares and bustling townsfolk. Merchants hawked their wares with loud voices while the aroma of freshly baked bread wafted from a nearby bakery, and the sound of children laughing as they played between the market stalls reached my ears.

I was drawn in by the savory aroma of roasting meat. A food stall offered skewers of seasoned meat, sizzling over a crackling fire. My stomach growled, and I realized how hungry I still was after the meager meal from the previous night. After a moment of hesitation, I handed over a few coins and took a skewer, savoring the warm, smoky flavor as I continued to walk.

Wintmorian life was on full display—The town seemed to be a place where old and new intertwined—aged stone buildings sat next to newer wooden structures, and colorful banners hung across the narrow lanes. But I could see the signs if I looked closely— the somber looks on some of the traders' faces, the occasional whispered conversation that stopped abruptly as I passed, and the worn expressions of people just trying to get by. War had left its mark on Eldermist, even if it hadn't brought destruction to its doorstep.

In a quieter corner, the hustle softened. Small stalls sold herbs, potions, and other more obscure items. An old woman sat behind a display of glass bottles, each filled with liquids of different colors. Her sharp, knowing gaze followed me as I passed, but I kept moving, not wanting to draw any attention. At the square's center, water spilled from the hands of an ancient, bearded deity carved in stone. I sat by the fountain, watching children chase each other, their laughter filling the air. For a moment, I allowed myself to relax. It felt good to be around people again, to feel the pulse of life that seemed almost forgotten in the war-torn lands I had traveled through. But I couldn't linger too long. I stood, adjusting the strap of my pack, and went on my way.

\*\*\*

I moved slowly through the narrow streets, my eyes scanning the buildings and signs for any hint of the Crimson Merchant Alliance guild tavern.

I walked past rows of stone buildings, their thatched roofs peeking over market stalls, and kept an eye out for anything that matched the description Lilah had given me. The tavern would bear the emblem of intertwined gears and arrows, a distinct symbol of the Alliance. As I moved deeper into the town, the streets became less crowded, and the shouts of the market faded into the background, replaced by the clatter of carts and the occasional sound of laughter from a distant window.

Turning a corner, I spotted a group of soldiers chatting animatedly as they ate from bowls of hot stew. I tensed for a moment, recognizing their armor—Wintmorian soldiers. They wore the signature dark furs and heavy cloaks that marked them as warriors of the northern kingdom, and their weapons hung visibly at their sides. My heart pounded as I instinctively pulled the hood of my cloak lower. I had almost walked past them before one of them—a broad-shouldered man with a friendly face—caught sight of me and called out.

"Hey, traveler!" he shouted, his voice carrying across the street, halting me mid-step. His large frame was impossible to ignore, and his tone—while warm—still carried an under-current of authority. "You look half-starved. Sit with us and have a bite!"

I hesitated. Instinct urged me to move on, to avoid any unnecessary interaction. But their eyes were already on me. The others—two men and a boy who barely seemed old enough to hold a sword—watched with curiosity rather than hostility. I took a steadying breath and approached, offering a polite smile.

"Thank you," I said evenly, accepting the bowl of steaming stew he offered. My fingers tightened around it as I sat on the edge of their circle, their gazes still weighing me. I felt their eyes on me, so I measured my responses, careful not to reveal anything that might hint at my identity.

"Long road behind you, huh?" His tone was casual, though his eyes studied me closely.

"Yes," I replied, keeping my focus on the bowl as I took a deliberate sip. The stew was hearty, its warmth spreading through my chest. The younger one watched me with open curiosity. "Where are you from?" he asked, his voice lacking the guarded tone of the older men.

"Far enough that it doesn't matter," I said, keeping my tone light. "Just passing through."

"What's your business in Eldermist? Not many wander here without a reason." The huge soldier laughed, but there was a subtle edge to it, a soldier's instinct for prying out truths.

I lifted my head, meeting his gaze with what I hoped was the right balance of honesty and reserve. "Just looking for someone," I said simply, keeping it vague. "Thought I might find answers here."

He nodded, his expression softening. "A lot of folks come here for that. Eldermist is a good place to get away from the fighting, at least for a while. My name's Harwin, by the way." He extended a hand, and I took it, shaking it firmly.

"Kael," I replied, offering only part of my name.

The other soldiers introduced themselves—Bran, a tall, lanky man with a quick smile, and Toren, the youngest one.

The tension eased as they spoke of long patrols and bitterly cold nights in the mountains, their words offering glimpses of lives that felt disarmingly human—almost at odds with the image I had grown up with: Wintmorian soldiers as ruthless savages, driven by bloodlust and an unyielding hatred for Centralia. Harwin spoke of his family—how he hoped the war would end soon so he could return home to see his sister. Bran joked about the cold nights in the mountains, and how Toren's struggle to stay warm despite all the furs they carried. They laughed, teased each other, and shared hopes and fears in a way that felt disarmingly familiar.

It was unsettling to realize how alike they were to the soldiers I had trained with in Centralia. They weren't the barbarians I had been taught to hate. They were just men, caught in the same nightmare of war, trying to survive and dreaming of a better future.

As the conversation continued, I found myself relaxing. I shared a few vague stories about my travels careful not to reveal too much. They seemed content with my company, unaware of who I truly was.

Eventually, Harwin clapped me on the shoulder. "You seem like a good man, Kael. If you ever need help, we're stationed here for a while," He grinned. "Just steer out of trouble, eh?" I smiled and nodded. "I'll keep that in mind. Thank you for the meal."

With that, I handed the empty bowl back and offered a polite nod to the soldiers before continuing down the street.

But, emboldened by their unexpected kindness, I turned back toward the soldiers, my brow furrowed slightly.

"Actually," I called out, catching their attention again. The soldiers turned. "Do you know where I can find the Crimson Merchant Alliance guild tavern?" I asked.

Harwin raised an eyebrow, his expression shifting to one of mild surprise. "The Merchant Guild, huh? Odd lot to seek out. Most don't look for them unless they're desperate— or hiding something. What's your angle?" I hesitated for a moment before deciding that honesty would be the best way forward. I took a deep breath. "I'm looking for my brother," I said, my voice sincere. "He was a trader, traveled with the Crimson Merchant Alliance. I think that if I can find someone there, they might know what happened to him."

The soldiers exchanged glances, their expressions softening. Bran let out a sigh and stepped closer. "A lost brother, huh? That's a tough thing. War tears families apart, but maybe you'll find some answers there."

Harwin nodded, his gaze sympathetic. "The guild tavern is past the well, right at the crossroads. Look for a sign with gears and arrows intertwined. Watch yourself in there, mate." He paused, a slight smirk tugging at the corner of his lips. "Those merchants play by their own rules. They'll help you if they can, but rarely for free."

I nodded, grateful for their kindness. "Thank you. I appreciate it."

Toren, the younger soldier, gave me a small smile. "Good luck, Kael. I hope you find your brother. And remember, if you need anything, we'll be around."

With one last nod of thanks, I turned and continued on my way. I carefully followed the directions Harwin had given me, walking down the cobbled street until I came to a large stone well that stood at a crossroads. Taking the right turn, I moved deeper into the town, the streets growing narrower, and the buildings more densely packed. My eyes scanned every corner, searching for the symbol of the guild tavern, my heart pounding in my chest.

At last, I found it—a swinging sign etched with intertwined gears and arrows. The wooden tavern exuded warmth, the scent of spiced ale wafting through its worn facade. I pushed the door open and stepped inside, the warmth of the room hitting me instantly. The noise of the tavern washed over me—laughter, chatter, the clink of mugs. I swept my gaze over the room, searching for someone who might help.

My eyes swiveled past groups of travelers sharing stories over drinks, merchants negotiating deals, and the occasional guild member speaking in hushed tones. The atmosphere was lively, filled with the energy that only a place untouched by the frontlines of war could hold. I took another deep breath, stepping further into the room, I studied every corner with a sense of urgency.

And then, near the back of the room, my gaze froze. A man sat cloaked in the half-light of the tavern, his rugged features partially obscured, the fabric of his travel-worn cloak frayed at the edges. My heart stuttered as recognition struck like a thunderclap.

It was Malik!

# CHAPTER
# 7

Malik was the young guard from the Crimson Merchant Alliance caravan—the one I had met months ago when I had first started searching for my brother.

"Malik!"

His gaze flicked up as recognition flashed across his face.

"Kaelan! By the gods," Malik said, a surprised smile spreading across his features. "You've survived the journey, I see."

He stood, extending his hand, which I took in a firm shake.

"Not without some difficulty," I replied with a smile, relief washing over me as I looked him over. "I never expected our paths to cross here."

His clothes bore travel-worn and lines of premature wear marked his face. He gestured to an empty chair, and I sat down, leaning my pack against the table. We exchanged courtesies, recounting brief tales of the paths our lives had taken over the past several months.

"It's good to see you again," I continued. "I've been searching for news about my brother, Eamon. You said you were part of the caravan he was with, but I lost your trail after we parted ways."

Malik's expression grew more serious as he nodded. "And I've kept my ears open ever since," he said, his voice dropping to a hushed tone. "You know, the war's shadow leaves many tongues tied. But I did hear something recently—something that might be of use to you."

I leaned forward. "What is it?"

Malik took a sip of his drink.

"Kaelan," he began, his tone cautious, "what I must tell you will not sit well."

My chest tightened. "What is it? Is it about Eamon?"

Malik glanced away, his fingers drumming on the table. "There's talk of him. But... well, it's hard to know what's true these days."

"What..."

"Someone saw him. Or someone who looked like him. In Edmundshire."

"Edmundshire?" My heart fell into my stomach. "You're certain?"

"No," he admitted, meeting my gaze. "But it's the best lead I've got."

I clenched my fists until my nails dug into my palms. Edmundshire—of all places. The heart of the Wintmorian Empire, the capital itself where tensions were at their highest. What was he thinking? Of all the places to run to... Malik glanced at me sympathetically.

"Edmundshire isn't just trade and gold, Kaelan. It's shadows, too. Spies. Soldiers. People like us don't last long there. If he is there, you need to find him. You know that."

I took a deep breath, my mind racing with the possibilities, the dangers, the hope. "Thank you. You've done more for me than I could have asked."

His eyes flicked up to meet mine, and for the first time, I saw something unguarded there. "There's something I owe your brother, Kaelan. Something I've never spoken of." I raised my face to look at his. "Your brother did something for me once—something I can never repay," he admitted, his voice low but steady. "The weeks after we left Central, I was caught in the middle of a Wintmorian raid on a caravan. Let's say I wouldn't be sitting here if it weren't for him."

The weight of his words settled between us, and I nodded, understanding now why he'd been so helpful. It wasn't just Eamon's sacrifice for the Crimson Merchant Alliance, it was personal for Malik. I was touched.

"You don't owe him this, Malik. You've already done more than enough."

He snorted, shaking his head. "You don't get it, Kaelan. It's not about owing him—it's about doing what's right. I never got to thank him properly. Helping you find him... it's the least I can do."

"Thank you, Malik."

"If you need provisions or help before you head out, let me know. The Crimson Merchant Alliance might not be saints, but we look after our own—and that includes friends of the caravan."

I stood, clasping Malik's hand once more. "Thank you, truly,"

"Be vigilant, Kaelan," Malik replied, giving me a firm nod. "And may fortune favor you on the road ahead."

I rose from the table and wove through the crowded tavern, the clamorous voices and hearty laughter dulling to a distant hum as my thoughts swirled. Malik, though I had not noticed, followed close behind and reached me just as I stepped outside into the cool breath of Eldemist's evening air. A quiet reprieve from the noise within and the turmoil in my mind. As soon as I saw him come up behind me, I smiled and clasped his hand. The streets were still busy, and we silently watched merchants and townsfolk go about their day. Suddenly, Malik gave me a nudge, a knowing grin spreading across his face.

"Come, Kaelan. Let's walk awhile. You've earned the right to hear all I know, but let's take it slowly, aye? You look like you could use a moment to catch your breath."

I managed a smile, nodding in agreement. Malik had acquired a certain hard crust and shrewdness since the last time I saw him. He was no longer the fresh-faced, gangly youth I had met months ago when our squad was on our way to the Wintomorian fortress, but a wiry man with a sharp tongue and an eye for trouble. Now, we walked along the cobbled streets, Malik leading me through the winding lanes of Eldermist.

We came toward a quieter part of town, past the main market and along a narrow street lined with small workshops and homes.

"So," Malik began, glancing at me as we walked, "I believe it's time I told you what I've learned of your brother," He paused to gauge my reaction before continuing. "As I mentioned, someone claimed to have seen him in Edmundshire, tending to goods at one of the larger merchant yards just beyond the capital's gates. The man even recalled his name, saying he was overseeing the guild's wares—but that was some time past."

My brow furrowed, a storm of hope and uncertainty swirling within me. "How long ago was this?" I asked, my voice almost hesitant, fearful of what the answer would be.

Malik rubbed his chin, his eyes narrowing as if searching his memory. "It was about six weeks ago."

"Maybe seven," Malik said again, "It was very chaotic because of the war. If Eamon was there, he'd have had plenty of opportunities to slip into the crowd unnoticed."

My heart pounded as I tried to imagine Eamon in the bustling streets of Edmundshire. Six or seven weeks wasn't long, but it was enough time for him to move on—or for something to happen to him.

"If he was there during the festival," I said slowly, "then he's either still in the city... or long gone."

Malik nodded looking at me earnestly. "I wish I had more to offer you, but it's something, is it not? Better than nothing, at least."

My gaze dropped to the ground as we continued walking. Edmundshire was the last place I wanted to go.

We stopped in front of a small stone fountain, the gentle trickle of water providing a peaceful backdrop to our conversation. I looked at Malik, my expression grave.

"Edmundshire is a dangerous place, Malik," I said. "If I go there and they find out who I am, I won't get out alive."

Malik nodded, his expression grim. "I know. That's why I wanted to meet you here, to talk about it before you make any decisions. There are ways in, but none of them are without risks." He hesitated for a moment and leaned closer. "There's a group—smugglers, mostly—but also spies, dissidents, and those who live in the shadows of the empire. They move people and goods in and out of the capital. They know the routes, the safehouses, and all the back alleys and blind spots."

My eyes widened slightly. "And they'd be willing to help someone like me?"

Malik leaned forward, lowering his voice even further. "Listen, Kaelan, they're not the sort you want to cross paths with if you can help it. But they're the only ones who can help you without catching the attention of the Wintmorian guards. If they believe aiding you will line their pockets or further their goals, they'll take you in."

"And what happens if they decide I'm not worth the trouble?" I asked.

Malik's lips twisted into a grim smile. "Then you will wish the guards found you first."

He hesitated. "A few years back, there was a merchant—Harlin, I think his name was. He made a deal with the smugglers to move a shipment of spices across the border. Only, he didn't have enough coin to pay them when they delivered." Malik's voice dropped lower, and he leaned closer. "They left him tied to a tree in the middle of the Redwood. By the time anyone found him, well..." He let the sentence trail off, the implication clear.

"And you want me to trust these people?"

"Trust?" Malik shook his head. "Certainly not! You deal with them the same way you deal with a cornered wolf—carefully, and with something sharp in hand. They're neither loyal to Wintmore nor Centralia. They're loyal to coin. But if you want to find your brother, there's little choice in the matter."

I exhaled slowly. "How do I find these smugglers?"

Malik gave me a long look before nodding. "I thought you might ask that," he said, reaching into his cloak and pulling out a small piece of parchment. "There's a tavern near the edge of the town—The Broken Horn. The people there know how to find them. Just mention that you're looking for a way into 'The Heart of Winter.' They'll understand."

I took the parchment, tucking it away safely. "The Broken Horn," I repeated, nodding. "Yes."

Malik placed a hand on my shoulder, giving it a reassuring squeeze. "Listen, I know this will not be easy, nor will it be without peril. But I have faith in you, Kaelan. You have borne trials that would break the strongest of men, and still, you stand. You shall reach Edmundshire, and you shall find your brother."

I looked at Malik, gratitude welling up inside me. "You've my thanks, Malik. Without your help, I would be lost."

Malik grinned, his eyes warm. "Just promise me one thing, will you? When you find him, you both get out of there alive. I'd not relish the thought of coming to seek the both of you."

I tilted my head, the tension easing just a little. "And if I don't, feel free to send a search party. But make sure they bring better directions than yours."

We laughed as I thumped him on his back briefly before parting ways. Malik headed back toward the bustling heart of Eldermist, while I turned in the opposite direction, the small piece of parchment with the tavern's name tucked safely inside my pocket.

Navigating the winding streets, I made my way toward the edge of town. The sun had begun its slow descent and the air grew colder with each passing moment. I kept my hood low, staying aware of those around me, making sure not to draw too much attention.

Following Malik's directions, I found myself in a less frequented part of Eldermist. The streets here were narrower, the buildings older, their facades rougher and worn by time. Fewer people lingered, and those who did gave me quick, abrupt glances before hurrying on their way. I knew I was close.

At last, I spotted it—a worn sign hanging above a door that had seen better days. The symbol on the sign depicted a horn, cracked down the middle, and beneath it was scrawled the name in faded paint: "The Broken Horn."

# CHAPTER
# 8

The building itself was perched at the edge of the lane, a crooked, sagging structure with shutters that hung askew as if the building itself were trying to keep its secrets locked away. Its windows were dimly lit from within, and the low murmur of conversation seeped out into the street. I took a deep breath, steadying myself before pushing open the door. A creak echoed through the small room as I stepped inside. The tavern was a far cry from the bustling guild tavern I had just left. The air reeked of salt and stale ale, mingled with something foul that I couldn't quite place—a sickly sweet tang that made my stomach churn. The dim light of oil lamps struggled to cut through the thick haze of smoke, casting flickering shadows that danced across the grimy walls. The floorboards creaked under my boots, their protests swallowed by the low murmur of voices.

My gaze swept across the room, lingering on the patrons. They were few, scattered across the room in small groups or sitting alone, nursing their drinks. A pair of sailors hunched over a game of dice, their faces drawn and gaunt. At the far end of the bar, a man with a jagged scar running from his temple to his chin drained his cup and slammed it down, his one good eye gleaming like a predator's. The bartender, a stocky man with graying hair, glanced up as I approached, his eyes narrowing slightly.

"What can I get for you?" he growled, wiping a stained rag over a chipped tankard. I leaned in slightly, keeping my voice low. "I'm looking for a way into the Heart of Winter." The bartender paused, his eyes narrowing as he locked onto mine as if weighing my intentions. The tension at the moment seemed to stretch out, and I could feel my knees nearly buckle under me. After a moment, he set the tankard down and nodded toward a door at the back of the room.

"Through there," he said simply.

I let out a sigh and with a nod of thanks made my way toward the door. I could feel eyes on me as I crossed the room. I kept my face impassive, and my strides long. I reached the door and pushed it open, stepping into a narrow hallway that led further back into the building.

At the end of the hallway was another door, this one slightly ajar, the light from within casting a thin line on the floor. I approached it cautiously, taking a deep breath before stepping inside.

The room was small and dimly lit, with a table at its center surrounded by a few chairs. Two men and a woman sat at the table, their attention turning to me as I entered. Their eyes were sharp as they scrutinized me. One of the men, a wiry figure with an ugly scar running across his cheek and an eye covered by a patch, spoke first.

"Who are you?" he asked, his voice gruff and impatient.

I straightened my posture, meeting the man's gaze evenly. "My name is Kaelan. I need a way into Edmundshire. It was said you could help."

The three people exchanged glances, their expressions unreadable. The woman leaned back in her chair, crossing her arms as she studied me, a scowl on her face. "Edmundshire, huh?" she said, her tone skeptical. "You're not the first one to come asking, but it's not an easy trip. Why do you want to go there?"

I hesitated for a moment, then decided to tell a part of the truth. "I'm looking for my brother. He was last seen in Edmundshire, and I need to find him."

The scarred man narrowed his eye. "Your brother? That's a bold reason to wager your life in the wolf's den. Do you even understand what you're asking? This isn't some idle ramble through the countryside."

"I know the risks," I said firmly. "I would not be here if there was another path to take."

The room fell silent for a moment, the three smugglers considering my words. I could feel the tension, the weight of their scrutiny pressing down on me. Finally, the scarred man leaned back in his chair, a faint smirk curling his lips. "You speak boldly, Kaelan," he said, his voice low and rough like gravel scraping against stone. "But bold words often crumble under the weight of reality."

He paused, studying me, his good eye narrowing as if he could see straight into my soul. "The path you seek is not for the faint of heart. You'd do well to consider that there are dangers in this world far worse than death. If you're still eager to throw yourself into the Fowler's net, perhaps you should prove you're not just another fool chasing shadows."

The woman made a sound that sounded like a snarl, her arms crossed as she leaned back in her chair. "We've seen many like you—desperate souls with fire in their eyes. Most don't make it past the first step."

"I'm not most people." I clenched my jaw impatiently. "Tell me what I must do." My voice was steady, though I could feel the tension coiling in my chest.

The scarred man exchanged a knowing glance with the others, his smirk widening. He leaned back in his chair, his eyes never leaving mine. The room seemed to grow quieter, the only sound the flickering of a lantern that hung from the low ceiling.

"Have you ever heard of the Lost Cities, stranger? Places older than the stories of your people, buried deep beneath the earth's very bones?"

I hesitated. "I've heard whispers. Legends."

"Not just legends," the woman interjected, her voice sharp like the crack of a whip. "People have found them— well, parts of them. And those parts? They're rife with things that have little love for visitors."

"There's one," the man said, his voice growing more somber. "An ancient city buried deep beneath the earth. A maze—an old, forgotten kingdom that thrived long before Wintmore. It is said that many of the kingdoms and empires of today first took root in those very places."

I listened intently, the weight of what he was saying beginning to settle in. The woman at the table leaned forward, her eyes narrowing as she studied my reaction. "We need something from that place. An artifact—a treasure, if you will. It's a chalice. Silver, etched with markings said to be older than any we know today. Some claim it's cursed, others say it holds secrets of those ancient empires. All we know is that it's of great value. We've tried to retrieve it before, but none have returned with it."

"And why's that? What's stopping them?" I pressed, my pulse quickening.

The third man, who hadn't spoken until now broke his silence. He looked up from his cup as if waking up from a deep slumber.

"People go in, but they don't come out," he muttered, tracing the rim of his empty cup. "Whatever's down there doesn't take kindly to visitors. But that chalice... it's of great value to us. We care not for anything else you might find—treasures, relics. They're yours to keep—but the chalice must be returned to us." His eyes were dark. And cold.

I nodded slowly, dread curling up my toes. It was the price I had to pay to get into Edmundshire.

"And what do you need this chalice for?" I asked, for want of something to say. The question was met with cold, humorless laughter.

The woman's smile curved, but it was tight, almost forced, and her eyes darted to the scarred man for a fraction of a second before settling back on me. "That's none of your concern. Bring it to us, and we'll hold up our end of the bargain."

The scarred man leaned forward, his hands clasped tightly on the table. "Let's just say it's valuable enough to change things for you," he said, his voice low.

He relaxed back in his seat. "If you're wise, you won't ask any more questions."

The third man let out a soft snort, shaking his head. "Or maybe he should ask," he muttered, staring into my eyes.

"See if he's still so eager once he knows what he's walking into."

The woman shot him a sharp look. "That's enough," she snapped, then turned back to me, her expression hardening. The scarred man leaned forward again, his gaze challenging. "So, Kaelan, what will it be? Now's the time to turn back."

It was quiet as I regarded them. Fear slithered through my stomach, but I ignored it, focusing instead on the image of my brother, on the hope of finding him again. My palms were damp against the rough wood of the table, and I clenched them into fists, willing the tremor in my fingers to stop. This was dangerous. It wasn't just a task; it was a grave waiting to be dug. My heartbeat thundered in my ears, the rhythm quick and unrelenting, and for a fleeting moment, I wondered if I was already in over my head.

But then Eamon's face surfaced in my mind, as clear as the day he'd left—his grin cocky, his voice full of plans he never bothered to explain. The memory hit me like a fist to the chest, stealing my breath. He wouldn't give up on me, I told myself. So how could I give up on him? I exhaled slowly, the weight in my chest shifting—not lighter, just more focused. The fear was still there, coiled tight in the pit of my stomach, but alongside it, something fiercer burned: determination. My brother needed me, and no ancient ruin or lurking creature was going to stop me. I met the scarred man's gaze, my voice steady.

"I shall do it. Just tell me where this ancient city is, and I shall get you your chalice."

***

I headed northeast into the hills. The landscape grew more desolate as I moved further from the town. The well-worn paths began to fade, replaced by rugged trails barely distinguishable from the untamed wilderness. The trees that lined the edges of the hills grew sparse, their branches twisting as if resisting the cold wind that swept through the area. The stillness around me felt unnerving—no birdsong, no rustling of leaves, just the crunch of my own footsteps and the occasional whisper of the wind. I pressed on, my eyes sharp as I scanned my surroundings. The terrain was littered with the remnants of the past—stone foundations of ancient buildings that had long since crumbled, their outlines barely visible beneath the undergrowth.

Occasionally, I came across a fallen column or a broken archway, the stone etched with faded carvings that spoke of a civilization lost to time. These were the markers, I knew— the signs that I was getting closer to the ancient city.

But it wasn't just the ruins that caught my attention. As I walked, I began to see more unsettling sights—burned-out remnants of caravans, their wooden frames blackened and charred, scattered along the path. The scent of smoke lingered in the air, though the fires had long since died out. The ground was littered with broken crates, torn fabrics, and the remains of supplies that had been left behind.

I paused by one of the ruined caravans, my eyes narrowing as I studied the scene. The damage wasn't recent, but it wasn't ancient either. Whatever had happened here, had been violent, and it left a lingering sense of unease in the air. I knelt, brushing aside some of the debris, my fingers grazing over a broken wheel, its spokes shattered.

The wagons looked as though they had been attacked—by whom, I couldn't tell. Bandits? Wintmorian soldiers? Whoever they were, they hadn't left much behind. My gaze shifted to the path ahead, my sense of caution growing with each step forward. If something had happened here, then there was a chance those responsible could still be nearby. I moved cautiously, my hand resting on the hilt of my sword, ready for whatever might come.

A low creak sounded from one of the caravans. My hand tightened around the hilt, heart pounding, but nothing moved. Still, dread prickled at the back of my neck. I glanced around, scanning the shadows. "If anyone's there, show yourself!" My voice rang hollow in the vast silence.

Nothing answered but the wind.

Gritting my teeth, I pressed on. There was no time to waste. If the stories were true, I was stepping into a place not just forgotten by time, but haunted by the echoes of old and new conflicts.

The sun began to dip lower in the sky, casting long shadows across the hills, and I knew I must be getting close. I kept my eyes peeled for the stone markers the smugglers had mentioned, my heart pounding as I navigated the twisting paths through the ruins. The ancient city lay ahead, buried beneath the hills, waiting for me to find its entrance. And with it, the treasure.

Before the sun completely sank beyond the horizon, I caught sight of something up ahead—a pair of tall, weathered stones standing like sentinels among the ruins, each one marked with faint carvings that were nearly indecipherable. They glinted faintly in the dying light, their ancient symbols defying the erosion of time. As I traced a finger over the markings, a faint hum seemed to echo in the still air. The air grew colder, as if the stones themselves were alive, and the wind carried with it a whisper of something ancient, guarding secrets long buried.

The smuggler had whispered, her breath on my face, "You'll know you're near when you come upon the old stone markers. The entrance is well-hidden, but if you're keen-eyed, you'll find it."

This was it. I had found the entrance to the ancient city.

# CHAPTER
# 9

Drawing a deep breath, I gripped the torch I had fashioned from a stout branch, bound tightly with a piece of cloth. With a strike of flint, I brought the torch to life, its flame sputtering and casting long, wavering shadows along the entrance. I took my first step down into the darkness, the narrow passageway descending into the earth. The stone beneath my feet was worn smooth from centuries of use, and the air grew even colder as I descended further.

The narrow passage soon opened up, the walls spreading outward. The stone that formed the hallway was carved from the mountain itself—carefully laid blocks, their surfaces aged and cracked. Creeping vines had wound their way through the chamber, their tendrils prying through the seams between the stones, twisting and curling in the dim light. Spiders scuttled along the dark walls, their webs hanging like lace, shimmering in the flickering glow of my torch.

I could feel a chill shrouding me as I moved deeper inside. The air was heavy, thick with the scent of damp stone and earth, and each step seemed to echo faintly, as though the ancient city itself were listening. Eventually, the passageway began to widen, revealing an archway that led into a larger chamber. I stepped forward, my torch casting light into the room beyond, and my eyes widened at the sight before me.

The first chamber of the ancient city opened up before me, a vast space with high, vaulted ceilings. The walls were carved with intricate reliefs, their images depicting long-forgotten kings and warriors, mythic beasts, and scenes of battles that had taken place ages ago. They were faded, worn down by time and neglect, yet there was something undeniably powerful about them. The floor of the chamber was uneven, with cracked stone shifting beneath my feet.

In the center of the room stood a raised platform, its edges softened by the passage of time. I approached cautiously, my footsteps echoing faintly in the vast space and my eyes sweeping over the carvings on its sides. They depicted a figure holding an object aloft, though the details were too worn to make out clearly. I studied it closely. It could have been a crown, a staff... or perhaps the chalice that I sought. I knew that whatever secrets lay here would not give themselves up easily.

The chamber's far walls were lined with niches, each holding what appeared to be relics of the past—ceramic vessels, small metal statues, and tablets carved with symbols I could not decipher. I approached one of the alcoves, carefully examining the items that lay within. The inscriptions on the tablets were unfamiliar, and I couldn't help but wonder who had carved them, and what stories they told.

A rustling sound broke the silence, and I froze, my heart pounding as I turned to face the darkness beyond the reach of my torch. The flickering light cast long shadows across the chamber, and for a moment, I thought I saw something move—a shape slipping through the shadows, there and then gone. Sweat trickled down my back. My grip tightened on the hilt of my sword, the metal cool against my palm.

This accursed place seemed intent on playing tricks on my mind. I shook my head, trying to steady myself. I couldn't afford to be unsettled by every noise, every shifting shadow. I turned my attention back to the dais, running my hand along the smooth stone surface. There was nothing here that resembled the chalice I sought, but I knew that the ancient city would not give up its secrets easily.

Slowly, I made my way to the far side of the chamber, where an archway led further into the depths of the city. I raised my torch, the flame flickering as I stepped through the archway and into the unknown. The darkness ahead was thick and impenetrable, and I could feel the chill of the stone beneath my feet as I moved forward, the sense of unease growing with each step.

A vast chamber lay ahead, its towering pillars etched with symbols that hinted at long-forgotten mysteries. Shadows shifted with every step, the silence pressing closer, amplifying every faint creak and breath. I took a tentative step into the room, my eyes sweeping across the vast space. The pillars stood in neat rows, stretching into the darkness on either side, their surfaces worn smooth by time. The chamber felt almost like a forest of stone, each pillar a tree that had grown from the bones of the mountain itself.

The dry snap of a bone beneath my boot sent a shiver down my spine. Around me were the skeletal remains of those who had come before me; those who had perhaps come to seek what I now sought; their remains tangled in silent heaps, their crumbling skeletons bleached pale by years of decay. Fingers, still curved as if reaching for salvation, now grasped only dust, their jaws frozen in a mockery of terror. A bead of sweat traced my temple despite the cold. My grip on the torch tightened as the silence pressed in on me. I was beginning to crush under the weight of fear.

And then, I saw it—a glint of metal, the faint reflection of the torchlight against something embedded in the floor. I knelt, holding the torch close, revealing a thin line of metal that ran across the stone surface—a weighted stone, the type that yielded to unseen forces.

My heart quickened, the realization sinking in. The room was filled with traps.

My gaze over the floor, seeking further signs of hidden danger. The stone beneath my feet was lined with small, almost imperceptible gaps—weighted stones, waiting to be awakened. I followed the lines, noticing how they criss-crossed the chamber in a seemingly random pattern, a web of hidden dangers that would punish any misstep.

Raising my gaze, I caught something else—a thin thread, nearly invisible, stretched across one of the pillars, just at chest height. I swallowed, carefully sidestepping away from the thread, mindful that a single misstep might awaken whatever cunning trap lay concealed within. The ceiling, too, held secrets—dark openings, barely visible in the gloom, that seemed to suggest something hidden, waiting for centuries, just waiting for someone to awaken them.

My chest tightened as I inhaled, steadying my nerves. Yielding to fear would serve no purpose but to hasten my doom. I knew I must find a path across the chamber, a way that would not stir the ancient traps slumbering in the shadows My eyes moved over the rows of pillars, searching for some hidden order in their arrangement.

Thin strands, like gossamer threads of steel, nearly invisible in the dim torchlight, stretched taut across the chamber. Each step demanded precision, my movements measured against the chamber's silent threat. The stone floor was riddled with hidden triggers, their edges blending seamlessly with the surrounding rock, waiting for the unwary step. My foot hovered over one for a moment, then moved just slightly to the side, landing on what I hoped was a safe spot.

The air was thick with tension, and I could feel my pulse pounding in my ears. Every inch I moved, I had to account for what lay ahead and what might be hidden. I kept my eyes on the torch, adjusting its angle to catch glimpses of glinting metal or subtle shifts in the stone—anything that might reveal the presence of a trap.

I moved slowly, ducking under one of the treacherous cords strung between the columns. My body was low, almost crouching, as I passed through the gap, my hand resting on the nearest pillar for balance. For a moment, my eyes strayed upward, and I saw the holes in the ceiling, black voids that promised danger if stirred. I swallowed hard, refusing to let fear grip me.

One step, then another—each one deliberate, my weight shifted slowly so as not to disturb anything that might lay hidden in the stone.

Suddenly, I heard it—a soft click, the faintest sound, barely audible over the crackle of the torch. My breath caught in my throat as I froze, my eyes darting down to the floor beneath my foot. A hairline seam ran along the stone, barely visible, but there. I must have brushed against it.

I held my breath, waiting, listening for the telltale sign of something shifting, some mechanism springing to life—but nothing came. I stayed motionless, counting the seconds, my muscles tense, ready to spring into action.

One... two... three...

Nothing.

Slowly, I exhaled, my breath shaky. Whatever I had done, was not yet the end of me. I reached a narrow gap between two pillars, the space just wide enough for me to pass through. I paused, inspecting the floor and walls, searching for any sign of a trap. The floor appeared free of weighted stones, but as I raised the torch, the light caught on a thin, nearly invisible thread running across the gap.

I safely stepped over it and came to the center of the room. Here, a series of symbols were carved into the stone floor—an elaborate design that resembled a riddle. The markings were faint, partially obscured by the dust and grime of centuries. With my free hand, I swept away the dirt, uncovering the design beneath.

The pattern formed a path, winding its way across the floor toward the far side of the chamber. My eyes narrowed as I realized what it was. It was a safe route—a way to navigate the traps without triggering them. I traced the path with my eyes, committing it to memory, before rising to my feet.

My muscles ached my body tensed from the effort of moving so slowly, so deliberately. Sweat trickled down my brow, my breath coming in controlled, shallow exhales. I moved forward, one step at a time, following the winding path until, finally, I reached the far side of the chamber.

There, standing before me, was the door—an ancient slab of stone set into the wall, its surface carved with the same intricate designs that adorned the rest of the chamber. I let out a slow breath, relief washing over me. I had made it through the gauntlet, past the traps that had claimed many before me.

I studied the door. There were no handles, just a solid surface of stone, the carvings faded and worn. I traced my fingers along the stone, my eyes searching for any clue to unlock it. Then, my fingers paused, brushing against an indentation—a small, shield-shaped slot carved into the stone, almost as if it were meant to hold something. I narrowed my eyes, inspecting the indent. It looked familiar.

A sudden realization struck me, and my hand went instinctively to my chest. I pulled off my amulet and its dark metal surface glinted in the dim torchlight, the small emerald set in its center. The indent in the door was almost the same size and shape as the dent in the amulet.

I hesitated for a moment, the amulet in my hand. Slowly, I placed it into the slot and twisted it. It didn't fit. The edges were too sharp, the curves slightly mismatched, as though I'd made a mistake. Anxiously, my hands working fast, I pressed harder, the metal cold beneath my fingers. I was about to give up when I felt it shift—a subtle, almost imperceptible adjustment like the door itself was resisting. Then, without warning, the emerald fractured and a thin crack spread across its surface like lightning frozen in glass. My stomach dropped. The faint light within the gem flickered, not glowing steadily, but erratic—chaotic. A low hum resonated from the door, deep and guttural, as though the mountain itself was growling. Symbols carved into the stone began to shift and rearrange, moving with the sluggish persistence of grinding gears. The amulet grew warmer, then hotter before the force within it yanked me from my feet and threw me to the other side of the dank room.

The amulet stayed embedded in the slot, pulsing, throbbing, as the fractured emerald leaked tendrils of green mist. The mist spiraled into the air like living smoke, swirling around the door before seeping into the cracks between the stones. A tremor shook the chamber, dust falling from the ceiling as the door slowly began to part, the sound of ancient mechanisms scraping and groaning filling the room. I sat where I had fallen, my heart pounding, my mouth agape.

The amulet's emerald finally dimmed, now a dull, fractured husk, as if it had sacrificed its essence to open this gateway. Whatever lay beyond was no longer locked.

# CHAPTER
# 10

Dust rained down from above as the heavy stone slab slid to the side, revealing the passage beyond. The light from my torch flickered, illuminating the darkness ahead and revealing another chamber beyond the door. As the door opened, I slipped the fading amulet back into my pouch and took a hesitant step forward. The thrill of discovering the hidden door quickly waned and I noticed a lingering unease in my chest. Raising the torch high, I stepped through the doorway, its light cutting into the shadows beyond. It grew colder as I entered the next chamber, the torch's glow faltered, smothered by the oppressive void ahead.

It was vast and sprawling—a maze of narrow corridors, winding paths that twisted and turned into the darkness beyond. The corridors were tight, the stone cold and damp beneath my fingertips as I moved forward, the air thick with the scent of moss and fear. I moved slowly, my eyes scanning the stone floor ahead of me and my ears straining for any sound beyond the crackle of the torch. Each step I took echoed in the confined space, bouncing off the walls and disappearing into the labyrinthine corridors that stretched ahead and merging with the distant trickle of unseen water, a sound that seemed alive, shifting as I moved. I paused at an intersection, the pathways splitting like a spider's web into twisting corridors. A thought flitted through my mind—was this maze constructed to guard a treasure or to ensnare the reckless, or something even more sinister?

Suddenly, my thoughts were interrupted by a sudden, heavy sound from behind me—a deep, grinding noise that resounded through the narrow corridor. I spun around, holding the torch high, just in time to see the stone door sliding back into place with a dull thud and sealing off the entrance through which I had come, leaving me alone in the darkness.

In the silence that followed, the trickle of water grew louder, cascading now, echoing off the walls as if it came from every direction and reverberating off the stone walls as if the entire maze had suddenly come alive.

I panicked as I saw water pooling around my boots — cold, dark, and rising with an unnatural speed. The dry stone floor was now awash with a shallow layer that was spreading and increasing with every passing moment. My eyes swept the dimly lit corridor. I saw no way out. I forced myself to breathe, to think. I needed to find the door, an exit—anything that could get me out of the maze before it became my watery tomb.

The torchlight flickered as I moved, the flames reflecting off the rippling surface of the water, now ankle-deep and rising fast. The once eerie silence of the maze was now filled with the deafening cacophony of water cascading from unseen sources. I moved through the maze, desperate. I splashed through the rising water, its icy grip clawing at my legs. The water was at my knees now, dragging at me, each movement more arduous than the last. I fought to keep afloat as I came around the corner the torchlight casting flickering shadows that made the walls seem alive. I had risked every-thing to reach this place, but now, as the water clawed at me, I wondered if it had been folly—a man's arrogance leading to an unmarked grave.

And then, I saw it—a stone door, partially obscured by vines, set into the far wall of the chamber. Hope surged through me like a lightning strike. I surged forward, the water, now at my waist, the current threatening to sweep me off my feet. My fingers found the cold, unyielding surface of the door, my eyes darting over it for a way to open it. No handle. No latch.—only a narrow seam where it met the wall.

The weight bore down on me like a living thing, the water swirling in angry currents around my waist, pulling at my legs, threatening to drag me under. Desperation surged as I pressed my palms against the door. Something shifted beneath my touch. A faint warmth pulsed from the symbols, a response to my presence. With one final effort, I leaned my weight against the slab, and it began to rise with a grinding protest. The stone groaned in protest, ancient and unyield-ing, but it moved—a fraction. Inch by agonizing inch, the door rose, the opening just wide enough. With a final, gut-tural cry, I heaved upward and I threw my weight forward, slipping through the gap and into the space beyond. The door crashed back into place behind me, sealing off the rush-ing water with a deafening thud.

I collapsed onto the cold stone floor, gasping for air, trembling, with the torch clutched in my grip as its flames sputtered weakly. My heart slammed against my ribs, my mind reeling from the narrow escape—but I was alive.

*** 

I took a moment to catch my breath, my eyes closing as the sound of the rushing water faded into the background, replaced by the stillness of the new chamber. I was safe, for now, but the ancient city had made one thing clear—it would not let me pass easily.

Slowly, I pushed myself to my feet and looked around. I was in what appeared to be a grand hall. The ceiling stretched high above me, the stone vaulting decorated with carvings that had once been magnificent. The hall was immense, its walls lined with arched doorways that led to smaller rooms beyond, each one a dark void that seemed to hold the memories of those who had once lived here.

The air here was different—less damp than the maze, though still carrying a chill that made me pull my wet cloak tighter around my shoulders. I walked slowly, peering into the rooms that branched off from the main hall. They were small, modest—living quarters, perhaps, for those who had called this place home. The furniture was long gone, but I could still make out the shapes of where beds had once been, the outlines of tables and shelves, reduced now to little more than dust and shadows.

It was hard to imagine that this place had once been alive, filled with the sounds of people living their daily lives. The silence was overwhelming now, the emptiness echoing through the grand hall. There were markings here too—symbols carved into the stone, similar to those I had seen in the previous chambers. They were faded, the meaning lost to time, but they looked like they were meant to be a guide, a message left by those who had come before me.

At the far end of the hall was a set of grand double doors, their surface adorned with carvings far more elaborate than anything I had ever seen. The doors were larger than any I had encountered so far—heavy and formidable, their frames decorated with scenes of warriors, beasts, and grand battles, each detail painstakingly etched into the stone. Despite the passage of time, the carvings remained vivid, the figures almost seeming to move in the flickering torchlight.

. My fingers brushed against the cold stone, feeling the grooves and ridges of the carvings beneath my fingertips. I pressed my hands against the cold stone and exerted all my strength. The door creaked and groaned, the sound echoing through the grand hall as it slowly swung open, revealing the chamber beyond. I stepped forward, my torch high, the flickering light casting dancing shadows across the room. The chamber was vast, and I knew immediately that this was the throne room. The ceiling stretched high above, arching gracefully, the stone walls adorned with murals. At the far end of the room stood a large stone throne, raised on a dais, its surface intricately carved with images, each bearing scenes of triumph and despair, etched with artistry so life-like it seemed as if the figures might step out of the stone. Surrounding it were jars and goblets, both large and small, wrought from pure gold and silver. Scattered among them were fine jewels and ornaments and glittering substances the likes of which I had never beheld before. They still sparkled, seemingly untouched by age. Above the throne, on a pedestal built into the wall, sat the object I had come searching for—

the treasure that would give me access to my brother. It was unmistakable. The chalice gleamed even in the dim torchlight, its surface etched with patterns that caught the flicker of the flame, reflecting it with an almost ethereal glow. The emeralds embedded in its sides shimmered with a deep green hue, and I felt a strange sense of awe as I took in the sight before me.

I took a tentative step forward, my eyes locked on the chalice. It seemed almost unreal, the way it shimmered, untouched by the passage of time. It sat there as if waiting for someone to lay claim to it, to awaken whatever power it might hold. My heart pounded in my chest. I moved cautiously, my eyes scanning the room, taking in every detail, every shadow, every flicker of movement. The throne room had an eerie, forgotten beauty to it, a testament to a once-great kingdom that had long since vanished. As I neared the dais, unease coiled in my stomach. This was too simple. The chalice's beauty was a snare, a lure to draw in the unwary.

Yet, the chalice held my focus.

My foot brushed against something thin and taut. A faint vibration shivered through the air. Blood drained from my face as realization struck—It was a trap.

The chamber seemed to hold its breath, the silence pressing in like a weight.

Click.

The sound was like a hammer blow, and the room erupted into motion. My heart jolted and my eyes darted frantically around as I searched for the source. Suddenly, the walls of the chamber came to life. Torches, hidden in brackets along the walls, burst into flames, one after another, their light flaring to life in a sequence that illuminated the room in a brilliant, almost blinding radiance. The murals along the walls seemed to writhe in the sudden light, their anguished faces turning toward me as if to warn of what was to come.

Beneath my feet, the ground trembled, slabs of stone grinding against one another as they began to shift. Cracks spidered across the floor, revealing dark chasms below. From within the depths, the glint of metal spikes emerged, sharp and glistening—and then, as if in response to some ancient mechanism, they burst into flame.

I had awakened something—something ancient that had long lain in wait for an intruder to disturb it. My heart raced, and I leaped backward, narrowly avoiding one of the openings as it widened. The roar of the fire filled the chamber, and the heat from the flames licked at my face. The floor continued to shift, the gaps widening, leaving only narrow pathways of solid stone between the pits of flaming spikes.

I moved—if I hesitated, I would fall.

The room became a maze of treacherous pathways, narrow strips of stone suspended above the pits. Flames erupted from the spikes below, their heat rising in waves that threatened to consume everything. My heart thundered as I leaped onto a narrow ledge, barely maintaining my balance as the ground behind me crumbled away. I darted to another thin slab, my eyes scanning the shifting floor, searching for a path that would take me to the throne.

Ahead, the chalice remained untouched, the emeralds glinting in the firelight, its glow almost mocking in its serenity.

Gritting my teeth, I pressed forward, each step a calculated risk as the stone beneath me shifted unpredictably. I shifted my weight, my arms outstretched to keep my balance as I carefully made my way forward, the flames from the spikes roaring beneath me, the heat almost unbearable. But I focused on the prize, blocking out the chaos around me.

The floor moved erratically, the stones grinding as they quickly slid away. I jumped forward, landing on another section of stone just as the slab beneath me disappeared into the darkness below. The fire roared up around me, the flames leaping toward my body, and I ducked, my heart pounding in my chest.

I could almost touch the throne now, the dais only a few steps away. The floor beneath me shifted again, and I jumped, my body twisting as I leaped across one of the widening gaps, my feet landing on the dais. I almost cried with relief.

I grasped the edge and hauled myself up. The air here was still, untouched by the raging inferno below. My breath came in ragged gasps as I stood before the chalice, its brilliance overwhelming. Slowly, I reached out, my fingers brushing against the surface of the chalice. It was cold, unnaturally so, and the moment my skin made contact, the flames behind me roared higher, as though the chamber itself recognized my audacity. The ground beneath the dais quaked violently, but I held my ground, and lifted it from its pedestal.

Suddenly, the room fell silent and the flames extinguished as abruptly as they had started. In the suffocating stillness that followed, I felt the weight of the chalice in my hands—and only time would tell, the extent of what I had unleashed.

But for now, I had survived. All that was left was to claim my prize —the treasure that the ancient city had hidden away for centuries.

# CHAPTER
# 11

I had taken nothing else from the chamber, neither gold nor silver though the words of the smuggler echoed in my heart.

The chalice is the only prize we seek. Everything else, you may keep.

But nothing mattered to me more than the chalice. It felt solid in my grasp, its smooth surface etched with intricate symbols that seemed to pulse with a life of their own, the chamber illuminated only by its sparkle. As soon as I covered it with my cloak, darkness immediately swallowed the chamber. My breath hitched, and I stood still, straining to hear any sound beyond the frantic pounding of my heart.

.A deep rumble echoed through the throne room. I spun around, half-expecting another trap to spring, but the sound was more ancient and deliberate, as though the chamber itself was stirring from a long slumber. Dust fell from the ceiling, catching in my throat as I coughed, and the walls seemed to hum with life. My eyes darted around in the pitch darkness, seeking the source of the sound. At first, there was nothing.

But then, a faint line of light appeared on the far wall, so thin it might have been a trick of my weary mind.

The rumble grew louder, and the sliver of light widened, splitting the stone wall with a deliberate, grinding slowness. The faint scent of fresh air crept into the chamber, mingling with the musty odor of ancient stone.

I approached the opening, each step careful and deliberate, my boots scuffing against the uneven stone floor. The doorway yawned wider, spilling pale light into the chamber. A chill breeze brushed against my face, finally carrying with it a sense of relief and the promise of freedom.

I had made it.

***

The treasure now mine, I began to make my way across the throne room. By the doorway, the light grew brighter and the fresh scent of the forest replaced the musty, stale air of the ancient city. I stepped through the threshold and the cold air hit my face. I blinked, my eyes adjusting to the brightness as I stepped out into the open.

The sky above was a dull gray, the sun hidden behind thick clouds, but the light was enough to guide me. I took a deep breath, the cold air filling my lungs, invigorating me after the trials I had faced below. I glanced down at the chalice in my hand, the emeralds glinting in the pale light of day, and felt a surge of triumph. I held the treasure that would take me to Eamon.

My boots crunched against the frost-covered trail as the shadow of the ancient city loomed behind me. The wind stirred, carrying with it a memory as vivid as the frost beneath my boots. I could see him as clearly as if he stood before me—grinning, soaked to the skin, and utterly fearless. "I didn't drown, Kaelan. I'm fine," he had laughed, brushing off my worry as though being swept downstream was little more than an inconvenience. I was ten, maybe eleven, standing ankle-deep in the river, my arms burning from the effort of pulling Eamon out of the rushing current. My older brother had sat on the bank, soaked and laughing, as though he hadn't just been swept halfway down the stream. I planted my hands on my hips, water streaming from my tunic as I glared at him. "You almost drowned!" I burst out, almost in tears, and still shaky from the experience. "What would I tell Ma, then?" Eamon had waved me off, shaking water from his hair like it was nothing. "I didn't drown, Kaelan," he said over and over, grinning as if the whole thing had been an elaborate joke. The branch he'd grabbed in his heedless quest to save a squirrel from the water had snapped just as I reached him. But he looked entirely unbothered, the scrape on his arm already forgotten. He was careless. And that carelessness scared me. How could Eamon laugh after something like that?

"You're not fine!" I had shot back, my voice breaking. My fists clenched as I stepped closer, glowering at him. My wide eyes must have betrayed more than anger because Eamon's smile faltered and his gaze softened. He ruffled my damp hair. "Don't worry about me, little brother." Then, he started walking toward the village.

"Someone has to," I muttered.

Eamon turned, "What did you say?"

"Someone has to worry about you, Eamon."

I had always worried for Eamon. My brother, ever bold, carried a spirit larger than life itself, soaring through his days with no sense for his own safety. Since he told Ma, Pa, and me at the table that he was venturing into the war-torn area for trade, I had worried. And even more so, when his letters ceased to come. Now, he was in the most dangerous place in the empire, and the thought of what he could be doing there frightened the wits out of me. But each step closer to Eldermist and the smugglers made my feet lighter as though the weight of every promise I'd ever made to Eamon had clung to my boots. Even the forest seemed different now— less threatening, more open. The dread that had shadowed me was gone, replaced by a sense of calm, of quiet triumph. Yet, I was aware of my frailty, and I could feel the exhaustion creeping into my muscles, each step an effort, but it was a welcome fatigue.

So, I trudged on, mindless of the snow inside my boots. The chalice felt heavier with every passing hour, but the thought of finding my brother kept me steadfast. The promise of rest mattered little in comparison.

***

Relief flooded me as the gray stone walls of Eldermist loomed ahead, their surfaces dusted with snow, and the tall gates stood partially open, guarded by a handful of sentries. The wind funneled through the narrow gap between the gates, blasting me with icy gusts that stung my cheeks. I pulled my cloak lower, trying to shield my face as I approached. The guards glanced in my direction, their eyes lingering briefly on my weather-worn cloak before waving me through without a word. I stepped beneath the archway, the echo of my footsteps muted by the snow that covered the cobblestones. Eldermist was bustling as usual, even in the depths of winter. The market square was alive with activity. The townsfolk moved in hurried groups, their faces flushed from the cold. I kept my head down, moving quickly through the crowded streets, scanning the faces around me. I couldn't afford to draw attention to myself. Each face that passed was a potential threat, each shadow a danger lurking just out of sight.

The bustling market faded behind me as I turned into one of the narrower streets.

Suddenly, there was a scuffle of movement behind me, quick and sharp. I spun around and saw three figures emerging from the shadows, their faces obscured by scarves. They moved with purpose, and I knew at once that they weren't just passing through. My pulse quickened as they closed in, their hands reaching for weapons. There was no time to think. I turned on my heel and ran, my boots slipping on the icy cobblestones as I sprinted through the narrow alley. The shouts of my pursuers echoed behind me, their footsteps pounding against the frozen ground.

I rounded the corner, my breath coming in ragged gasps, my lungs burning with the cold air. They were close. Too close. My eyes scanned the alley ahead. There—a stack of crates piled against the side of a building. I ran towards them clambering over the crates, the wood creaking beneath my weight. I landed hard, pain jolting through my knees, but I kept moving, forcing myself forward. I could hear them behind me, closer now.

I ducked into another alley, this one narrower, the walls closing in on either side. I risked a glance over my shoulder, catching sight of the lead pursuer, his eyes locked on me, a knife glinting in his hand. My heart pounded in my ears, fear driving me onward. I darted to the corner, just outside his line of sight. I spotted a low-hanging beam just ahead —my only chance. I leaped, my fingers barely catching the rough wood. My muscles screamed as I hauled myself up, legs scraping against the stone. I pulled myself up, scrambling onto the roof, my limbs trembling. I lay flat, trying to catch my breath, my body aching from the exertion.

Below, the men rushed into the alley and their eyes scanned the ground, confused. The lead pursuer's knife glinted as he cursed, his fingers grasping at empty air. I held my breath and watched as they moved past, their footsteps fading into the distance. I let out a shaky sigh, rolled onto my back, and stared at the darkening sky. I couldn't stay here. Slowly, I made my way across the rooftops, careful not to make any noise.

Eventually, I climbed down, to an empty alley. I pulled my cloak tighter around me, the chalice pressing against my chest, and hurried to the Broken Horn. Soon, the old wooden sign came into view, creaking in the wind, the faded image of a broken horn barely visible beneath years of grime.

Raucous laughter and conversation spilled out from behind the door, along with the distant strumming of a lute. I pushed the door open. The warmth of the tavern hit me immediately, a stark contrast to the biting cold outside. I stepped inside, closed the door behind me, and paused, taking in the scene before me. The Broken Horn was as dreary as ever. Two patrons sat at the far end of the tavern, casting dice and quaffing ale, while the barman held his post, pouring a draught for a man who swayed unsteadily before him. I kept my face straight and strode past them toward the door at the back. I could feel their eyes upon me, yet none made any move to stop me. At the end of the hallway, I yanked the door open and entered. One of the smugglers, the one with a scar and one eye, looked up as I approached, his eye narrowing in anger before recognition flickered across his face.

And a grin spread across his face as he nudged the man beside him, nodding in my direction. My eyes darted around for the robust woman I had met earlier. She wasn't there.

"Well, well, look who finally made it back," the man called, his voice was uncharacteristically high-pitched. "I was almost convinced we'd never see you again, lad. Thought maybe that old place had consumed you."

I approached the table and my hands trembled as I pulled the chalice from beneath my cloak and set it carefully on the rough wooden surface. The emeralds embedded in its surface caught the flickering firelight, their glow drawing every eye at the table. The other smuggler's grin widened. "By the gods," he muttered, reaching out to touch the chalice. His fingers hovered just above the metal, then brushed against it with reverence. He looked up at me in wonder. "You actually did it."

I kept my posture stiff, my gaze steady. "I kept my end of the deal," I said, my tone sharp. "Now, let's see if you'll keep yours."

The smuggler chuckled, leaning back in his chair. His fingers drummed lightly on the table as he exchanged a knowing glance with the other man. "Easy now, lad. A deal's a deal, and we're not in the business of breaking them."

I didn't relax. My eyes flicked between the men—rough men with calloused hands and questionable motivations. "I'll hold you to that," I said, my voice low.

The smuggler smirked, his gaze briefly returning to the chalice. "You don't trust me," he said, almost amused. "Smart lad. But we're men of our word—today, at least. Aye. You brought us what we asked for, and we'll get you what you want."

# CHAPTER
# 12

"Edmunshire." The smuggler chuckled, his good eye glittering in amusement. "You've had a long journey. Let's get you something to eat, and then we'll talk about the next steps."

I sat, grateful for the rest while I eyed them warily. A mug of ale was slid in front of me, the dark liquid sloshing slightly as it came to a stop. A barmaid suddenly materialized with a bowl of soup and warm bread before me. They eyed the chalice greedily while I wolfed my food down.

"Tell me how I can get into the city," I said, glaring at them.

He glanced at his companions around the table, the grin fading as his expression turned more serious. "Getting in there won't be easy, but it's not impossible. We've done it before." I leaned in, listening intently as the smuggler lowered his voice to a near-whisper. "There's a caravan leaving Eldermist in three days. Officially, it's carrying textiles and spices—trade goods, nothing that would draw too much attention. Unofficially, it's got a few other things on board, things that people in Edmundshire are willing to pay a pretty price for." He gave me a knowing look. "We'll be smuggling you in with that caravan. You'll be hidden among the crates, covered up, and when we get to the city, you'll slip out and make your way to wherever you need to go."

I frowned considering the risks. "And the guards? Won't they search the caravan when we get to the city?"

The smuggler nodded. "Aye, they might. But that's where a bit of coin and a bit of charm come in handy. The driver's one of ours—he knows how to handle the checkpoints. He's got a way with words, and enough silver to make sure the guards don't look too closely. It won't be without risk, but it's your best shot."

I took a sip of my ale, my mind racing as I considered the plan. I didn't like it at all—but it was my chance.

"Once we're inside the city," I began, "How do I find who I'm looking for?"

The smuggler exchanged a glance with his companion before turning back to me. "Edmundshire's a big place, lad. Finding someone there won't be easy, especially if they don't want to be found. But the Crimson Merchant Alliance has a presence there. They've got a guild house, and if anyone's got news, it'll be them. You must keep to the shadows until you can get to them, but once you do, they might be able to help."

I clenched my fist beneath the table, feeling the tension in my muscles. The smuggler's gaze softened. "But you need to understand, lad—once you're in Edmundshire, you're on your own. We'll get you there, but after that, it's up to you. The city's crawling with Wintmorian soldiers, and if you make any misstep, you will lose your head. "

I swallowed and wiped the sweat on my palms. I knew the risks—I had known them from the start—but hearing them spoken aloud made them feel more real. Still, I couldn't stop. I was too neck-deep to stop. Moreover, I couldn't forget the promise I had made to myself, to my family, to find Eamon, I had no mind to break it. The fear rippled beneath the surface; yes, but it only sharpened my focus, making my resolve even clearer.

I looked up, meeting the smuggler's gaze. "I understand," I said, my voice steady. "I'll take care of myself once I'm inside. Just get me there, and I'll do the rest."

The smuggler studied me for a moment, then nodded, a faint smile tugging at the corner of his mouth. "All right, lad. In three days, then. Be ready. We leave at dawn."

I murmured my thanks before taking a final spoonful of the stew. I was exhausted. My body ached from the journey, and the promise of rest was too alluring to ignore. I stood up, sliding the chair back under the table, and nodded to the smugglers once more before heading toward the door. The sun had already dipped below the horizon, leaving the streets illuminated only by the dim glow of lanterns hanging above the doorways of shops and homes. The bustling noises of the market had faded, replaced by the murmur of people heading home, their faces weary from the day's work. My heart was filled with rambling thoughts as I made my way down the narrow streets. I needed a place to stay—somewhere warm, with a hot meal, where I might bide my time for the next three days until it was time to leave Eldermist. My steps were slow and deliberate, exhaustion settling into my bones, but my eyes remained alert. I passed by shuttered shops, the faded signs swaying gently in the breeze, and could hear the faint murmur of conversation and laughter from within the houses I passed.

The streets were winding, twisting in ways that made it easy for a newcomer to get lost. Each corner I rounded felt like a risk, with constant danger lurking in the shadows. My eyes darted to every movement, and my ears heard every faint whisper of sound.

As I turned another corner, my eyes caught sight of a sign hanging above a doorway, the wood worn but still legible. The Lantern's Rest, it read, and said it was an inn. Beneath the sign, the door was slightly ajar, the golden glow of candlelight spilling out onto the cobblestone street. I paused, eyeing the building. It looked modest, but good enough to shelter for a few nights. The muffled sound of conversation came from within, and I could make out the faint scent of roasted meat and bread.

I glanced over my shoulder before pushing the door open and stepping inside. The Lantern's Rest was a refuge carved out of the unforgiving night, a place where the world seemed to soften its edges. Warmth enveloped me as I stepped inside, the soft glow of lanterns lining the walls casting a golden light across the room. Thick wooden beams stretched across the ceiling, their rough-hewn edges giving it a rustic charm. There were a handful of patrons in the common area—travelers warming themselves by the fire and a few townsfolk sitting together at a table. Here, laughter rang freely, and the weight of the outside world faded to a distant hum. The worn oak tables bore the marks of countless travelers, etched with names, sigils, and memories. In the corner, a bard perched on a stool near the hearth, cloaked in a threadbare mantle patched with care. He strummed a lute, his soft voice weaving tales of distant lands and battles long past.

It spoke of battles fought and lost, of soldiers separated from their families, of lands scarred by conflict. The words had a haunting quality to the tune, and stirred an ache in my chest, as though the song had been crafted solely for me. I turned my attention to the counter at the far end of the room, where the innkeeper stood pouring ale into a wooden mug. He was a barrel-chested man with a thick beard and a hearty smile who greeted me with a grin that crinkled the corners of his eyes. I made my way to the counter, pulling my hood down as I approached. The innkeeper's warmth seeped into the air, slowly unwinding the tight knot of tension in my shoulders.

"Good evening, traveler," the innkeeper beamed. "Looking for a place to stay, are you?"

"I need a room for a few nights. Somewhere quiet."

The innkeeper raised an eyebrow, his gaze flicking briefly to my cloak, noting the wear and tear of my clothing. "You've had a long journey, I see," he said, his tone sympathetic. "We've got a room available. Two silvers a night, and that includes supper and breakfast."

I reached into the pouch at my belt, pulled out the coins, and placed them on the counter. The innkeeper reached beneath the counter, retrieved a small iron latch to secure the door, and handed it to me.

"Up the stairs, will you? First door on the left," he said, with a hint of sympathy. "There's a washbasin in the room, and if you're hungry, there's stew in the pot by the fire. Help yourself."

The room was small but comfortable—a narrow bed with a thick woolen blanket, a wooden chair in the corner, and a wash basin set on a small table by the window. The soft glow of the lanterns outside filtered through the frosted glass, throwing a gentle light across the room. I closed the door behind me and leaned back against the wooden surface for a moment as I took a deep breath, the weight of the past days finally catching up to me.

I was here. I had a place to rest, if only for a while. For now, the room's warmth offered a welcome respite from the cold. My entire body ached from the journey—the tension in my shoulders, the soreness in my legs—but for the first time in days, I felt a flicker of comfort.

As I lay on the bed, my eyes immediately grew heavy and for the first time in what felt like forever, I surrendered to sleep, my burdens momentarily forgotten.

# CHAPTER
# 13

Morning arrived too quickly, with the soft light of dawn filtering in through the frosted window. I woke with a start, my body stiff from the previous day's exertion. The quiet room was a rare comfort. I allowed myself a moment to just breathe, savoring the warmth of the bed and blanket.

I splashed cold water on my face, the chill snapping me awake. I dressed quickly, pulling on my worn cloak, and went downstairs. The common room was filled with the scent of bread and tea. The fire crackled, and the bard strummed his lute. I moved toward a table near the fire, sitting down and listening to the bard's mournful song. Suddenly, the door swung open, and a group of Wintmorian soldiers entered, their laughter echoing through the room. The sudden noise made me stiffen immediately, turning my head toward the entrance. My eyes widened slightly as recognition settled in. It was Harwin and his friends, the soldiers I had met the day I arrived in Eldermist. Harwin, with his easy smile and warm eyes, immediately spotted me near the fire, and he beamed.

He nudged one of his companions and pointed in my direction.

"Look who it is!" Harwin called, his voice carrying across the room as he made his way toward me, his heavy boots thudding against the wooden floor. His friends followed, their cloaks dusted with snow. Their faces flushed from the cold and their laughter filled the warm space.

I greeted Harwin as he approached, his grin widening as he pulled up a chair and sat down across from me. His companions gathered around, some leaning against the counter, others pulling up chairs of their own. The innkeeper, seeing the new arrivals, gestured to the barmaid to prepare a round of drinks, and soon enough, mugs of ale were being around.

"Good to see you again Kael," Harwin bellowed from across the table. "Still in Eldermist? Found your brother yet?"

I shook my head. "Not yet. But I've got a lead. He might have been seen near Edmundshire. It's a long shot, but it's all I've got."

Harwin's expression softened. He took a deep gulp of his ale. "Edmundshire, eh? The capital itself. Not an easy place to get to, especially at this time." He glanced at his companions, who were listening quietly. "But you're determined, aren't you?" I smiled. "He's my brother. I can't just..."

My voice faltered as I spoke, my gaze dropping to the table. I swallowed hard, suddenly overwhelmed. The silence stretched between us, thick with all the things I couldn't say.

"I'm still not sure where he is," I muttered, the weight of those words sinking deeper. 'And that's the hardest part—the not knowing. It's like I'm stumbling through the dark, hoping for a light to show me the way. The uncertainty...

It eats at me…" My voice trailed off, careful not to say anything that would betray me. Harwin reached out, giving my shoulder a reassuring pat. "I understand," he said, his voice gentle. "Family's everything. And you've got more courage than most, setting out alone to find him. Not many would do that."

One of Harwin's companions, a tall, lanky soldier with a crooked smile, spoke up. "You know, I've been to Edmundshire. It's busy—traders, merchants, always something happening. If your brother's there, you might have a good chance of finding him." I managed a small smile. "That's what I'm hoping for," I said. "I've heard there's a guild house for the Crimson Merchant Alliance there. If anyone has information, it'll be them."

Harwin nodded thoughtfully, taking another sip of his ale. "You're right. The Crimson Merchant Alliance has eyes and ears everywhere. If your brother's in Edmundshire, they'd know." He paused, glancing at me with a thoughtful expression. "But you'll need aid to get there. Edmundshire isn't a welcoming place for a stranger, least of all, one without allies. "

He casually reached into his belt pouch, pulling out a handful of coins. The clinking of metal against metal was clear in the warm room, drawing the attention of those around us. Harwin extended the coins toward me. "Here," he said, his voice gentle. "It's not much, but it might help you on your way. You're doing something noble, Kael. And if I can help, even a little, I will."

I stared at the coins. My hand hovered over them for a moment and my fingers trembled slightly. I could feel the weight of the gesture—the weight of Harwin's generosity—

but it didn't sit right with me. Gratitude bloomed in my chest, but it was quickly stifled by a knot of pride. I was a proud Centralian, and he was a Wintmorian soldier— an enemy. But the truth was, my pockets had never been emptier. I had also anticipated hostility from Wintmorian soldiers, mistrust at best, but here they were, offering me kindness, showing me generosity. I looked up, meeting Harwin's gaze. "Thank you," I said quietly, letting the coins spill into my palm. "This means more to me than you know."

Harwin smiled, his eyes crinkling at the corners. "It's the least I can do." He leaned forward, his elbows resting on the table, his voice quieter than before.

"I know what it's like, not knowing if you'll see a loved one again. My mother... she vanished when I was but a lad, during the days of the Civil War. Never found a trace of her." His gaze met mine, a shared silence between us. "So, when you say you must seek out your brother, I understand. Truly, I do. Just be wary on your journey, all right? These lands have grown perilous, especially for one who travels alone."

He was gregarious and we drank noisily. He raised his mug, His face red, "To finding your brother, Kael. May your journey be swift, and may fortune favor you."

I clinked my mug against Harwin's and his comrades and knocked down my drink.

Harwin's leaned towards me with a curious expression.

"Kael, if you don't mind me asking—where's that name from?"

My heart skipped a beat, as the men fell suddenly quiet, waiting for my answer.

"It doesn't sound very Wintmorian. I'd almost think it's Astari, but you sure don't look like an Astari."

I hadn't considered how my name might give me away, and now Harwin's curiosity had caught me off guard. "Ah, well," I forced a thin smile, "my father was from southern Noble. My mother's Wintmorian, but I guess my name comes from that side of the family. My father always said it was a common name where he was from."

Harwin's face lit up, a broad smile breaking across his features. He reached out, clapping me on the shoulder with a friendly laugh. "Noble, huh? Well, that explains it! You've got a mix of both worlds then," he said, his eyes gleaming with enthusiasm. "My grandparents were from Noble too, before they moved here. That makes us almost kin, eh?"

He gave me a hearty pat on the back and I managed a chuckle, the tension easing slightly. "Indeed," I said, relief washing over me. Harwin stood, adjusting his cloak as he did. "Well, Kael, it's been good seeing you again. I hope our paths cross once more, and when they do, I hope it's with good news about your brother."

His companions began to gather their things, pulling their cloaks tighter as they prepared to leave. I watched them, my eyes lingering on the way they moved—the camaraderie between them, the easy laughter. There was a warmth in their friendship, one that made me ache for what I had lost. Harwin cast me one look.

"Take care of yourself out there. Remember, you've got friends in Eldermist," he said.

"Thank you, Harwin. For everything."

He turned to his friends, giving them a quick wave. "Come on, lads, let's leave our friend here to his rest."

They left as loudly as they had come. As the door swung shut behind them, I leaned back in my chair, taking a deep breath. I had not yet found what I sought yet, but favor had found me. Perhaps, it was sheer luck or the gods had me on their backs. Or perhaps, it was a sign that I was on the right path. I had to hold on to that hope—it was all I had.

# CHAPTER
# 14

The morning sun broke over Eldermist, its soft light illuminating the frost-covered streets. In the quiet of my room at the Lantern's Rest, I packed my belongings with measured care— my cloak, the provisions I had purchased with Harwin's gift, and a worn map that Lilah had pressed into my hands. I had carried that map, though I no longer needed it. I kept it because it bore the faith of my journey, or perhaps it served as a reminder of the one who had given it to me—the hope of life she had instilled within me.

My glance lingered on the bed that had offered comfort for a night. But I couldn't afford to wait— time was against me, and every moment risked discovery. With a deep breath, I slung my pack over my shoulder and headed for the door. Soon, I stepped into the chill morning air, leaving behind the comforting warmth of the common room and the scent of fresh bread. The streets bustled with vendors and lively chatter as Eldermist woke. The city seemed peaceful, unaware of the war beyond its borders.

My breath was visible in the cold air as I made my way through the streets, heading toward the northern edge of the city. The smugglers' directions were clear—they'd gather at an old caravan stop, away from the prying eyes of the city guards. I moved purposefully, watching the crowds as I meandered through the winding streets. As I approached the northern gates, the city's noise gradually faded, replaced by the quiet of the open road and the rustle of bare branches swaying in the winter breeze. The trees stood like silent sentinels, their skeletal forms a testament to the harshness of the season.

My steps quickened, the path ahead leading me further from Eldermist's safety and toward the unknown. In the distance, I spotted the caravan rest stop—a collection of worn wagons and crates, the area partially hidden by the trees that bordered it. Figures moved around, their cloaks blending in with the shadows. The horses tied to the makeshift posts snorted as they stomped their hooves against the frozen ground. I adjusted my pack nervously as I approached. The smugglers were gathered near one of the larger wagons, their faces partially obscured by their hoods. As I drew closer, one of the men turned, his gaze meeting mine before giving a nod of acknowledgment.

"Right on time, lad," he said, his voice a low rasping growl. He gestured toward the caravan. "Get over here. We're making our final preparations."

I stepped closer to the group looking around warily. The smuggler eyed me for a moment longer, then turned back to his companions, his hands moving deftly as he tied down a tarp covering one of the wagons. I couldn't help but feel a pang of fear—the fear of the unknown, of my traveling companions, and of what I might face once we crossed into Edmundshire. One of the smugglers—a burly man with a wooden peg for a leg—caught my eye and gave me a nod. "You ready, lad?" he asked, his voice brusque.

I swallowed, nodding. "I am, sire," I replied, my voice steadier than I felt. He grunted in response before turning back to the wagon.

The others were busy, securing supplies, checking the horses, and making sure everything was in place. I moved to help where I could, my hands fumbling slightly as I tied down a rope, the cold making my fingers stiff. The smugglers worked quickly, their movements practiced and efficient. They had done this before, and their confidence was reassuring, even if only slightly. As I finished securing the rope, my gaze swept over the scene before me. The battered wagons, the weary horses, and the long shadows cast by the skeletal trees upon the frozen ground—it all felt strangely surreal, as though I was watching myself from a distance. I clenched my jaw, grounding myself in the moment.

"All right, everyone, mount up!" the one-legged smuggler called, his voice cutting through the quiet. He clambered onto the driver's seat of one of the wagons, the others following suit. I moved toward the back of one of the wagons, pulling myself up and settling in among the crates. The space was cramped, the smell of hay and leather filling my senses, but it was enough. I pulled my cloak tighter around me, trying to find warmth as I settled in for the journey ahead.

The caravan began to move, the wheels creaking as they rolled over the frozen ground. I felt a jolt as the wagon lurched forward, my body swaying with the motion. This was it. There was no turning back now. I was going to find Eamon, no matter what it took.

The trees lining the road seemed to close in as we moved further away from Eldermist, their branches arching overhead like a canopy. The world outside the wagon was quiet, the only sounds being the creaking of the wheels and the occasional snort from the horses. I kept my head low, my body tense, acutely aware of the possibility of danger. I tightened my grip on the edge of the wagon, the cold seeping through my gloves, and took another deep breath. One step at a time.

The city of Eldermist slowly disappeared behind us, replaced by the vast, open expanse of the winter landscape. The path ahead was uncertain, but my resolve was unbroken. I resigned myself to whatever lay ahead.

\*\*\*

Soon, one of the smugglers leaned in, a wiry little man, and handed me a tattered blanket. "Keep yourself covered. We don't want any guards getting too curious," I didn't have to be told twice. The interior of the wagon was dim, and the space was cramped, lined with wooden crates that carried unknown goods. I immediately slipped into the narrow space between the crates, wedging myself in as best I could. Then, I pulled the blanket over my body, the rough fabric scratching against my face as I settled into the dark, confined space. The smell of dust and wood filled my nostrils, but I focused on steadying my breathing, ignoring the discomfort.

The first few hours were filled with the steady rhythm of the wagon wheels, the creaking of wood, and the occasional low murmur of the smugglers talking amongst themselves. I kept still, focusing on the sounds around me—the crunch of snow under the wheels, the steady clops of hooves, and the eerie calls of strange birds. Every sound sent my nerves on edge. The hours dragged on. My body throbbed with discomfort, my legs tingling as though pricked by a thousand needles from the long hours of confinement. The cold floor of the wagon pressed against me, its unyielding surface sapping the last remnants of warmth from my limbs. Despite my best efforts, fatigue crept in, my eyelids growing heavier with each passing mile. In the darkness of the wagon, time became meaningless—a blur of movement and muffled sounds that blended into one another. It was a battle to keep my mind from drifting to dark places—to fears of dangers unknown. Soon, the wagon's sway became almost hypnotic, lulling me into a fitful sleep.

# CHAPTER
## 15

A sudden, sharp turn jolted me fully awake, my heart racing as the crates shifted around me. My fingers clenched the edge of the rough blanket, my breath catching in my throat. Outside, the muffled voices of the smugglers grew louder, their tones low and urgent. I strained to hear, pressing myself further into the crates as the wagon came to a gradual halt.

My heart fluttered as I strained to listen to the murmurs. I tensed myself, ready to spring into the night if need be. Or to fight for my life. Cold sweat formed on my brow and I clenched my fists. A few moments later, the back of the wagon opened, the tarp swiftly yanked back, and my heart jumped into my mouth.

"You can come out now. We're stopping here for the night." It was the one-legged smuggler—his face half-hidden beneath his hood, a rough smile tugging at his lips. I could have cried with relief. He looked me over for a moment in amusement. "Are you well, lad?"

"Aye, aye."

He extended a hand to me. I took the offered hand, and he helped me climb out of the wagon. The cold evening air hit me immediately, the chill biting into my skin after the stale warmth of the wagon's interior. I took a deep breath and stretched my arms, wincing as my stiff muscles protested the movement. It felt good to finally be able to move, to feel the ground beneath my feet.

"Name's Bran," he said, barely looking at me. "Come on, there's a fire going. You'll want to warm up and eat something."

The promise of food and heat was too tempting to refuse. I followed Bran to a clearing just off the road, where a small fire flickered, holding back the encroaching darkness. The other smugglers moved around, tending to horses and gathering firewood. The air carried the enticing aroma of something cooking, and my stomach growled in eagerness.

The other smugglers cast occasional glances at me, their faces unreadable, masks of practiced indifference. They were used to this—hiding, moving under the cover of darkness, smuggling goods and people as it suited them, and avoiding the eyes of the law. It was a life I was slowly becoming familiar with, whether I liked it or not. Bran gave me a curt nod, his eyes flicking toward the others as they worked to set up camp. The rest stop was simple—a clearing just off the main road, sheltered by the thick trees that surrounded us. The smugglers gathered firewood, their cloaks pulled tight against the cold as they moved about their tasks. Bran led me over to where a fire was being built and handed me a bowl of stew.

"Eat up," he said, his voice gruff but not unkind. "You'll need your strength for what's ahead."

I nodded, my lips curling into a faint smile. "Thanks, Bran."

The stew, though simple, warmed me from the inside out. The heat spread through me, easing the hunger that had gnawed at me. Around me, the smugglers settled into a rhythm—their voices low, their laughter subdued but genuine. They seemed at ease, unlike me, who restless and on edge.

Bran eased himself down beside me, propping his good leg against a gnarled log, his steaming bowl of stew balanced in his hands. He stared into the fire, his expression thoughtful. Then, he turned to me.

"Takes guts to do what you're doing," he said quietly, almost to himself. "Heading into dangerous territory, risking your life for family."

I met his gaze, the firelight casting his rugged features into sharp edges. "It's not a choice," I replied, my voice low. "He's my brother. I can't leave him out there, not knowing if he's alive or dead."

Bran nodded slowly ladling a spoonful of stew into his mouth.

The fire crackled between us, its sound blending with the rustling of the wind through the trees. The smugglers shared stories of close calls and near escapes. I listened to their tales—their accounts of past journeys, narrow escapes from soldiers, and how they always managed to stay a step ahead of those who sought to hinder them. I felt the tightness in my shoulders slowly ease. Their voices blended into the sounds of the night, and for a fleeting moment, I allowed myself to feel a semblance of safety. And I shared the fire with these men, these smugglers who, despite their line of work, had shown me kindness.

The stars above began to emerge, the sky deepening into a velvety darkness as the flames danced, casting flickering shadows across our faces. One by one, the smugglers finished their meals, their voices growing quieter as the fatigue of the day set in. Bran stood, stretching his arms above his head, his eyes meeting mine.

"Best get some rest, lad. We've got another long day ahead of us tomorrow," Bran said. He gestured to a bedroll that had been set up near the fire, the blanket neatly folded.

I lay down and closed my eyes, letting the sounds of the night lull me into a light sleep. The crackling of the fire, the rustling of the wind through the trees—it was almost enough to make me forget where I was, to make me forget the danger that surrounded me. Almost.

Suddenly, my eyes snapped open, my senses jolted awake by a distant, rhythmic sound. Drums. The deep, resounding thud of marching drums echoed through the stillness of the night, growing louder with each passing moment. I pushed myself up on my elbows, straining to listen. It was the Wintmorian regiment. And they were close.

My breath caught, the realization hitting me like a punch to the gut. I turned my head, glancing toward the road beyond the clearing, where the distant glow of torch-light flickered against the darkness. The drums continued, a steady, relentless beat, and I could already hear the tramp of heavy boots against the frozen ground. I scrambled to my feet, my gaze darting around the camp. Bran barked low, urgent orders to the others, and they obeyed, their movements swift and fluid.

Without hesitation, I moved quickly, slipping into the wagon and pulling a blanket over myself. The darkness enveloped me, my breaths shallow as I tried to calm my racing heart. My breaths came in jagged pants under the darkness of the wagon, which wrapped around me like a cloak.

Outside, the sounds grew louder: the clanking of armor, the snorting of horses, the heavy thud of boots on frozen ground. The air was thick with the strain of the moment, every sound amplified by the stillness around us.

The regiment was close now—too close.

Then, a sharp voice cut through the drumbeats, "Caravan ahead! Halt and identify yourselves!"

The soldiers had arrived.

# CHAPTER
# 16

If the soldiers saw me, it was over. The wagon shifted slightly as the smugglers moved around outside, the creaking of wood echoing in the silence that followed the soldier's order. I heard Bran's voice, calm and measured, answering the call, though the words were muffled, lost beneath the relentless pounding of the drums.

I closed my eyes, my body tense as I waited, every second feeling like an eternity. I prayed the smugglers knew what they were doing, that the spirits of my people would guide me, and that I would not die before I found Eamon. Outside, the sounds grew louder—the crunch of boots on the snow, the clang of weapons and the snorting of horses. The regiment had halted, and I could hear the muted murmur of the soldiers, accompanied by the faint clatter of their gear as they moved.

I strained to listen to the voices outside. The distinct voice of one of the soldiers grew clearer.

"Your letters of passage," the soldier demanded, his voice sharp. There was a pause, followed by the sound of shuffling as Bran moved to comply. I could hear Bran's voice, calm but cautious, as he handed over whatever writs they had prepared.

"What are you doing here?" the soldier continued, his tone suspicious. "Why have you stopped on this road?"

Bran cleared his throat, his voice steady. "We're traders, sire, moving goods from Eldermist to Edmundshire. The road was rough, and the horses needed rest. We stopped to set up camp and rest our bones for the night. We'll be moving again by first light."

There was a moment of silence, and I could almost picture the scout's face as he weighed Bran's words, considering whether to believe them.

"Hmm," the soldier finally muttered, and I could hear the sound of rustling parchment as the scout examined their writs. "It seems in order... but these are troubled times. We've been charged to inspect any caravans we encounter on the road. We can't take any chances."

My blood ran cold at the words. I held my breath, my heart hammering in my chest.

"Very well," Bran replied, his voice level. "Search what you will, good sire, but know this—we're but simple traders. There's nothing among our goods that would warrant the attention of a soldier." The scout ignored Bran's plea and turned to one of the soldiers at his side. "Check the wagons," he ordered, "See that they're telling the truth."

My heart sank. I closed my eyes, trying to think of any way I could get out of this. But there was nothing I could do. I was at the mercy of fate, and whatever story the smugglers could sell.

I heard a soldier step forward, his boots crunching against the frozen ground as he approached the wagon. The creak of the wood was loud in my ears as the soldier climbed up.

The blanket that covered me itched my skin. The tight space of the wagon felt even more suffocating and the scent of the wood and damp earth suddenly made me nauseous. But I couldn't move.

I heard the soldier grunt as he stepped into the wagon, I held my breath, my entire world narrowing to this one moment, to the sound of the soldier moving closer, the feeling of the wagon shifting beneath the weight of another.

I could hear every creak of the wood, every rustle of fabric, every breath the soldier took. He searched methodically. I heard the sound of barrels being opened, the scrape of metal against wood as the lids were pried loose, and the distinct thud as they were dropped back into place. I could picture it all in my mind— the soldier rifling through the barrels, his hands moving swiftly, searching for anything that didn't belong. Each sound seemed to stretch into an eternity, the silence between each movement heavy and oppressive as I fought to keep my breathing even, to remain absolutely still.

He moved further back, the wagon creaking beneath him as he made his way closer to where I lay hidden. I heard the soft rustle of a tarp being pulled back. I thought of what I'd do.

Do I beg for my life?

Do I stand defiant and dare them to do their worst with my silence?

Do I fight like a proud Centralian?

The soldier muttered something under his breath, the sound barely audible, lost beneath the rustle of the tarp as he tossed it aside. I could hear my heartbeat, loud in my ears, the rush of blood drowning out everything else.

And then... the grip loosened.

The soldier paused, muttering something to himself, his fingers slipping from the fabric. He let go of the blanket and his attention shifted elsewhere. I listened, frozen, as the soldier stepped back, his boots moving away from where I lay.

"I've found something not on the list, sire!" the soldier called out, excitedly.

My eyes flew open beneath the blanket, my pulse racing even faster now. What had they found? What would happen next?

There was a brief pause, the sound of footsteps approaching, and then the scout's voice cut through the night air.

"What did you find?" the scout asked, his tone suspicious.

I heard the soldier rummaging through the barrel, followed by the sound of something being pulled out and displayed. The scout's footsteps grew louder, and I knew he was now beside the wagon.

The scout spoke again, his voice cold. "This isn't on the ledger. Care to explain, trader?"

I strained to hear Bran's response. I could only imagine Bran standing there, his face impassive, doing his best to remain calm under scrutiny.

Bran cleared his throat, his voice carrying a practiced ease as he answered, "These barrels of fabric must have been left over from the last shipment, sir. We took on some new cargo in Eldermist and must have forgotten to sort everything properly. My apologies. It's an honest mistake. Nothing more, I assure you."

There was a pause, an agonizing silence, as I waited to hear the scout's response. My fingers tightened on the edge of the blanket, the fabric crumpling beneath my grip.

"Hmph." The scout sounded unconvinced, but his voice was reluctant as he spoke. "See that it doesn't happen again. We can't have discrepancies, not with tensions as high as they are."

"Yes, of course, sir. It won't happen again," Bran replied, his voice level and calm.

The scout let out a grunt and I heard the sound of his armor clinking as he turned away. "Leave the wagon," he ordered, and I heard the soldier stepping back, his boots thudding against the wooden floor as he climbed out of the wagon.

My heart finally began to slow, and the tension that had been building for what felt like an eternity began to ease. I listened as the soldier's footsteps faded, the muffled voices outside growing more distant as the Wintmorian soldiers began to move away.

I lay there, listening as the sounds of the Wintmorian soldiers began to recede. Relief washed over me like a wave, and I let out a shaky breath, my entire body relaxing for the first time since the soldiers had arrived. The camp around me began to stir again, the murmurs of the smugglers rising, the clinks and clatters of them resuming their work. Moments later, Bran lifted the tarp, his face appearing in the dim light, "You're still in one piece?" He muttered, a hint of a smile tugging at the corners of his mouth. He reached down, helping me sit up, the cold air rushing in as the blanket was lifted away.

"I'm fine," I murmured, my voice steady despite the thundering of my heart. "That was close, though."

"Closer than I'd like," Bran replied. He glanced around the darkened camp. "Those soldiers weren't fooling around. But we're in the clear now."

I looked at Bran, my voice filled with gratitude. "Thanks for covering for me. I know it's not easy—putting yourselves at risk like that."

Bran waved a hand, brushing off the thanks. "You've earned your place, lad—whether you like it or not, you're one of us now." He gave a wry grin, then his expression turned serious again. "Get some rest, if you can. At first light, we move out, no more stops. Not till we're where we need to be."

I shifted back into my hiding spot and pulled the rough blanket around me. "Get some sleep if you can." I heard him say, "It will be a trying few days ahead."

With that, Bran turned, climbing out of the wagon, the tarp falling back into place behind him. The camp settled once more. The sounds of the smugglers preparing for their departure faded into the night. I closed my eyes and offered bashful thanks to the gods.

# CHAPTER
## 17

I woke with a start, the sudden jolt of the wagon beneath me jerking me from a restless sleep. The wheels clattered against the uneven road, each sharp bump sending a shiver through my tired body as I tried to make sense of my surroundings. It was still dark, the faint light of dawn barely beginning to filter through the blankets.

The smugglers hadn't wasted any time. Just as Bran had said, we were making our way toward Edmundshire without stopping, pushing forward into the heart of the Wintmorian Empire.

The road was unforgiving, each bump jarring my sore body, the cold seeping through the blanket and into my bones. I tried to distract myself, focusing on the rhythm of the wheels, the steady sway of the wagon, anything to take my mind off the discomfort. But it was hard—the cramped space, the darkness, the fear that we could be discovered at any moment. It weighed on me, a constant pressure that refused to let up.

Every so often, Bran or one of the others would climb into the wagon, offering me a scrap of bread or a cup of cold soup. It wasn't much, but it was enough to keep me from losing my mind, holding me together a little longer and drawing me from the edge of completely losing my mind. The second day was much of the same—the endless rhythm of the wagon, the muffled conversations of the smugglers outside, the jolts and bumps as we navigated the rough terrain. I tried to sleep when I could, though it was difficult. The constant movement of the wagon, the cold seeping in through the wooden gaps, and the strain that kept my body rigid made rest nearly impossible. But I forced myself to close my eyes, take deep breaths, and let my mind drift whenever possible.

The third day dawned. Light filtered in through the narrow slits in the wood, painting thin lines across the wagon's interior. I felt close to my breaking point, yet a shift hung in the air—a sense of nearing our destination that pricked at the edges of my weariness.

I could hear the smugglers talking excitedly. The road beneath us had grown smoother, the noise of the wheels had lessened, and I knew we were nearing civilization.

The wagon slowed, the horses snorting as they were pulled back, the creaking of the wheels growing quieter as we approached our destination. I shifted slightly, my heart pounding in my chest as I listened.

And then, through the muffled layers of wood and fabric, I heard it—the distinct sound of voices raised in command, the sharp clank of metal, the unmistakable presence of soldiers. The caravan had stopped, and we were at the gate.

Edmundshire.

\*\*\*

Wintmorian soldiers called out to the smugglers, demanding their tokens of passage. I closed my eyes, my fingers tightening around the rough fabric of the blanket.

The wagon came to a stop. There was a low murmur of voices outside, followed by the distinct clank of armor. I could make out the soldiers' orders as they demanded that the caravans provide their identification.

The soldiers stepped in front of our cart, their boots crunching on the gravel. "Present your writs!" A curt voice barked. I held my breath as I strained to listen. The smugglers were ready, just as they had been before. I heard Bran's voice, calm and steady, answering the soldier, followed by the rustle of parchment as they handed over their writ.

There was a moment of silence, followed by the shuffling of footsteps, and the unmistakable sound of metal armor as one of the soldiers moved closer.

"This mark here..." the soldier began, his voice suspicious. "You were inspected a few days ago? There were discrepancies in your cargo?"

My fingers tightened on the blanket as I listened, every muscle in my body tense.

Bran's voice came next, still as calm as ever. "Yes, sire, that's true. We were inspected a few days back. There was an item left over from a previous shipment—an honest mistake, I assure you. We were cleared to continue once we explained."

The soldier paused, and I could almost feel the weight of the silence that followed. After a moment, the soldier spoke again. "Honest mistake or not, you're at the capital now. Mistakes don't go unnoticed here."

Bran said something indecipherable. There was a long pause as parchments crinkled and boots crunched on the gravel. Finally, the lead soldier muttered, "You've been busy, merchant," He didn't sound happy. "Strange, though… these stamps look older than they should be. Almost as if—"

He paused and I heard him walking around the crate I was in. Suddenly, he paused and walked toward Bran. "What are you hauling?" His voice dripped with suspicion.

Bran's voice was calm, but I heard the faintest edge beneath it. "Fabrics like fine linen and silk. And spices; ginger, clove, saffron. Imported goods from Port Oviella."

The soldier's companion, a younger man with sharp eyes and restless hands, stepped closer, peering at the tightly sealed crates. "Mind if we take a look? Just to be sure."

My pulse thundered in my ears. From my hiding place, wedged between the crates, the smell of burlap and sawdust did little to mask my rising fear. I could feel every creak of the wooden planks above me. Any shift, any stray movement, and the soldiers would notice.

Bran stepped forward, his voice a bit patronizing. "You're welcome to inspect them, Captain, though I'd advise against it." He leaned in slightly, lowering his voice. "Saffron's a delicate cargo. One wrong move and the merchant guild will be at your doorstep faster than you can draw that sword. I've seen it happen before—ugly business, I tell you."

The captain hesitated. My heart pounded in the uneasy pause that followed. For a moment, it seemed the bluff wouldn't hold. Then, with a grunt, I heard more crinkling of parchment and the soldier said, almost regretfully, "Get moving." He stepped back. "And watch yourself, merchant. Roads aren't safe these days."

Bran tipped his hat, guiding the cart forward with unhurried ease. Only when the soldiers were well behind them did he let out a breath, his knuckles still white on the reins. I heard the low murmur of the smugglers as they thanked the soldiers, and the creak of the wagon as Bran climbed back into the front.

"You breathe yet, Kaelan?" he muttered with a chuckle. And I let out a relieved sigh.

The horses snorted, their harnesses clinking as they were urged forward, and the wagon began to move once more as the gate of Edmundshire slowly opened before us.

We were through. I was in the heart of Edmundshire, the capital of Wintmore.

We had made it.

***

The city was alive with movement, the streets bustling with people, soldiers, merchants, and townsfolk alike. The clamor of the capital reached me even through the blanket—the sounds of the market, the calls of vendors, and the distant clatter of a blacksmith's hammer.

The smell was different too—rich, pungent, filled with smoke and spices, and the scent of so many people living so close together. There were voices in every direction, vendors calling out their wares, children calling for their mothers, and soldiers barking orders at one another.

The wagon began to slow, the creaking of the wheels lessening as we moved off the main road. Bran's voice finally called.

"We're stopping here. Unload what needs unloading, and then we move on."

I waited, and soon, I felt the tarp being pulled back. Bran's face appeared with a smirk of satisfaction.

"Come on, lad. We're here. You can stretch your legs," Bran said, his voice low enough that only I could hear.

Grateful, I swung myself out of the wagon in one swift motion. The light of day hit me, the bustling scene of the trading post opening before me. The cobblestone square was filled with people, carts, and merchants haggling over goods. The noise was deafening, a cacophony of life and business that surrounded me.

Bran gave me a nod, gesturing to the side. "You did well, Kaelan." I managed a faint smile. "Thank you, Bran. I wouldn't have made it without your help—all of you." I looked around at the other smugglers, each of them busy with their tasks, unloading crates and barrels from the caravan. Bran gave a curt nod, a small grin tugging at his lips. "You've got spirit, lad. Just see you keep out of trouble, eh?" He gave me a firm pat on the shoulder. "You're tougher than you look, lad." His lips twitched into a faint grin, though his eyes crinkled with weariness. "Most would've cracked after the first night in that coffin of a wagon."

I smiled too. "I thought I might. If not for the soup, I'd probably be mad by now."

"Ah, the soup!" Ben chuckled, a dry gravelly sound, "Not my finest work, but if it kept you from losing your mind, maybe, I should bottle the stuff."

We laughed and I regarded him. He was less taciturn now than when we were on the way to the city. He gesticulated, chatting cheerily with the other smugglers. I hesitated, searching for the right words. "Truly, Bran. I'd not have endured without your aid. I owe you more than words could ever repay."

Bran's grin faded slightly, his gaze shifting toward the bustling square. "Don't go trading with smugglers, lad. We are not the noble sort." He sighed, then added more softly, "You remind me of my boy. Not in your looks—he's got his mother's nose—but in the way you cling to hope, even when the world seems to crumble around you. Such a thing is rare in these times."

I blinked, caught off guard by the unexpected compliment. "You've got a family?"

"Had." His voice dipped, just enough to make my stomach twist. "Lost them long ago, before fate led me to this wretched life. That's why I warn you—stay vigilant. This city has no care for hope. It will chew you up and spit you out if you're not careful."

"I'll be careful, I assure you."

Bran clapped me on the shoulder. "Good. Now get moving. You've got a brother to find and I've got crates to unload. Just don't forget what I have said."

Bran then turned back to the wagon, joining the others as they unloaded. I watched for a moment, then turned away. I was on my own again, and whatever came next, I would have to face it alone.

The city of Edmundshire sprawled out before me—its narrow streets winding through a labyrinth of stone buildings, its crowded alleys filled with people, each with their own lives, their own stories.

Now, it was time to find my brother.

But first, I needed to get my bearings.

I glanced back toward the caravan, my eyes searching for Bran. I made my way over to him again. He was directing some of the other smugglers as they unloaded the crates.

"Bran," I called, catching his attention. He turned, raising an eyebrow, his expression questioning. I hesitated for a moment, then came closer. "Where would you recommend I start looking? I know it's a long shot, but...He's a merchant, or at least he was."

Bran stared at me for a moment, then let out a small laugh, shaking his head slightly. "Well, lad, I don't know your brother, but if he was a merchant, there's a good place to start," he said, his tone light but genuine. He gestured toward the western side of the trading post. "There's a merchant's guild hall a few streets down. It's where most traders pass through to register their goods or meet with buyers. You might get lucky and find someone who knows him—or at least someone who's seen him."

I nodded, grateful for the advice. "The merchant's guild hall. Aye, I've got it," I said, a flicker of hope sparking in my chest. It was something—somewhere to start. Bran gave me a nod, his smile faint but encouraging.

"Just keep your head down, and don't draw too much attention to yourself. This city's full of people who'd be more than happy to see a stranger like you get lost for good."

The streets of Edmundshire were busy, filled with merchants and townspeople going about their business. I wove my way through the crowds, my eyes hovering on the signs above the shops, the stalls filled with goods, and the bustling people that surrounded me. The city felt overwhelming—the sheer number of people, the noise, the sights and smells—it was all so different from the quiet of the forests and fields I had grown up in.

I kept my hood pulled low, my eyes forward, as I maneuvered through the winding streets, asking for directions here and there—but eventually, I found it. A large stone building, its entrance marked by an ornate wooden sign depicting a balance scale, the symbol of the merchants' guild of Wintmore. I stood before the imposing building and took a deep breath. It was time to look for my brother.

# CHAPTER
# 18

The air inside the guild hall was warm, tinged with the scent of parchment, ink, and exotic spices. It bustled with activity—merchants moving from table to table, clerks carrying stacks of ledgers, and guild members conversing in hushed voices. The walls were lined with tall shelves, filled with parchments and scrolls detailing the various trade routes, shipments, and the merchants sworn to the guild.

I approached a clerk sitting across a long table stacked with parchment. He was bent over a ledger, his quill moving quickly across the page.

"Excuse me," I began, keeping my voice low. The clerk looked up, his eyes narrowing slightly as he assessed the stranger before him. "I'm looking for someone—my brother. His name is Eamon. He's a merchant, or at least he used to be."

The clerk studied me for a moment, then shook his head. "Eamon, you say? Sorry, lad, but I can't help you. We have too many merchants pass through here—too many to remember individual names," he replied before returning his attention to the ledger.

I nodded, trying to hide my disappointment. I thanked the clerk, moving away, and my eyes swept the room once more. I approached another guild member, this time a middle-aged man standing near a map pinned to the wall.

"Have you seen a man named Eamon?" I asked, my voice hopeful. "He's my brother. He might have come through here recently."

The man frowned, shaking his head. "Eamon? No, can't say I've heard of him. We've got a lot of traders coming in and out, but that name doesn't ring a bell. Sorry, lad."

I nodded, forcing a small smile. "Thank you," I said, though my heart sank a little deeper each time I heard the same response. I turned away, searching for anyone else who could help.

I approached another man, a younger guild member who was sorting through a pile of scrolls, and began asking my questions. But as I spoke, I felt a strange sensation—a prickle at the back of my neck, the unmistakable feeling of being watched.

My words faltered mid-sentence, and the clerk frowned, muttering something I didn't hear. Slowly, deliberately, I turned my head, my pulse quickening. There he was. A figure cloaked in dark fabric, standing partially hidden behind a row of shelves, his hood pulled low over his face. He wasn't just looking in my direction—he was staring. Watching. Unease coiled in my stomach. His presence was too deliberate to be a coincidence. The air seemed to shift between us, thick with unspoken tension. My mind raced with questions. Did he know who I was? How long had he been following me? Was he a spy—Centralian? Wintmore? Or something worse?

As soon as my gaze met his, the figure moved. A subtle shift at first, his head tilting slightly, the faintest suggestion of acknowledgment. And then, in one fluid motion, he turned on his heel, his cloak swirling like smoke behind him as he strode swiftly toward the exit.

The spell broke. My instincts screamed at me to follow. Before I knew it, I was moving. "Hey!" I called out, shoving past merchants and guild members, my eyes locked on the figure slipping toward the far door. Whoever that person was, he knew something. I could hear the surprised murmurs of those around me, but I didn't care. I dashed across the guild hall, my cloak billowing behind me as I moved. I shoved the door open and stepped outside, my eyes sweeping the street for any sign of the figure.

There—just ahead, slipping into a narrow alley, the edge of his cloak vanished around the corner.

My heart pounded, the urgency of the chase propelling me forward. I sprinted toward the alleyway, the bustling noise of the marketplace fading behind me, replaced by the echo of my own hurried footsteps. I rounded the corner, breath coming in short gasps, my boots skidding slightly on the uneven cobblestones.

I halted abruptly, my gaze darting around, as I took in the narrow passage ahead. The alleyway was dark, the high walls on either side blocking out much of the sunlight. It was a narrow, winding corridor, lined with old wooden doors, stacked crates, and piles of refuse. Small windows sat high up on the stone walls, with most of them boarded up or covered with grime, leaving the passage shrouded in shadows.

And there was no sign of the figure.

My breath came in ragged gasps as I skidded to a halt, the damp air of the alley clinging to my skin like a second layer. My eyes darted frantically around for the hooded figure, but the realization hit me like a stone: the figure had vanished. A cold frustration gnawed at me, tightening my throat. Whoever he was, he had been watching me. He knew something. And now, because I hesitated, he had slipped away. My fists curled as I fought the urge to scream. I leaned against the wall, panting, letting the damp chill seep into me.

Get it together, Kaelan.

There was no time for mistakes. Not now. I turned to follow the alleyway deeper into the bowels of the city when a commotion behind me made me turn.

A group of four soldiers was hustling a woman from a cart as she protested wildly. She refused to follow forcing the soldiers to drag her willy-nilly. I slipped further into the shadows. It was dangerous for the soldiers to see me. I was a Centralian after all. But something about that girl made me turn one more time.

It was Lilah!

My breath hitched as I saw her—Lilah, bound and defiant, her slender wrists rubbed raw by the ropes biting into her skin. The sight of her struggling against the soldiers sent a jolt through me, and a tangle of anger and fear twisted in my gut. My mind screamed at me to stay hidden, to turn away and disappear into the shadows like the soldier I once was. A Centralian revealing himself here was as good as making a death wish. But my chest tightened with a different instinct, one I couldn't ignore: Lilah needed me. She was reckless, infuriating, and too stubborn for her own good—but she was an ally. I watched her—Lilah, defiant even in chains—and something in me refused to stay silent.

My feet moved before my mind could stop them. "Wait!" The word tore from my throat, loud and sharp, slicing through the chaos of the alley. A part of me—the soldier in enemy territory—immediately regretted it. Every step closer to those Wintmorian men felt like walking a tightrope over an open flame. But another part of me, the iron-willed part, refused to let fear keep me hidden. My fists clenched at my sides as their hard, suspicious eyes turned to me. "You're a fool, Kaelan," I muttered to myself. But fools still have to protect their friends.

The soldiers turned to me, their expressions hard and suspicious. "Who are you?" one barked. He was bald with a wicked glare.

I swallowed hard, willing my voice to be steady. "My name is Kael. She's my sister," the lie tumbled easily from my lips. "Please, let her go. Whatever she's done, we can settle it."

The lead soldier narrowed his eyes. "Your sister, huh?" His voice dripped with suspicion as he dragged Lilah closer. "She's a thief. Stole from one of us and refused to return it. We're taking her where she belongs—to the dungeons here in the capital. Let's see how long her sharp mouth lasts there."

My pulse roared in my ears. Prison! In the capital!

"I'll pay," I blurted, the words rushing out before fear could clamp my throat shut. My hand trembled as I reached for my pouch, my movements fast and clumsy. "Whatever she took, I'll pay for it. Just let her go."

The soldier's sneer deepened. He didn't move, his gaze boring into me. "You'd pay for this wench? She doesn't look worth the coin."

I forced myself to meet his eyes. "She's my blood," I said, my voice firmer now, though my hands still shook. "Family is worth everything," I reached into my pouch and pulled out the last of my savings. I held it out, my hand trembling slightly. "Take it. This should cover it."

The bald soldier exchanged glances with his comrades. The silence stretched as I held my breath. Finally, he snatched the pouch from my hand, spilling the coins into his palm. "Fine," he spat. "But if we catch her again—no amount of coin will save her."

He untied Lilah and shoved her forward. She stumbled into my arms, and I caught her, wrapping my arms around her. As the soldiers stalked away, I felt their eyes linger on me for a moment too long. My breath hitched, and I forced myself to look away, focusing instead on Lilah. Her lips were curled in fury as she rubbed her raw, reddened wrists.

"Well," she muttered, her voice laced with sarcasm, "that was fun. Thanks for the rescue, brother Kael. Though you shouldn't have bothered. I was taking care of it."

"What are you doing here, Lilah?" I said, my voice a mixture of surprise and exasperation.

She raised an eyebrow, her expression dancing between sarcasm and something softer—something almost like concern.

"Oh, you know me," she drawled, pushing off the crate and stepping closer. "I just love running through dangerous cities for no reason at all." Her tone was light, but her eyes lingered on me "I'd ask you the same. I thought you'd be in Eldermist."

I sighed, running a hand through my hair. "I got news that my brother was seen here. I reduced my voice, "So I found a way and brought myself here."

"She raised an eyebrow. "You don't love your life, do you, Kaelan? Oh, wait. You are Brother Kael of Wimtmore nowadays."

"What are you even doing here, Lilah?" I asked again, my voice softer this time.

She hesitated, her gaze flickering away for the briefest moment before she sighed. "I followed you. From Eldermist."

My eyebrows shot up. "You what?"

Lilah rolled her eyes. "Don't get all sentimental about it. Someone has to make sure you don't get yourself killed running off on these perilous quests."

A small smile tugged at the corners of my lips. "You're worried about me."

"Worried?" she scoffed, though a faint blush crept into her cheeks. "Let's not get carried away. It's just... inconvenient when you're not around to annoy me, that's all."

Her words were light, but there was a tenderness beneath them, a quiet affection she tried to mask.

I chuckled, shaking my head. "Well, I appreciate your... inconvenience." My voice grew sterner. "What I don't appreciate however is stealing. And from Wintmorian soldiers!" Lilah was outrageous. In a way, she reminded me of Eamon.

"Why did you steal from them, Lilah?" I asked, my voice quieter now.

She shrugged, looking away. "One of them; the one with a bald head and beady eyes; was bullying a father with his two little sons on that path leading to the market at Eldermist. Took the poor man's basket of fruit and left him with nothing. Let's just say…I got the basket into the hands of the owner."

I laughed. "You're impossible."

"And you're predictable," she shot back, but there was no malice in her tone. Just a faint, unspoken gratitude.

For a moment, we just stood there, the chaos of the alley melting into the hum of the city beyond. My heart was still pounding, my head spinning with the risks I'd just taken. I wanted to tell her—about the hooded figure, about the questions clawing at me since I'd entered Edmundshire, about the sharp-edged fear that kept me awake at night. But the words lodged in my throat. Lilah stood there, brushing at the marks on her wrists, her usual defiance masking anything deeper. She didn't need my burdens, I told myself. She didn't need to know how much her being here both terrified and grounded me in ways I didn't fully understand. But the words I needed to say caught in my throat. Instead, I forced a smile and said, "Let's get out of here," the words feeling like a shield against everything I wasn't ready to say.

Lilah nodded, her smirk returning. "Lead the way, hero. You're the boss, Brother Kael. Try not to trip over your noble intentions on the way."

A burst of laughter came out of me and I unconsciously took her hand. Together, we disappeared into the crowd, leaving the alley and its shadows behind.

# CHAPTER
# 19

The streets of Edmundshire seemed narrower as the sun dipped below the horizon, the golden hues giving way to the deep blues and grays of dusk. The warmth of the marketplace had been replaced by a biting chill. My pouch felt unnervingly light against my side, its weight—or lack thereof—a reminder of the coins I had just surrendered. The reality was stark: I had no money left for an inn or even a decent meal.

"Where might we be heading?" Lilah asked, her voice amused as she tried to keep up with my determined strides.

I didn't look at her, my eyes grazing the streets for an idea—any idea. "Someplace quiet," I muttered. "I require a moment to think."

"Ah, yes," Lilah drawled, her tone dripping with sarcasm. "The infamous Kaelan and his brooding ways. Should I brace myself for some profound wisdom or just more of your grunting and furrowed brows?"

I shot her a half-hearted glare and continued down the alley in long strides. She ran after me throwing jabs. The alley was suffused with a biting cold that crept through every seam of my tunic. The scent of rotting produce and damp wood filled the air, and the occasional scurrying of a rat reminded me that this was no place for anyone to linger, least of all Lilah. It was a quiet alley with crates stacked on both sides. I sat down on one of the crates to stretch my legs. She plopped down beside me, her presence both grounding and irritatingly distracting. Her usual smirk faltered as she drew her knees to her chest to stave off the chill.

The streets were quieter now, the buzz of the marketplace replaced by the distant hum of taverns and the occasional rattle of a passing cart. A shadow moved in the corner of my vision, and I stiffened instinctively, but it was only a stray dog sniffing at an overturned barrel.

Lilah's voice broke the silence, light but edged with impatience. "You don't mean to have me sleep here, do you? I've endured worse, true, but must we tempt fate?"

I hesitated, my mind racing.

"You're really making a habit of these glamorous accommodations," she teased, gesturing to their surroundings. "First the woods, now a pile of crates. Should I start calling you 'Sir Kaelan of Nowhere'?"

I chuckled softly, the sound surprising even me. I leaned forward, resting my elbows on my knees. "I will find a way. But this isn't quite how I envisioned things unfolding," I admitted, my voice quieter now.

Lilah tilted her head, her teasing smile fading just a fraction. "What troubles you, Kaelan?"

I hesitated, feeling unused to unburdening myself. But Lilah's gaze was steady, expectant.

"Earlier at the guild hall, I sought news of my brother," I began, my voice dropping to a hushed tone. "But there was a man—cloaked in shadow. He followed me, Lilah. He was watching my every move."

Her brow furrowed, her teasing demeanor slipping away entirely. "Watching you? Did he speak a word to you?" Her voice was tight with concern, her gaze sharp as if trying to read the answer on my face.

I shook my head. "No. He disappeared before I could get to him. But it wasn't random, Lilah. He knew who I was—what I was."

"Did he carry any weapon?" she asked, her tone sharp now, her eyes scanning the alley as if she thought the cloaked figure might emerge at any moment.

"None that I saw. "I replied glad that she was concerned for me. "But it wasn't just his presence—it was how he looked at me. Like he'd already decided something about me, something I didn't want to know."

Lilah frowned as she considered my words. "If he wanted to hurt you, he's had his chance. No, Kaelan, this is different."

"He's waiting—watching. And that's almost worse."

Lilah leaned closer, her voice softer now but no less resolute. "Then, maybe it's time to stop running, Kaelan. Maybe it's time to face whatever—or whoever—this is."

A shadow flickered at the mouth of the alley, drawing both our eyes. For a heart-stopping moment, my breath hitched, but it was just a passing figure, a merchant hurrying home before the night fully claimed the streets.

I swiped at a fly that buzzed in my face, "I don't want them to get me before I'm able to find my brother."

Her face relaxed into a smile.

"Even in the face of danger, you still care more about others than yourself. You care too much. You won't admit it, but it's true."

I opened my mouth to argue but stopped. She wasn't wrong. I did care—about her, about Eamon, about things I'd long tried to bury under layers of guilt and anger.

"Yes, I care," I admitted quietly, my gaze meeting hers. "Which is why I don't want you out here on the streets tonight."

\*\*\*

Lilah walked beside me, her usual smirk firmly in place, but her eyes darted around the bustling streets, skimming every shadow as if she expected trouble to leap out at any moment. She was quiet for once, but I could feel her curiosity simmering just beneath the surface, ready to boil over with questions about what we would do next.

I tried to think. We couldn't stay on the streets, not with the Wintmore soldiers still lurking about. I couldn't risk being seen—or worse, recognized. But where could we go?

"Kaelan," Lilah finally broke the silence. And I glanced at her, relieved that she had not called me Brother Kael.

"Tell me, do you actually have a plan, or are we just wandering about until the city spits us out?" Her eyes danced with mischief and her tone was playful but carried the legendary sharp edge.

Her teasing brought a reluctant smile to my face. "I'm thinking."

"Well, think faster, oh wise leader," she quipped. "I'm starving. And I'd rather not sleep under a cart tonight."

"There's a place," I said at last, the words heavy on my tongue. "It's not ideal, but it's safe."

Lilah turned her head, curiosity sparking in her eyes. "Oh, do tell. Is it another pile of crates, or are we moving up in the world?"

There was one place we might go. Times were desperate.

Lilah raised an eyebrow. "Oh, this should be good. Where, please tell?"

"The House of Mercy," I replied keeping my head straight.

Her eyebrows shot up, the smirk vanishing from her face. "The temple of Oerhzn?"

I shrugged. The House of Mercy was a humble temple on the outskirts of Edmundshire, tended by a group of red-robed clerics who served one of the lesser Wintorian deities, Oerhzn. They offered aid to travelers and the destitute. It wasn't much—just a few rooms and a shared hall where they served watery soup to the needy—but it was better than nothing.

"Don't tell me you've found religion," Lilah said, her tone dripping with sarcasm. "Because that would truly be the strangest thing I've seen today."

"Come on," I replied, suppressing a grin. "They won't ask too many questions, and it's a roof over our heads for the night."

The walk to the House of Mercy felt longer than it was, the silence between us punctuated by the occasional whisper of wind or distant shout from the city's main square. I kept my hood low, my eyes peering into every shadow for signs of danger. If Lilah noticed my tension, she said nothing, though her hand rested a little too casually on the hilt of her dagger.

As we neared the outskirts of Edmundshire, the city's noise faded, replaced by the faint, mournful strains of a hymn carried on the breeze. The House of Mercy came into view, and Lilah stopped and gazed at it.

"Not exactly a castle, is it?" Lilah said, her voice light but her eyes scanning the area with practiced caution. "But I suppose it beats the alley."

***

The House of Mercy sat at the edge of the city, a squat, unassuming building with weathered stone walls and a wooden sign creaking in the evening breeze. The glow of candlelight spilled from its narrow windows, casting warm pools of light onto the cobbled path.

A priest with white markings on his forehead greeted us as we entered, his warm eyes flicking over our disheveled appearances. "Welcome," he said, his voice gentle. "You're travelers, yes? You're welcome to stay, though our accommodations are humble."

"Humble is fine," I said quickly, my voice firm but polite.

"My husband and I are looking for a quiet place to rest," she said with a smile so disarming it could have melted iron. She looped her arm through mine leaned and into me with an air of practiced ease. "It's been a long journey, and he's always so concerned about my comfort. Don't you, my love?" she teased, her eyes sparkling with mischief. I blinked, caught off guard. "Uh… yes, of course," I muttered, glancing sideways at her.

I scoffed internally. Lilah was indeed a character.

The priest beamed at her, "We don't often see married folks around here. I'll give you our finest room."

He led us up some twisting stairs, his thin legs barely making any sound on the sturdy wood. I shot Lilah a fierce whisper. "That was... unexpected."

She smirked. "You're welcome. And pray, try not to look like a hare caught in a snare. It does little for our wedded reputation."

The old priest led us down a hallway where he showed us to a small room, little more than two narrow cot and a bench. The walls were bare, save for a single wooden symbol hanging above the bed.

"It's not much," the cleric said, his expression apologetic.

"It's perfect," I assured him.

Once he shuffled out, Lilah dropped onto the bench with a dramatic sigh. "Well, this is cozy," she said, kicking off her boots. "I guess I can survive one night without luxury."

I leaned against the wall, exhaustion tugging at my limbs. The events of the day had taken their toll.

"You didn't have to follow me, you know," I said after a moment, my voice quiet.

Lilah looked up at me, her smirk softening into something more sincere. "And let you get yourself killed? Not a chance. You're too interesting."

"Is that why you...?" I trailed off, struggling to find the right words. I wanted to ask why she had claimed we were married—did it mean anything to her, or was it simply another jest? My gaze met hers, and for a moment, I faltered. "Might there be a chance... you could..." My voice faded again, lost in the uncertainty.

Lilah stared at me for a moment, her expression unreadable. Then, as if unable to resist, she grinned. "What, the great Kaelan of Centralia is at a loss for words? Should I alert the town crier?"

I groaned and scrubbed a hand over my face. "You make it impossible to be serious."

"That's my charm," she quipped, but her voice was gentler now. "You don't have to say anything, Kaelan. I already know."

I looked at her then, my eyes searching hers for some hint of mockery or dismissal, but there was none.

"Regardless of what you think at this moment," she said, her smirk returning, "someone must keep you alive long enough to figure out how to wield that grand, noble heart of yours. Might as well be me until you can find that damn brother of yours."

I let out a soft laugh, shaking my head. "You're unbearable, Lilah!"

"And you're too stuck in your ways," she shot back, leaning closer, her voice dropping to a mock whisper. "But don't worry—I find it oddly endearing."

Her words caught me off guard, and before I could respond, she reached out and gently poked my chest.

"And you're stuck with me now, Brother Kael, or is it Husband Kaelan?" She said, teasing. "Might as well get used to it."

I opened my mouth to respond, but she was already standing.

"Come on, Kaelan. Let's find something to eat before I waste away."

***

We returned to the main hall, where the clerics silently served bowls of steaming soup to a small gathering of travelers. Lilah grumbled about the thin broth but ate every last spoonful, and polished off mine too.

As the evening deepened, the hall grew quieter, the other guests retiring to their rooms. Lilah and I lingered at the table, the flickering candlelight casting shadows across her face.

For the first time since we'd reunited, she seemed… vulnerable.

Lilah leaned back against the hard chair and regarded me. "You're better than the rest of them," she said suddenly, appraising me.

I blinked, caught off guard. "What?"

"You Centralians," she clarified, her voice laced with dry humor. "Self-important, cold, too obsessed with their shiny boots to notice when they're stepping on someone's neck. But you? You're…" She waved a hand vaguely in my direction. "You're different."

I snorted, shaking my head. "Thanks for the glowing endorsement."

"I'm serious," she pressed, her tone softening. "You're not like them, Kaelan. You care. You don't want to admit it, but you do."

"Centralians care."

She scoffed and I opened my mouth to argue but stopped. At least, she wasn't entirely wrong. I did care—about her, about Eamon, about things I'd long tried to bury under layers of guilt and anger.

As I watched her talk, banter, and tease me, I felt a strange pull—a deeper, more consuming emotion that tugged at the edges of my carefully guarded heart. I didn't have the words yet—not the right ones, at least. But for now, her laughter and her presence were enough.

As the night deepened, we leaned against the wall, the tiny bed forgotten, the sounds of the city fading into the background. For the first time in what felt like forever, I let myself breathe.

# CHAPTER
# 20

When I woke, Lilah lay still, fast asleep, curled beneath the threadbare blanket. In the soft light of dawn filtering through the temple's high windows, she seemed almost serene—vulnerable, even. For a moment, I lingered, watching her chest rise and fall in a steady rhythm before I drew myself away. Rising slowly, I moved with care, determined not to rouse her. This was my burden to bear. Whatever danger awaited, it was not hers to share. Lilah had said her piece, but I would not risk her safety—not for this.

I slipped from the small chamber into the quiet of the temple's halls, passing by a statue of the deity propped on a wooden table in the hallway, the faint echo of my steps swallowed by the stillness. Outside, Edmundshire unfolded before me, cloaked in the half-light of dawn. The streets were yet hushed, the city only beginning to stir, as the first tendrils of morning light crept across the stone.

This time, I left my hood lowered, my face bare to the crisp morning air. If the figure sought me, whoever they were, they would find me. I needed to know who the figure was and why they lingered in my wake. I went through the narrow lanes and cobbled alleys, the city's labyrinthine streets as much a test for me as for them. Past sleeping market stalls and shuttered windows, I walked deliberately, each turn a quiet invitation.

I moved with purpose, senses taut as a bowstring, hoping for the shadow to appear—or daring him to let himself be seen.

As soon as my eyes caught sight of the figure, I moved without thought, darting after him at once. He fled, his dark cloak billowing behind him like smoke in the wind, as he weaved through the labyrinthine streets of Edmundshire as fast and silent as a phantom. My chest tightened, every instinct screaming not to lose him—not again.

Suddenly, he slipped into the same alley where he had vanished the day before, and disappeared. I skidded to a halt at the mouth of the alley, my breath sharp in my chest. Taking a cautious step forward, I let my gaze sweep the shadowed alley, every muscle tensed. I refused to believe he was gone again—not this time. My eyes combed every corner, searching for movement, a flicker of their presence, anything to prove that the figure wasn't simply a ghost haunting my steps.

I moved cautiously, peering into every corner, every shadow that might conceal the cloaked stranger. There were so many places to hide—so many nooks and crannies, piles of old crates and refuse, darkened doorways that led who knows where.

My eyes narrowed as I approached a stack of crates, the wood aged and splintered, piled high against the side of the alley. I pushed them aside and peered behind them. Nothing. I turned, looking up toward the rooftops, half-expecting to see the figure climbing up the wall, disappearing across the roofs of the city. But there was nothing—just the narrow strip of sky above, a dull gray of the winter light.

Frustration bubbled up inside me, my hands clenching into fists. I had been so close. Whoever that figure was, he knew something. I could feel it in my gut. This wasn't just about the figure. It was about Eamon. About every mistake I had made, every moment I had hesitated when I should have acted. The memory of all my losses clutched at my chest. I had not kept those I loved safe. I hadn't kept us together. Eamon was gone, my friends were gone, and I was here, chasing shadows through the streets of a city I barely knew, grasping at shadows.

If I let this lead slip through my fingers, what then? Another dead end? Another sleepless night, haunted by the thought that I wasn't fast enough, clever enough, or strong enough to protect the people who mattered most.

I couldn't lose again. I wouldn't be able to bear it.

And what would I tell Lilah? That I had risked everything and come up empty-handed? That I had dragged her into this, only to let her down, too?

But just as I was about to give up, a faint scuff mark caught my eye, and a trail led to a stack of crates against the wall.

I moved closer. The crates were old and splintered, and as I pushed them aside, I saw it—an arrow, its tip buried in the wood, pinning a folded piece of parchment, yellowed and frayed. My hand trembled slightly as I pulled the arrow free, the parchment fluttering loose. I unfolded it, my eyes narrowing at the hurried words across the page.

Where the Centralian wolf hides among black sheep, the shadows will meet, and the truth will sleep.

My fingers tightened around the note, my breath catching in my throat. I knew now that I was onto something—something far bigger than just my brother. It wasn't just a message—it was a warning, and whoever had left it wanted me to find it. And that was what scared me the most.

# CHAPTER
# 21

I folded the note carefully and slipped it into my cloak, my mind racing with possibilities.

The paper was brittle in my hands, and the ink faded and smeared in places. I flattened it against the cobblestones and read the words again, my brow furrowing as I tried to make sense of them. There was indeed danger; a danger so great it must be veiled in riddles and shadows.

Where the Centralian wolf hides among black sheep, the shadows will meet, and the truth will sleep.

I stared at it, the riddle dancing in my mind, twisting, but not falling into place. I frowned, repeating the words silently, trying to make sense of them. Centralian? Who, besides Lilah knew I was Centralian? And Centralian wolf. The words hung there, mocking me. I knew the term Centralian well enough—my land, my people, a name whispered with both reverence and disdain—but the mention of a wolf? That unsettled me. Wolves had their place in tales of cunning and carnage, yet what place they held among Centralians, I could not say. A wolf? What did that have to do with what I sought, or the men trailing me? Was it symbolic? A metaphor, perhaps? And why hide among black sheep?

I shifted, my mind racing, trying to catch a thread, a clue, anything. The black sheep—that part was clear. Everyone knew the term around here. The outcasts, the ones who didn't fit the mold, those who lived in the shadow of the city's power. Wintmore's castaways.

But the wolf?

My fingers drummed against the paper, my thoughts circling like a trap I couldn't escape. Black sheep... a wolf hidden among them? No, that didn't make sense. Why hide a wolf? A wolf was the danger, the predator. It didn't hide.

I squinted at the words again, the riddle pressing down on me like a weight. It felt important. Whoever had left this message had wanted me to figure it out. But what was it?

Then, a fleeting memory brushed my mind. The Centralian wolf—no, wait. The Centralian wolf!

My heart skipped a beat. The stories I had heard as a child, whispered by travelers and merchants in darkened taverns. The Centralian wolf wasn't just a myth. He was a figure—a name spoken with a chill in the air. A ruthless merchant who came from the southern lands, a man with a shadow as dark as his deeds and known for deception.

Suddenly, the riddle seemed to settle into place. The wolf wasn't an actual animal. It was a Centralian—a wolf in human form, hiding among black sheep... It was a metaphor. A man whose true nature was hidden in plain sight. Was it me? Or was there another Centralian hiding here in Edmundshire, disguised among the Wintmorians? And the shadows meeting—was that a place, or a time? My mind turned over the words again and again, but they remained as elusive as ever, their meaning just out of reach.

The shadows will meet, and the truth will sleep.

I began to walk back toward the busier streets of the city, observing the bustling crowds as I moved. I needed answers—I needed to figure out where to go, and what to do next. But Edmundshire was massive, a maze of narrow streets and alleys, filled with people whose lives were as tangled and complicated as the city itself. Finding one person—one lead—seemed like an impossible task.

I moved through the market square, the noise of vendors and townspeople washing over me, their voices a dull roar in my ears as I tried to concentrate. I passed a group of merchants gathered around a cart, their voices animated as they haggled over the price of goods. I glanced toward them, wondering if any of them might have heard something—if there were rumors of a Centralian hiding here in the city. But I didn't stop, the riddle still consuming my thoughts.

The Centralian wolf hides among black sheep—

My eyes narrowed as I considered the words. It sounded like someone in disguise—someone hiding in plain sight, blending in with those around them. Perhaps, someone who was passing themselves off as a Wintmorian. But where would they be hiding? And how could I find them?

I paused, leaning against the wall of a nearby building, my eyes closing for a moment as I tried to think.

The shadows will meet—

What did that mean? Was it a place, a time, a symbol?

I opened my eyes, looking around the street, my gaze falling on a small group of children running past, their laughter ringing out as they chased each other through the market square. They darted between the stalls, their small forms disappearing and reappearing in the shifting light. I watched them for a moment, something stirring in my mind.

The shadows will meet...

I looked up, my eyes narrowing as I scanned the rooftops and the narrow alleys between the buildings. Shadows meeting—was it a place where the light didn't reach, a hidden spot where someone could meet without being seen? It was possible—there were plenty of places in Edmundshire that fit that description. I just had to find the right one.

I straightened, my breath quickening. The shadows... that was it. The man—or woman, would be somewhere hidden in the shadows of the city, a place where secrets were buried. The truth was there, waiting, but it was dormant— just as the riddle had said.

I clenched the paper tighter, my resolve hardening. This was no ordinary lead—it was a clue. A dangerous one. The kind of thing that would pull me into the depths of Wintmore's secrets.

But who had left it? Why? And what did they want me to find?

I had no answers yet. But I would find them.

I passed an old tavern, its sign swinging slightly in the breeze, the name faded and worn. I paused, my eyes narrowing as I considered it. Taverns were places where secrets were exchanged and where people went to disappear. It was as good a place as any to start.

I took a deep breath, trying to calm my racing thoughts. I needed to think—to focus. The answer was there, hidden within the words of the riddle. I just had to find it.

I had wandered into a less desirable part of the city, an area where people averted their gazes, their cloaks pulled tightly around themselves as they hurried along. The energy here was different—guarded, wary. It felt right.

I stopped in front of a small tavern tucked between two taller buildings. Its sign was weathered and broken, hanging on a single rusty chain. The name was barely legible. It was called The Black Sheep.

*** 

The name gave me pause, my brow furrowing slightly.

The Centralian wolf hides among sheep...

A chill ran down my spine as I stared at the sign. Something about it felt right. The way it sat, hidden in the shadows of the buildings, made me think twice.

I pushed open the door and stepped inside. The air was thick with the scent of stale ale and smoke, the dim light barely illuminating the room. A handful of patrons were scattered throughout the tavern, most of them hunched over their drinks, their eyes flicking up as I entered, then quickly turning away.

I moved toward the bar, and the barkeep—a tall, lanky man with a beautiful face—looked up, his eyes narrowing slightly as I approached.

"Looking for something, stranger?" he asked, he smiled but his eyes were wary.

I hesitated for a moment, then nodded. "I need you to tell me something," I said, keeping my voice low. "I heard this is the kind of place where people go to... keep things quiet." It was a quiet plea.

The barkeep's eyes narrowed further, his lips pressing into a thin line. He looked me up and down, then leaned forward, his voice dropping to a whisper. "Depends on the kind of secrets you're seeking," the man said, his voice low and edged with a sly undertone. "And, of course, what you're willing to offer in return."

"I am a Wintmorian merchant with a score to settle," I replied my gaze fixed on the barkeep's. "I'm looking for someone who knows about the Centralians in Wintmore. Someone who knows where the shadows meet."

His expression remained impassive, but I saw a flicker cross his eyes. "Knowledge, aye," he said, leaning forward, his voice low and sharp as a whetted blade. "But wisdom carries a price, same as anything else. The question is—what can you afford to part with?"

I straightened, my voice calm though desperation simmered beneath the surface. "I have come from far, and my coin is spent. But I give you my word, I will return with a payment equal to the worth of the news you give me."

His eyes narrowed, and he leaned back with deliberate ease. "You want to buy ale, sire?" he asked loudly, his tone mocking as his eyes blazed with disdain. "If not, I suggest you leave this place at once."

Desperation clawed at me, tightening my chest. "Help me, I beg you. I shall reward you," I said, my voice quiet but firm.

The barkeep leaned forward again, his voice dropping to a low snarl. "If you don't leave now, there are men here who will see to it that you don't live to see sundown."

I glanced around at the patrons. Most seemed preoccupied with their drinks, but the tension in the air was unmistakable. I wasn't willing to test his threat. With a heavy sigh, I stepped back, the barkeep's mocking whistle following me as he scrubbed a goblet with exaggerated vigor.

I had come to a dead end. The thought that my brother might never be found stirred and took root in my weary soul. The dissipation of hope I once cherished melded with a sharp disdain for myself. I turned and stepped out into the brisk street, leaving the clamor of the tavern fading behind me. The sting of failure coursed through me like poison, leaving little time to gather my thoughts before a sharp, familiar voice rang out.

"How dare you, Kaelan!"

I turned sharply. Lilah stood before me, her fiery gaze locked onto mine. Her eyes blazed with fury, and I knew without a doubt—I was in bigger trouble.

# CHAPTER
# 22

"**D**o you think so little of me that you didn't even feel the need to tell me you were leaving?" Lilah's voice trembled with fury, her eyes wide and blazing. "You think I'm a burden to be left behind, Kaelan?"

I opened my mouth, but no words came. What could I say?

"That old priest of Oerhzn told me my husband had left at dawn to run errands in town," she continued, jabbing a finger at me. "But I knew you were gone!" Her voice angry, and her accusation cut deep. I stood in front of the tavern as she glared at me. A deep weariness settled in my bones, a burden I could no longer carry. Sadness, loss and frustration—they intertwined, holding me in a chokehold and I realized I could no longer bear it.

"I'm sorry, Lilah." My voice was raw and stripped bare, and my words felt hollow against the weight in my chest. "But I have nothing anymore. Nothing I can offer you. I've been emptied—piece by piece, loss by loss. My brother... my land... my people... I've lost them all."

My hands rested uselessly by my sides. "I've watched brave men—Jarin, Cedric, Edric, Sir Gareth—men with whom I broke bread and shared laughter, men I trusted with my very life—fall like leaves in a tempest. Their faces haunt me still, Lilah. Every night, I see them. I hear them calling my name. I wasn't enough. I wasn't enough to save them. Don't you see? It's all for nothing. Either I die in this place or I wander around forever, searching for my brother. Either way, I've already lost."

My hands trembled, and I hid them behind my back, ashamed of the weakness they betrayed. "You're not a burden, Lilah," I said, my voice faltering, the words heavy in my throat. "You're the only thing that feels real in this shattered world. But even you, Lilah... even you—I cannot hold onto. I cannot promise that I won't fail you as I've failed everyone else. And the thought of losing you, —it terrifies me."

I swallowed hard, my chest tight as if bound in iron. "Look at me," I said, my voice trembling. "Nothing is as it should be, and the path I walk is fraught with peril. I can't—" My voice faltered, "I can't lose you, Lilah. Not you. If I do, there'll be nothing left of me worth saving."

We stood there on the cobblestone street, the air thick with words unspoken. She stared at me, her face unreadable. The cold air bit into my chest and I wondered if it would be better to give up; pack my things up and return to Centralia, rather than to feel the disappointment battering me relentlessly. But before I could stop myself, I said, "I didn't leave because you meant nothing. I left because I love you, Lilah, I don't want you die because of me."

The words hung between us, heavy and unbidden. The ache in my chest, like the pounding of a smith's hammer, began to ease, as though I had shed the boulders I had borne upon my back for what felt an eternity. I could not decipher the look upon her face. Surely, she would hurl her boots at me now or unleash some biting jest. That would mark the pinnacle of an already wretched night. Yet, she stood unmoving, her gaze locked with mine, her eyes unreadable in the dim light. She moved—a small shuffle of her feet. Then, in a flash she came up to me, her eyes filled with something I couldn't quite place.

The next moment, her fist crashed into my shoulder with enough force to make me stumble back a step. It wasn't the kind of punch meant to do real damage, but it carried weight—enough to make her point.

"I knew it," she said, shaking out her hand like she'd struck a brick wall. "Honestly, Kaelan, for someone who's supposed to be a brilliant soldier, you're terrible at keeping secrets. It's been obvious since we met."

I opened my mouth, but she cut me off with a smirk. "Oh, don't even try to deny it. The brooding stares, the whole 'suffering in silence' act—it's like you read a tragic romance and decided to live it." She crossed her arms, arching a brow. "You might as well have worn a sign that said, 'I love you, please notice me.'"

Heat flared up my neck, and I huffed out a breath. "You're insufferable."

"And you are a complete idiot." Her smirk faded slightly, replaced by something quieter. Something sharper. "You left me, Kaelan. At that damned temple."

I exhaled slowly, my chest tightening. "I didn't want to get you killed." The words felt weak now, brittle and worn from being spoken too many times in my head.

She scoffed. "Oh, sure, because clearly I'm safer when you abandon me in the middle of the capital. Brilliant strategy, truly. Tell me, did they teach you that in training?" She shook her head, something unreadable flickering behind her eyes. "You don't get to decide for me, Kaelan. You don't get to run off and play the martyr while I sit around twiddling my thumbs, hoping you come back in one piece."

I swallowed hard, forcing myself to meet her gaze. "I thought I was doing the right thing."

She rolled her eyes. "Well, congratulations, Sir Kaelan of Noble Sacrifices, you succeeded in making both of us miserable." Then, quieter, her voice losing its usual teasing lilt—"Next time, you don't get to make that choice alone."

For a moment, we just stood there, the weight of everything unspoken stretching between us.

Then she smirked again, punching my shoulder once more—softer this time. "Besides," she added, tilting her head. "If you really wanted to keep me safe, you should've let me just follow behind. Then I'd have an excuse to drive you insane from a safe distance."

Despite myself, I let out a breath of laughter. "That's probably the worst idea you've ever had."

"Give it time," she said breezily. "I'm sure I can come up with worse."

***

We sat by the side of the road still clinging to each other, her head on my shoulder, and my arms wrapped securely around her lithe body, and our fingers intertwined. She smelled faintly of lavender, a scent that brought with it a pang of familiarity and longing. In that moment, I felt at home—truly at home—for the first time in what felt like years. She reminded me of Elsenburg, of our farm, and the smell of the earth when it had been touched by dewdrops.  For the first time in days, I breathed freely, suddenly unburdened.

"Nobody is willing to help for nothing." I murmured. Quietly, I recounted my fruitless day—how the barkeep had stonewalled me, the futility of my search, and the hopelessness of my situation.  Lilah sat up abruptly, smoothing her clothes with unusual meticulousness.

"What…" I began, but she was already on her feet, her expression dark.

"Come on soldier boy," she marched toward the tavern door. Panic shot through me, and I scrambled after her. "Lilah, what are you doing?"

She didn't answer. The tavern door creaked as she shoved it open and strode inside. I followed, the smoky air stinging my eyes and throat. The hum of conversation faltered as patrons turned to watch us. The barkeep glanced up from wiping a mug, his wary eyes narrowing.

"Back again, are you?" he said, his tone sharp. "I told you, I don't have—"

Lilah's hand slammed onto the bar, cutting him off. Her dagger gleamed in her grip. She didn't brandish it but placed it on the counter with deliberate precision. The metallic clink silenced the room.

"You know what we seek," she said, her voice low but carrying an edge that made even me uneasy. The barkeep's gaze flicked to the blade, then to the tavern's corner, where a pair of rough-looking men sat watching us. "I don't want trouble," he muttered.

Lilah leaned closer, her voice dropping to a whisper that still managed to cut through the smoky air. "Neither do I. But if you don't tell us what we need, I'll make sure everyone here knows you sell secrets. Let's see how long you live after that. But if you tell us, I will gift you this." She slid the dagger across the table to his side.

The barkeep's hand stilled, the mug in his grip forgotten. "You've got a sharp tongue—"

"And you've got greedy eyes." She retorted.

The barkeep hesitated, glancing toward the patrons.

"Well? What is it going to be?" Lilah said with a little tilt of her eyebrows.

With a quick motion, he grabbed the blade and tucked it out of sight. Then, he cleared his throat, and rubbed his hands together.

We regarded him coldly.

"You didn't hear it from me," he muttered finally, leaning closer, "but there's a place." His voice was barely audible. "Down by the old warehouses, near the river. People go there when they don't want to be found. It's where the shadows meet."

Hope flared within me. Lilah cast me a glance and I nodded. "Thank you," I said, my voice steady, though my pulse pounded in my ears.

The barkeep jerked his head toward the door, his eyes on Lilah. "Get out of here." He still seemed a little jittery, "And watch your back. The people you're looking for... they don't like to be found."

Without another word, she turned on her heels and strode out, her arms swaying at her sides with a proud, unyielding grace. I followed close behind, watching her exit with an air of quiet defiance. The cold air of the alley hit me, biting into my skin, but I barely noticed it. My heart was pounding, with excitement. I stared at her, pride swirling in my chest. "There," she said. "We have our lead."

I stared at her. "You could've gotten us killed in there."

"We're not dead—and we have what we came for," she shot back, a wry smile tugging at her lips. "Now, are you coming or not?"

I smiled and took her hand. I had something —a place to go. And, by some stroke of fortune or grace, I also had her—a woman fierce and beautiful to call my own.

# CHAPTER
## 23

"What if you don't return… again?"

"Then know I am dead."

She let out an exasperated sigh. "Oh, fantastic. That's so reassuring. I'll be sure to tell your corpse 'I told you so.'"

I hesitated. "I don't want you to come," I murmured, my voice unsteady. "It's too dangerous."

Lilah crossed her arms, tilting her head. "Right. Because you're the only one allowed to do reckless, idiotic things. How silly of me to forget."

"Promise me, Kaelan. Promise you'll be back before dawn—then maybe I'll agree to this absolutely brilliant idea of yours."

I exhaled, shaking my head. "I can't promise that. But I'll return as soon as I can."

She swallowed hard, and for the first time since I had known her, a flicker of fear crossed her eyes—a fleeting shadow that gripped my chest like a vice. But just as quickly, she masked it with a scoff.

"Fine. Then at least promise you won't do anything spectacularly stupid, like getting yourself killed."

"I'll be back, Lilah," I said solemnly.

She huffed, rolling her eyes. "You'd better be. If you die, I will find a way to drag your sorry ass back just so I can kill you myself."

We stood in silence, the world around us fading into nothingness as we drew closer. I could feel her breath mingling with mine, grounding me to this moment—one I wasn't sure I'd ever get again.

Then, she stepped back and smiled faintly, her usual wit shining through the fear. "You'd better keep that promise— or I'll come drag you back myself. Even if you're a ghost."

I couldn't help but chuckle, though my chest ached. "I'd expect nothing less from you."

She tilted her head, her lips quirking in mock seriousness. "And, I'm taking the good blankets. You can haunt me all you like, but you'll do it cold."

I laughed softly, shaking my head. "Fair enough. It's a deal."

I leaned down and pressed my lips to hers. It wasn't just a kiss; it was a vow sealed in the quiet between our breaths. When we pulled apart, we touched our foreheads together, lingering in the connection.

And then, without another word, I turned and walked away, not daring to look back. The weight of her eyes followed me, a silent plea that burned into my soul.

\*\*\*

I moved quickly through the twisting streets of Edmundshire, forcing my mind to focus on the riddle. The shadows met there—down by the river, where people went to hide. It made sense now. The pieces were falling into place.

The streets grew quieter as I moved further from the heart of the city. The bustling noise of merchants and towns-folk faded, replaced by the distant clamor of carts rattling over cobblestones. The air grew colder, the darkness deeper, the shadows stretching across the narrow lanes as I made my way toward the river.

Soon, I heard the sound of rushing water, then the faint light of the moon reflecting off its surface. The warehouses loomed ahead, dark and silent, their windows broken, their doors hanging open. I approached cautiously, my eyes scanning the shadows, my hand resting on the hilt of my dagger beneath my cloak.

I moved between the buildings, the air cold against my skin, the shadows deep and endless. The city felt distant now, the faint sounds of life and movement barely audible. Here, it was too quiet—an eerie stillness that seemed to hang over everything.

My breath misted in the cold night air, my senses on high alert as I crept forward. I approached one of the warehous-es. It was large, with the door hanging crookedly from its hinges, the interior shrouded in darkness. I pushed the door open, the creak echoing through the silence, and stepped inside.

The air was stale, filled with the scent of old wood and mildew, and I could barely make out the outlines of crates stacked against the walls, covered in cobwebs. I moved from crate to crate, unsure of what I was searching for—perhaps a clue, a symbol, something that could lead me forward. But there was nothing.

Frustration bubbled up inside me. It seemed like another dead end. I leaned against one of the crates, my breath coming in short, heavy puffs. I needed to calm down, to think. There had to be something here—some reason that I was led to this place.

As I turned to leave, something caught my eye—a glint of metal in the moonlight filtering through a broken window. I turned, my eyes narrowing as I approached the source. It was a small piece of metal, wedged between two floorboards, partially hidden beneath a pile of old cloth.

I knelt and carefully brushed the cloth aside. And my breath caught in my throat. It was a Centralian medallion, old and worn, yet unmistakable—a dragon-lion, its wings unfurled, its mouth agape. .I reached out, my fingers curling around the cool metal as I lifted it, the intricate details of the dragon lion's scales glinting in the dim light.

This was no coincidence—this was either a sign or a trap. I turned the medallion over in my hand, my eyes catching sight of something etched into the back. A series of words, barely legible in the faint light.

Where the flag falls, the truth shall rise.

Another riddle.

My brow furrowed as I read the words again, my mind working to make sense of them. The flag of Centralia—was it referring to a specific place? Perhaps a location where a flag had once been taken down, a landmark of significance from the war? Or perhaps it was a landmark, somewhere significant, somewhere that would guide me to the truth.

I clenched the medallion in my hand as my mind ran wild. I was close—whether close to what I sought, or close to the trap that would finally ensnare me, I knew not. But I was close. I rose to my feet, slipping the medallion into my cloak.

Stepping back out into the cold night, I scanned the darkened streets, my heart pounding. The flag falling—where could that be? A place of significance, a place that was connected to Centralia and its history, but where?

I leaned against the wall of the warehouse, my fingers brushing against the medallion in my cloak, my mind turning over the words again.

Where the flag falls, the truth shall rise.

I closed my eyes, picturing the city in my mind—the streets, the landmarks, the places I had passed during my time here.

Where the flag falls...

It had to be a place that once held Centralia's influence. And then it hit me.

The old chancery.

My eyes snapped open. The chancery—once the Centralian Empire's embassy in Wintmore, a symbol of their presence in Edmundshire. When the war broke out, the chancery had been abandoned, the flag of Centralia ripped from its pole in a show of defiance by the Wintmorians. It was a place where the flag had literally fallen.

Where the flag falls...

I pushed away from the wall excitement bubbling in my stomach. I had a direction now—a place to go. Pulling my cloak tight around me, I moved swiftly through the streets, navigating the darkened alleys. The city was quieter now, the bustling market long gone, replaced by the eerie silence of the night.

I made my way toward the old chancery. My footsteps echoed off the cobblestones, as the narrow streets wound through the heart of the city. I kept to the shadows, my eyes searching the darkened windows, the empty doorways, every sense on high alert. I could feel it in my bones—I was close, closer than I had ever been.

*** 

The old chancery stood at the edge of a deserted square, its facade worn and crumbling, a forgotten relic of the past. The tall columns that had once marked its entrance were cracked, and ivy had begun to creep up the walls, reclaiming the building. I approached cautiously, my eyes darting around the dank ruins.

The windows were shattered, the doors sagging on their hinges. This had once been a place where emissaries gathered, where the affairs of nations had been negotiated. Now it was just another ruin, a forgotten chapter in the story of Centralia and Wintmore.

I moved closer, and as I did, I heard something—a whisper, the low murmur of voices coming from the shadows near the entrance of the chancery. I peered into the darkness. A group of figures stood huddled near the entrance, their faces obscured by the hoods of their cloaks. I could see them now, shifting and murmuring, their conversation hushed and urgent. I couldn't hear distinct words, just fragments of whispers drifting through the night.

I pressed myself against the wall, inching closer, my ears straining to catch more. But before I could make sense of their words, one of the figures suddenly looked up and their eyes met mine. My breath caught, and for a split second, everything seemed to freeze. The figure's face was partially hidden beneath the hood, but I could feel the intensity of their gaze. I knew I'd been spotted. A rush of blood surged through me, my muscles tensing as I prepared for whatever would come next.

"Hey!" one of them shouted, their voice reverberating in eerie echoes. The group shifted, their postures changing from casual to defensive in an instant.

I turned and fled. The sound of their footsteps followed almost immediately, the clamor of boots on cobblestones echoing in the empty square. My heart pounded in my ears as I darted out of the chancery building, down a narrow alleyway, my cloak billowing behind me. I could hear their muffled voices as they gave chase.

I raced through the winding streets, my eyes darting left and right, searching for a route that might give me an advantage. The alley twisted and turned, and I took each corner with as much speed as I could muster. I glanced over my shoulder, and they were there.

Promise me, Kaelan. Promise you will return before dawn.

I pushed myself harder, my lungs burning with the effort, the cold air searing as I gasped for breath. I'd return to Lilah. I'd not break that promise.

Ahead, I spotted a stack of old crates piled against the side of a building, leading up to a low rooftop. Without hesitation, I veered toward them, leaping onto the crates, my fingers gripping the edges as I scrambled up. The wood groaned under my weight, the crates shifting slightly. I sprinted across the rooftop, my knees grazing the rough surface. I couldn't stop to acknowledge the pain. I was swift, the tiles slick beneath my boots. The city opened up below me, a patchwork of uneven rooftops, winding streets and faintly glowing  lanterns. My footing faltered on the uneven surface, but I pressed on, each step sending jolts of pain through my legs.

I could hear the figures below, their voices growing more distant, the clamor of their pursuit muffled as I put distance between us.

There—an alleyway. I could hide there. I darted into the narrow passage, pressing myself behind a barrel, my breath coming in shallow gasps. I could hear their footsteps growing closer and I clenched my jaw, trying to steady my breathing.

The shadows deepened around me, and I heard them enter the alleyway, their boots crunching against the frozen ground. My heart felt like it would burst out of my chest. This was it—I would be discovered. There was nowhere left to run.

"Kaelan? A voice rang out, cutting through the tension.

The voice was familiar, and the shock of recognition washed over me like a wave. I froze, my heart pounding even harder as I peered around the barrel, staring at the figure who had spoken. The others turned to look at me too, their eyes searching the shadows.

Where had I heard that voice before? It was distant, like an echo from a past life—something I had almost forgotten amidst the chaos of war, of battle, and survival. But it was unmistakable, a voice I could never forget. There was only one person who had that voice.

Eamon.

# CHAPTER 24

It was unlike a feeling I had ever had before. My pulse roared in my ears as the realization slammed into me—Eamon. My brother. Alive?

The hooded figure stood just ahead, the dim light casting shadows over his face, but I knew. Somewhere deep in my bones, I knew. My vision blurred as I stumbled forward, my hands trembling at my sides.

"Kaelan? Is that you?"

The voice—hoarse, but achingly familiar—tore through me.

"Eamon?" I whispered, the name faltering on my lips as though saying it aloud might shatter the fragile hope. My voice broke on the name, disbelieving. I took a hesitant step forward, my vision swimming. The figure reached up, and as the hood fell back, my world tilted. There he was. Older, his face lined with wear and the weight of months I had not shared. His red hair matted and streaked with sweat, his eyes shadowed but unmistakably his. Eamon. My dearest brother, Eamon.

For a moment, time unraveled. I was back in Elsenburg. For a fleeting moment, the months fell away, and I saw the boy I used to chase through the meadows, laughing as he dared me to climb the tallest trees, the sun on his face.

"Kaelan…"

His voice cracked, and that single word broke something loose inside me. My legs moved before I could think, and suddenly I was running. His arms opened, and I collided into him. I was a little boy again, clutching him so tightly I thought we might both crumble. All the pain, the fear the suffering of the past several months fell off like scales and it was suddenly worth it.

"I thought—" The words stuck in my throat. I couldn't speak, couldn't think. The world blurred around us, swallowed by the only thing that mattered: he was here.

Eamon's arms wrapped around me, his grip unyielding, as if he feared letting go would undo it all. I felt his chest heave against mine, the weight of his breath as uneven as my own.

"I thought I'd never see you again," I choked out, my face buried in his shoulder. The scent of him—dirt, sweat, and the faintest trace of pine—was so achingly familiar it made my chest ache.

He pulled back just enough to grab my shoulders, his hands rough but steady. His eyes, wide and glassy, roamed my face as though trying to memorize every line, every scar.

"How…?" His voice wavered. "Why are you here?"

"Because I couldn't stop," I said, my voice raw. "I couldn't stop looking, Eamon. Not until I found you."

"When my men told me someone was meandering through Edmundshire, asking dangerous questions, you were the last person on my mind. I didn't…"

Eamon's lips trembled, and he pressed them together, his jaw tightening. For a moment, he said nothing, and the silence stretched between us, heavy and fragile.

"You're a damn fool," he muttered, his voice thick with something between a laugh and a sob.

I laughed too, a broken sound, and pulled him into another embrace. The weight of the past—the battles, the sleepless nights, the fear and hopelessness—fell away like a crumbling wall. For the first time in months, I felt light. Whole.

"How is Ma? Pa?"

"They are fine, as of when I left. But they were so worried. When your letters stopped…we thought of the worst."

"Kaelan…" he whispered, his voice raw. He stepped back, his hands still resting on my shoulders, and his eyes peering into my face. "You have changed. You look worn and weary."

I laughed, tears flowing down my face.

"And you look old."

We laughed some more, embracing each other.

"I thought I lost you," I whispered, my voice barely audible. "I thought—"

"You didn't," he said, his tone firm despite the tears brimming in his eyes. "I'm here. And so are you."

We stood there, two broken pieces of the same soul, holding onto each other as if the world might fall apart again if we let go.

***

Eamon held my face in his palms. "Little brother, you shouldn't be here. This city—it's dangerous. How did you even manage to get past the guards, the soldiers?"

I shook my head, a small smile tugging at my lips. "It wasn't easy," I admitted. "I had help—smugglers, the Crimson Merchant Alliance... I did whatever I had to do. I just had to find you, Eamon."

Eamon's eyes widened slightly at my words, a look of concern crossing his features. He glanced back at the others standing in the shadows, then returned his gaze to me, his brow furrowed.

"Kaelan, you don't understand. Things here are... complicated. I've been trying to lay low, trying to stay out of sight." Eamon's voice lowered, a hint of urgency creeping in. "There are people looking for me, people who wouldn't hesitate to—"

He stopped, shaking his head, his eyes filled with worry. He leaned in closer, his voice dropping to a whisper. "You being here puts us both in danger. "Come with me," he said, his voice calm but tense. "We need to move. It's not safe to talk here."

With that, Eamon turned, motioning for me to follow. I fell into step behind him, a strange sense of peace washing over me.

We moved through the darkened streets, slipping further into the city, away from the main roads and deeper into the narrow, twisting alleys. The air was biting cold, each breath visible as a puff of mist. Eamon moved with purpose, his steps quick and deliberate, and I followed close behind, my senses on high alert.

Finally, we reached a door, half-hidden in the shadows between two crumbling buildings. Eamon paused, glancing over his shoulder to make sure we hadn't been followed. I held my breath as I listened for any sign of pursuit, but all I could hear was the sound of the night. Eamon rapped lightly on the door. After a tense moment, the door creaked open, revealing a dimly lit interior. We stepped inside. Eamon closed the door behind us, sliding a heavy bolt into place.

The room was small and cluttered, filled with old furniture, maps, and other belongings scattered across a worn table. A fire burned low in the hearth, casting flickering shadows across the walls. The air was thick with the scent of wood smoke and something else—something musty and aged, as if this place had been hidden from the world for a long time. It felt like a sanctuary. The men there were dressed as he was; long cloaks with hoods. They stood at several points in the room with their weapons ready as if they were expecting an attack.

He turned to me, his face tense, and gestured toward a chair by the fire. "Sit," he said, his voice quiet but firm. I sank into the chair, the warmth of the fire a welcome relief from the cold that had seeped into my bones. I watched as Eamon moved across the room, his expression grave. He pulled another chair up across from me and sat down with a heavy sigh, his eyes never leaving my face.

There was a long silence, the only sound the crackling of the fire. Eamon looked at me as if he were trying to decide whether to include me in whatever he had been up to. The weight of whatever he was about to say was evident in his eyes. Finally, he spoke, his voice low and filled with a heaviness that made my chest tighten.

"Kaelan... there's so much you don't know. A lot that I haven't been able to tell you."

I frowned, leaning forward slightly. "What do you mean?" A part of me feared what he might say, but I needed to understand.

He sighed deeply. "I wasn't a merchant with the Crimson Merchant Alliance," he began, his voice carrying a hint of regret. He paused as if searching for the right words. "I was sent here by the Centralian Empire—by the Imperial Court itself."

My eyes crinkled in confusion. "Sent here? What do you mean, Eamon? What are you talking about?"

He leaned back in his chair, the shadows playing across his face. "I'm a member of the Centralian Imperial Spies. I was employed long before the war even began. My position with the Crimson Merchant Alliance was only a guise. The real purpose of my journey to Wintmore was never about trading goods. I came to gather tidings—secrets of their movements, whispers of their plans. The Empire needed someone who could slip through the shadows, unnoticed. Someone who could walk lightly, without stirring suspicion."

I stared at my brother, his words sinking in slowly. "You're... a spy?"

Eamon nodded, his face grim, the weight of his words settling heavily between us. "Yes," he said.

The memory hit me all at once—the first battle we fought in Wintmore, on our way to the Wintorian fortress. I recalled how one of their scouts had mistaken me for Eamon, calling me a Centralian spy before Cedric had taken his life. At the time, I'd been left dumbstruck, but now, I understood.

"And the reason I didn't contact you, why I couldn't return home, is because I was caught too deep in it. Things have grown more perilous here, Kaelan. There are those—those in power—who've caught wind of what's stirring. They know there are spies among them, and they've been hunting us like wolves."

Everything suddenly made sense—the secrecy, his disappearance, the rumors of tension in Wintmore. My brother hadn't just been caught up in the chaos of war—he had been part of it, working behind the scenes, risking his life every day. I clenched my jaw, my emotions swirling. Relief, anger, sadness—it was all there, tangled in a mess I couldn't unravel.

"But why didn't you tell us the truth?" I asked, my voice cracking under the strain of it all. "Why didn't you tell me? I could have helped you—"

Eamon shook his head, his expression softening. His eyes bore into mine, and I could see the pain behind them, a pain that spoke of sacrifices I couldn't even begin to imagine. "No, Kaelan. You couldn't have. It was my burden to bear. I had to do it alone, to shield all of you. If anyone had discovered—if they had known who I was, who I cared about—"

He trailed off, his voice thick with emotion, the unspoken words hanging between us like a heavy curtain. Part of me wanted to be angry, wanted to scream at him for keeping this from me, for making me believe he was gone. But more than that, I was just relieved. My brother was alive. He was standing in front of me, and that was enough.

"What now?" I finally asked, my voice barely above a whisper. "What do we do now?"

Eamon leaned forward, his eyes locking onto mine, fierce and determined. "Something is happening here, Kaelan. Something big. And I need to get you out of here before it all comes crashing down."

I shook my head, the words coming almost instinctively, driven by the stubborn fire inside me. "No," I said, my voice steady. "I'm not leaving, Eamon. I'm not going to turn around and run."

His expression darkened, his brow furrowing, frustration clear in the set of his jaw. "Kaelan, you don't understand. If they find out you're here, you are as good as dead."

I clenched my fists, the heat of anger boiling to the surface, my voice trembling as I spoke. "You think I'm unaware of the danger? That I haven't grasped the peril of all this? I know full well what I'm risking, Eamon. But I didn't journey here only to turn my back on you."

Eamon opened his mouth, his face contorting with the beginnings of another argument, but I cut him off, my voice rising. "You cannot fathom what I've endured to reach this place. You've no notion of the trials I've faced—nor the things I've lost." I paused, my chest heaving as I fought to steady myself. He needed to hear this—he needed to understand why I couldn't just leave.

"When you disappeared," I began, my voice steady despite the rawness I felt. "When your letters stopped coming, I thought you'd been trapped here. I took up arms with the Centralian Army in the hopes of finding you. We fought battles, Eamon—battles that tore men asunder and left friends lifeless in the snow. I watched comrades fall, men I had trained alongside. And then, when we were sent to Wintmore, I was abandoned—left for dead."

Eamon's eyes widened, shock flickering across his face, the pain evident as he listened to my words.

"I was trapped beneath the rubble of a fallen building, alone. I came close to death, but I survived. I clawed my way out of that ruin with nothing left save the faint hope that you might still be alive somewhere. And so I pressed on. I wandered through forests, and sickness took hold of me, but I found help from a stranger. I reached Eldermist and fell in with smugglers who dared to get me here, risking all to see me safely here."

"Oh, my little brother…"

My hands were trembling now, the intensity of my emotions spilling over, my gaze locked onto Eamon's. "Don't you see, Eamon? I didn't come all this way only to depart without you. Whatever the peril is, it matters not. I shall not leave you behind—not now, not ever."

# CHAPTER
## 25

The room was dimly lit, the flickering glow of a single lantern casting long, shifting shadows on the stone walls. Eamon's movements were quick and deliberate as he walked to the far end of the small room, where a worn map of Edmundshire and its surroundings was pinned to the wall. He motioned for me to join him, and I rose, following his gaze to the map. His face was taut, every line etched with a tension that made my chest tighten.

"We don't have much time," he said, his voice low but sharp. "I just received word—a rebel group tied to the Crown Prince's assassination is gathering tomorrow night."

The words hung in the air like a blade, sharp and cutting. My stomach twisted. "The assassination?" I echoed, my mind racing. "The same group that started this war?"

Eamon's jaw tightened as he nodded. "The very same. We've been chasing their shadow for months, Kaelan. They have always been one step ahead. But this time, it's different. This time, we know where they'll be."

He leaned over the map, jabbing a finger at a marked section near the city docks. "Here. It's an old warehouse tucked away in the district's back alleys. It's secluded, heavily guarded, and perfect for the kind of meeting they'd hold."

His brow furrowed. "There's something I need to show you," he said, pointing to a section of the city map—a district close to the old chancery where we had just been.

My eyes narrowed as I looked at the map. The district he pointed to was infamous—a labyrinth of crumbling buildings and forgotten pathways. It was the place one only ventured into if he didn't want to be found.

"How certain is this news?" I asked, though the urgency in Eamon's voice left little room for doubt.

"Certain enough to act. We've been on their trail for months, yet they always seem one step ahead. This may be our chance to uncover the truth—what truly transpired, who is behind it, and the reason for it all." I took a deep breath, the weight of the situation pressing down on me. The Crown Prince's assassination had been the spark that ignited the war between Centralia and Wintmore—the reason I had taken up arms, and lost so much. And now, the possibility of confronting the ones responsible loomed ahead of us.

"What's the plan?" I asked, my voice steady.

Eamon turned, his eyes locking onto mine.

"Kaelan, It's…This is too dangerous."

I set my lips. "We have already talked about this. I am going with you."

He regarded me for a moment and smiled faintly, then he grabbed a seat towards me and sat down. "First," he said, "we need to know more. The gathering is to occur on the morrow eve, in an old storehouse near the docks. It is fiercely guarded, and the number of their ranks is uncertain. We must proceed with great caution. If they suspect we are upon them, we'll lose everything."

I nodded, my mind already churning the possibilities, the risks. "We need to know their numbers, their defenses. We need to figure out the best way to approach without being seen."

Eamon gestured to the map again, tracing a route with his finger. "I've scouted the area a few times. There's an old canal that runs underneath the district—if we can get to it, we might be able to get close without being detected. It won't be easy, but it's our best shot."

I studied the map, my eyes following the route Eamon had outlined. It was risky but it was our only chance.

"We need to prepare," Eamon continued. "Supplies, weapons—whatever we can get our hands on. We have no idea what we're walking into, so we need to be ready for anything."

We set to work, going over the plan and discussing every detail. It was like old times again, we were like rangy children again conspiring together and driving our parents insane. By the time we finished going over the plan, the room was filled with a tense silence. The hooded comrades of Eamon's cause had long since retired, leaving the two of us. Eamon sat by the fire, absently poking at the embers with a stick. The soft crackle of the flames was the only sound, wrapping the room in an almost eerie stillness.

I leaned back in my chair, and for the first time in several months, I was enveloped in a feeling of peace. I had everything I had ever wanted.

"Eamon," I said quietly, breaking the silence.

He looked up, his gaze steady. "What is it?"

I hesitated, my fingers tracing the edge of the table. "There's something I need to tell you. Something I should've told you before now."

Eamon frowned, setting the stick aside. "Out with it, Kaelan."

I hesitated, the words catching in my throat. "There's someone..." I began, "Someone waiting for me. Her name is Lilah."

Eamon's expression softened. "A girl, huh?"

"She's Wintmorian," I said, looking into his face searching for any change in his countenance. "And I love her, Eamon. She's in the temple of Oerhzn, likely pacing the floor, worrying about whether I'll come back."

Eamon's eyes widened slightly, but he said nothing. I pressed on, my voice shaking. "I know it's foolish, Eamon. I know how it sounds. The woman I love belongs to the side we've been fighting against. But she is not like them. She's kind, brave, and she saved my life when she didn't have to."

For a long moment, Eamon was silent, his gaze searching mine. Finally, he spoke, his voice calm but firm. "Kaelan," he said, "I have been trying to say something to you. Wintmore might not be the enemy you think them to be. The true enemies are the ones who orchestrated the murder of the Prince. They are the ones that started this war."

I stared at him, stunned. "You believe that?"

"I do," he said firmly. "And if this Lilah of yours is the one who makes you happy—if she's the one who gives you hope, even amid all this chaos—then you owe it to yourself to fight for her. Don't let this war, or anyone else, take that away from you."

A lump rose in my throat, and I looked away, suddenly overwhelmed by his words. Eamon had always been the braver of us, the one who could see the truth when my doubts blinded me.

"Thank you," I whispered.

Eamon clapped a hand on my shoulder, his grip firm. "You're lucky, brother," he said, a rare smile tugging at his lips. "Not many people find love in a world like this. If you love this woman, then I'll do whatever it takes to help you get back to her."

I was suddenly ready to face anything; for the truth, for my brother, and for Lilah.

# CHAPTER
# 26

When I awoke, daylight was already seeping in through the narrow cracks in the walls, painting the room in muted gold. I rubbed my eyes and realized the stiffness in my body had drained away. Across the room, Eamon sat at the table, bent over the map, his brow furrowed in thought.

"Finally awake?" he murmured without looking up.

I grunted in response and joined him at the table. He looked pensive. He reached into his tunic and withdrew a small object dangling from a leather cord. With deliberate care, he placed it in my open palm.

"This is called the Heartguard," he said, his voice solemn. "Wear it around your neck. It will shield you from harm when courage falters."

The trinket rested heavy in my hand, its intricate carvings all too familiar. My fingers tightened around it, shock rippling through me.

"Eamon..."

His brows drew together. "What's wrong?"

Wordlessly, I reached under my tunic and pulled out my battered amulet—its surface dulled, its magic long spent. Eamon's eyes widened as he stared, disbelief etched into his features.

"How?" he whispered, his voice barely audible.

"An old peddler in Central gave this to me," I said, my words tumbling out. "He said it would guide me when courage failed… or something like that. I didn't believe him, but it saved my life…"

Eamon was silent, but his silence was weighty. His gaze flickered between my face and the worn talisman and I could see the gears turning in his mind, the pieces falling into place.

"Eamon?"

He exhaled sharply, running a hand through his hair. "Do you remember the day before I left home?"

"Yes?"

His lips quirked into a wistful smile. "We went to the market. You ran errands while I… I sought out Veylor, the thaumaturge. I made a pact with him. This amulet was crafted to find you and keep you safe until we could be reunited."

My heart thudded painfully in my chest. "You did this for me?"

His eyes glistened as he nodded. "The charm worked, Kaelan. It found you, protected you. And now, it's time it serves you again."

Gently, he took the mangled amulet from my hand and looped the Heartguard around my neck. It felt warm against my skin, the amulet's subtle hum of magic steady and soothing, as though it recognized me.

"This is yours now," Eamon said, his voice steady but thick with emotion.

The warmth of the amulet seeped into my chest, chasing away the last remnants of doubt. For the first time in what felt like years, I felt grounded—connected not only to my brother but to something greater.

\*\*\*

We spent the next few hours gathering supplies—torches, weapons, extra cloaks—reminiscing about home and talking about how he found me.

Eamon said that the moment I set foot in Edmundshire, he knew, but he didn't know it was his brother. His web of cloaked eyes stretched further than I could imagine and they had whispers of a stranger in the capital—someone asking after Eamon. They could not decide if I was a friend or foe, so they chose to watch me closely. They placed their marks along my path, subtle hints meant to lure me into their grasp.

Eamon had never ceased to amaze me. I stared at him, my mouth agape, while he grinned in his usual boyish manner. I saw layers of my brother I hadn't seen before, and my heart swelled with pride.

We talked and ate, and by the time evening approached, we were ready. Eamon pulled on a heavy cloak, wrapping it tightly around himself.

"It's time."

I pulled on my own cloak, making sure my sword was secure. We left the hideout, stepping into the cold night air. Edmundshire was alive with movement, but Eamon led me away from the busy streets and kept to the shadows. We moved quickly and quietly, the sound of our footsteps barely audible against the cobblestones.

The city seemed to grow quieter as we approached the canal, the noise of the bustling market and townsfolk fading into the distance. The entrance to the canal lay at the edge of the old district, partially concealed by the remains of an ancient archway. Eamon paused, turning to me, his eyes meeting mine in the dim light.

"This is it," he whispered. Then, he led the way forward, crouching as he slipped through the archway, the shadows swallowing him up. I followed closely, feeling the chill of the underground air wrap around me as we entered the canal.

It was dark, the air thick with dampness and the musty scent of stagnant water. The only light came from the torch Eamon held, its flame flickering and threatening to go off as we ventured deeper into the tunnels. The soft echo of our footsteps reverberated off the stone walls, the canal stretching out before us like an endless labyrinth.

We moved in silence, our eyes ever watchful as we went. With each step we took, the noise of the bustling city above faded further away until all that remained was the sound of water trickling and the occasional groan of ancient stone shifting in the darkness.

At a point, the tunnel split, branching off in several different directions. Eamon paused, studying the map, his brow furrowed as he traced the paths with his fingers.

"This way," he whispered, nodding to the left. I followed without question. The dim glow of the torch was barely enough to pierce the gloom that surrounded us. I kept close to Eamon, every sense heightened, the weight of my sword resting at my side, providing a small comfort. My nerves were on edge, my eyes darting to every shadow, every possible hiding place where danger could lurk.

The deeper we went, the colder it became. Eventually, we came to a narrow, low passage that led upward. The walls were slick with moisture. Eamon gestured for me to follow, and we moved forward, ascending a set of worn, uneven stone steps. At the top, there was a small, heavy door, the wood ancient and cracked, the iron handle covered in rust. Eamon paused, pressing his ear to the door, his eyes closed as he listened intently.

I held my breath, and listened too, my heart thundering in my ears. There were no other sounds beyond the door— no voices, no movement.

Eamon gave me a curt nod before slowly, carefully, pulling the door open just enough for us to slip through. I stepped in after him, blinking as we entered a darkened room. The floor was covered in layers of dust, the air thick and musty. It was an old storage area, long abandoned, except for a faint glow of torchlight leaking through the cracks around a large wooden door on the far side of the room.

Eamon motioned for me to keep low, and we moved together, avoiding the patches of light spilling from the gaps in the door. The flickering light cast eerie shadows across the stone walls, illuminating cobwebs and remnants of what once was a busy storage area.

I could hear it now—voices, muffled but urgent, coming from beyond the door. I exchanged a glance with Eamon and we moved closer to the door, inching forward until we were right beside it. Eamon crouched down, his hand resting against the doorframe as he leaned in, listening intently. I followed his lead, pressing myself against the cold stone wall, my heart pounding so loudly in my ears that I feared it might betray us.

The voices on the other side grew clearer now, fragments of conversation finally reaching us, distinguishable amidst the crackle of the torches. There was an edge to the voices—a sense of urgency, of planning. I could hear mentions of supplies, of strategy, and hints of something about to happen. My throat was dry, and I clenched my hands into fists to steady myself. Slowly, cautiously, Eamon leaned forward, easing the door open just enough to take a look inside. I mirrored his movement, peering through the narrow opening, my eyes adjusting to the dim light that spilled into the hallway.

What I saw made my breath catch.

The room was larger than I had anticipated, with a high ceiling supported by thick stone columns that cast long, dark shadows across the floor. Torches were mounted on the walls, their flickering flames giving off a muted, almost haunting light. In the center of the room stood a group of men—the rebels, I assumed—gathered around a table covered with maps and parchments. The tension in their stance, and the intensity of their discussion, all spoke of something imminent.

But it wasn't the assassins that held my attention—it was the others.

# CHAPTER
## 27

Figures draped in white and red hoods stood in a circle, their faces obscured by shadows cast from flickering torchlight. Their cloaks, stitched with strange symbols and tightened by leather straps crisscrossing their torsos, gave them the look of ritualistic soldiers. The room seemed to bow to their presence, their silent authority forcing even the hardened assassins to lower their heads in reverence. Every movement they made, every shift in the dim light, was deliberate, and calculated. They spoke in a low, rhythmic language that was foreign to me—almost melodic, yet brimming with menace. Standing next to them was a man, clearly an interpreter, who translated their words into the harsh Wintmorian dialect. The rebels listened intently, nodding eagerly, their eyes wide with fervor.

I leaned closer, straining to make sense of the conversation. The interpreter's voice was tense, urgency marking every word. They spoke of plans—movements, targets—of Centralia, of borders, and an upcoming assault.

I glanced at Eamon, crouched beside me, and saw the fear in his eyes. He recognized them. And the realization on his face said it all—this was far beyond anything we could have imagined. Whatever was happening here was bigger than a group of radicals plotting in secret. The figures in white and red spoke again, their voices calm, commanding, as if they held the upper hand; as if they knew they were in control of whatever was about to unfold. A chill ran down my spine, a deep sense of foreboding settling over me.

This wasn't just a group of rebels acting alone—this was part of something larger, more sinister. Someone—some force—had orchestrated the assassination of the Crown Prince, had wanted this war, and had manipulated both sides into conflict, costing countless innocent lives. I clenched my hands into fists, my heart pounding in my ears as I stared at the figures, their voices low and malevolent.

I glanced back at Eamon, whispering urgently, "Who are they?"

Eamon's face was pale. "They're the Astari."

The words hit me like a blow, and a cold shiver ran down my spine. The Astari. I had heard that name countless times—spoken in fear, whispered in hatred. The Astari had always been rivals of Centralia—a people divided by culture, by faith, by blood. We had once been part of the same clan, but centuries of conflict had turned us into mortal enemies. And now, they were here, in the heart of Wintmore, conspiring with our enemies to tear both empires apart.

I leaned in closer, straining to hear every word as the interpreter spoke, his voice cold and deliberate. "The time is approaching," he translated, his gaze sweeping across the rebels gathered around the table. "Once the Centralians are sufficiently weakened, our forces will move in to assist you in taking control of Wintmore. The current ruling family will be eradicated, and a new rule will rise—one that will lead Wintmore to greatness once again."

I felt my breath catch in my throat, my eyes widening as the full weight of the words sank in. In the end, the Astari would finally become the ruler of the two empires. It gave me chills.

"We will provide the support you need," the interpreter continued, his tone matter-of-fact. "Once the Empire of Wintmore is under your control, we will turn our sights to the true enemy. Together, we will eradicate Centralia, and we will take our rightful place in these lands."

A heavy realization settled over me like a lead weight, squeezing the air from my lungs. The Astari were the true enemy—the enemies in the shadows, pulling strings with cold precision. My hands trembled as the enormity of their scheme sank in. This wasn't just about strategy or power. It was about lives—countless lives torn apart by a conflict they had manufactured. My thoughts flashed to the faces of my family, my friends, and every innocent soul who had suffered and would suffer because of this war. The weight of my helplessness pressed harder, a visceral ache in my chest. How could we ever hope to stop something so calculated, so monstrous? My heart pounded in my chest, rage building as I watched the rebels nod in agreement, their faces alight with zeal. They were being used—puppets in a larger game, pawns in a scheme that would see both Wintmore and Centralia brought to their knees. I glanced at Eamon, feeling the tension radiating between us. His eyes were dark and smoldering. This was far beyond anything we had imagined—a conspiracy that went to the very heart of the war, a plot that threatened everything we had fought for, everything we had lost.

We had to do something. We couldn't let this happen. We had to find a way to stop it, to warn our people, to make sure that both Wintmore and Centralia knew the truth. Eamon's hand tightened around my arm, a silent signal—we needed to get out of there. Now. We'd heard enough. I nodded, my heart still pounding as I began to back away from the door, my eyes still fixed on the group in the room. And then—

A soft creak echoed in the silence, the old wooden door groaning under the shift of weight. The sound slithered through the chamber like a serpent, every head snapping toward it in an instant. My heart plummeted as the men turned, their eyes narrowing, like wolves catching the scent of prey.

"What was that?" one of them growled, his voice sharp with suspicion.

We were trapped, caught like a game in a snare, and the sheer inevitability of what might follow sent an icy shiver racing down my spine. Eamon's grip tightened on my arm, a silent plea to move. But before we could take another step, the door burst open and several rebels surged out, their weapons drawn and faces twisted in fury. "There!" one of them shouted, pointing directly at us, his voice echoing off the stone walls. "Spies!"

The narrow passageway erupted into pandemonium. Torches flickered wildly as shadows danced along the stone walls, the sharp ring of steel filling the confined space. My heart thundered in my chest as I drew my sword, my knuckles white around the hilt. Eamon and I exchanged a glance—an unspoken agreement. We couldn't run. The first rebel lunged, his cudgel, swinging in a deadly arc. I ducked, the rush of air brushing past my head, and lashed out with my sword. The blade carved into his side and he staggered back with a strangled cry.

Beside me, Eamon moved like a whirlwind, his blade slicing through the narrow space with precision, disarming an attacker in a single fluid motion.

"Move!" Eamon shouted, shoving me forward as more men poured into the passageway. We fought our way through the tight corridor, the walls closing in around us, the flickering torchlight casting wild shadows that danced with the chaos of the battle. Amidst the chaos, my eyes darted back to the chamber. The Astari were already moving. Like phantoms, they slipped through a hidden passageway at the far end, their white and red cloaks flowing behind them. The torchlight caught the strange symbols stitched into their garments while they disappeared, seemingly otherworldly, untouchable.

"No!" The word tore from my throat, raw with frustration. I blocked another blow, my sword flashing upward to counter. "They're fleeing!"

Eamon parried a strike and shoved me forward, his expression hard. "Let them go! We cannot follow—not now!"

I gritted my teeth, frustration and anger bubbling in my throat as I struck down another assailant. The Astari's deliberate movements, their calm amidst the chaos, burned into my mind. They vanished into the shadows as if the very walls had devoured them. It was as though they were apparitions; ghostly orchestrators of destruction who left no trace, no proof of their presence.

Eamon's shout cut through the melee. "The exit! It's near!"

I saw it—the faint light of the canal's mouth, a sliver of salvation in the suffocating darkness. My lungs burned, my limbs screamed for rest, but we fought our way toward the light. Behind us, the rebels hesitated at the threshold, their shouts echoing like a pack of hounds denied their quarry. The cold night air hit me like a jolt, and I stumbled out into the open, gasping for breath.

Eamon grabbed my arm, pulling me further away. I cast one last glance over my shoulder, toward the darkness of the canal The Astari's departure lingered in my mind like a splinter, their escape a haunting reminder of their power. They hadn't just fled—they had retreated on their terms, knowing they held all the cards.

And I hated them for it.

# CHAPTER
## 28

We ran into the streets, our feet pounding against the cobblestones. Shouts echoed in the distance, the rebels growling like cornered tigers. The cold night air bit into my skin and my breath clouded in the frigid air as we moved through the darkened alleyways. But the rebels had followed us. Perhaps they knew the stakes were too high. We knew too much. I could hear their footsteps, the clatter of armor, and the shouts and chatter as they closed in. Eamon and I ducked around a corner, only to be met with a group that cut us off.

"Eamon!" I shouted in desperation. Eamon turned just in time, his eyes widening as he saw the soldiers in front of us.

He growled and drew his sword.

The rebels lunged at us, their weapons glinting in the dim moonlight. I braced myself, my sword raised as I moved to intercept the closest attacker. The clash of steel echoed through the narrow street, ringing in my ears. An assailant's mace whistled past my head, the rush of air brushing my skin as I ducked just in time. I seized the opportunity and drove my sword into his side. He grunted in pain, his knees buckling as I twisted the blade. I felt the comforting heat from my amulet—my brother's gift. It guided my hands as I slashed and fought my way through.

Eamon was beside me, his sword flashing in the darkness, each strike precise and powerful. He parried a blow, his movements swift as he disarmed one of the soldiers, the clatter of a weapon dropped in the chaos. Another armed man lunged at him, but Eamon sidestepped, using the man's speed against him, sending him crashing into the wall.

Eamon's shout cut through the noise. "Keep moving!"

I nodded, my heart pounding, my body aching from the relentless battle. Everything was a blur— shouting, clanging steel, and desperate movement. More rebels appeared ahead, their faces twisted with hatred. The narrow street was chaos— steel against steel, screams, grunts of pain, everything echoing off the stone walls. Each clash of steel sent jolts through my aching arms. I couldn't fail—not here, not now. If I faltered, it wasn't just my life on the line. Eamon needed me, and the fate of Centralia and Wintmore lay in our hands.

I caught a glimpse of Eamon, his face set in fierce determination, his movements almost primal as he fought. My brother. He was my anchor amidst this chaos, and even outnumbered, I knew that if we could hold on together, we might have a chance. But the walls were closing in. More soldiers pressed forward, their footsteps an unending march of doom. We were losing ground, pushed back further with each second, and I could feel panic rising in my chest. The narrow street left us no room to move, no space to breathe, and the weight of each attack felt like it was crushing me. My breaths came in ragged gasps, my vision blurring from fatigue.

"Eamon!" I yelled, my voice barely audible over the noise.

He grunted, parrying a strike aimed at his head. His eyes darted around, desperate, looking for a way out. I could see the same exhaustion written on his face—the strain in his eyes, the sweat that streamed from his brow. He deflected a blow, his sword cutting deep into an assailant's chest, and I heard the man cry out as he fell to the ground. But more were coming. It felt endless—wave after wave, as if every shadow brought another wave of enemies to kill us.

The narrow alley twisted and turned, its walls too close together. Suddenly, the path ended and towering walls barred our way. 'We're trapped!' I gasped, panic surging. Eamon didn't pause, his fingers already working the stones. A shout behind us made my blood run cold—the rebels were closing in.

"There!" Eamon shouted suddenly, pointing toward a narrow alleyway to our right. It was barely wide enough for a person to fit through. My pulse raced as I cut down the soldier in front of me, my sword slicing across his chest. I pushed forward, forcing my way toward the alley. Eamon fought beside me, his sword a blur, cutting down anyone who tried to stop us. We carved a path toward the alley, each step feeling like a small victory against the overwhelming odds.

I reached the entrance first, slipping into the narrow space, my shoulders scraping against the rough stone walls. I turned back, my heart in my throat as I saw Eamon still fending off the soldiers. "Come on!" I shouted.

He blocked a final strike and turned towards me, his eyes wild. "Go!" he said, his voice strained.

No, I screamed inwardly. I couldn't leave him behind. I watched as he cut down the man beside him and quickly slipped through. I helped pull him in, and together, we pushed a heavy slab of stone over the entrance until we had completely blocked the rebels. We ran until the sounds of the soldiers faded behind us; until my legs felt like they would give out, and the pain in my side was almost unbearable. My breaths came in ragged gasps, but I didn't dare stop until I was certain that it was only Eamon and I, alone in the darkness.

Finally, we slowed, coming to a stop in a narrow, darkened space between two buildings. My legs gave out, my back hitting the wall as I slid to the ground. The pain in my side flared, but it was nothing compared to the relief of stillness. "We made it," Eamon panted beside me, the hint of a grin tugging at his lips.

"Barely," I said and coughed out a laugh. We had made it out, but the fight was far from over. It was just beginning.

# CHAPTER
## 29

It was now almost midnight, and the darkness was absolute, save for the faint glimmer of stars above. Eamon straightened and leaned into me. "Follow me," he said, his eyes darting through the shadows.

I got up and immediately followed close behind. He moved quickly, slipping into the twisting alleys. My senses were heightened—every shadow shifting, every distant noise, every sound of the wind was a threat. Each step we took was deliberate, our footfalls barely making a sound against the cobblestones.

The city was empty. The silence was thick around us, and the few windows we passed were shuttered tight. I kept my hood pulled low and rested my hand on the hilt of my sword. Eamon led us through the maze of backstreets, avoiding the main roads where the rebels would likely be searching for us. He ducked beneath an archway and slipped through a narrow passage that seemed to stretch on endlessly. I followed, trusting his instincts. We moved like ghosts, our breathing shallow as we crept through alleyways that seemed to stretch on forever. Suddenly, Eamon held up a hand, and I stopped dead, my heart leaping into my throat. I strained to listen and heard the faint sound of soldiers' boots in the distance, growing louder, closer. He gestured for me to follow him, and we ducked into a darkened corner, pressing ourselves against the wall. I held my breath and watched as some soldiers passed by, their shadows moving across the ground in front of us.

The footsteps receded, and Eamon glanced at me, nodding slightly before we moved again, even more silently this time. My legs ached, and my arm throbbed from the cut, but I pushed through the pain.

Finally, we reached a small, nondescript door tucked away in the shadows of a narrow side street. Eamon paused, his eyes roaming the street around us, making sure we hadn't been followed. Then he knocked on the door in a specific pattern—three quick taps, a pause, then two more.

There was a moment of silence and then the door creaked open. A pair of wary eyes peered out from the darkness, widening in recognition when they saw Eamon and me. The door swung open fully, revealing a young man with long, black hair.

"Rylan." Eamon greeted.

"Get in, quick," Rylan said, stepping aside to let us in. We entered and the door closed heavily behind us, the bolt sliding into place with a reassuring thud.

I let out a long breath. The room was dimly lit, and the flickering light of a few of the other spies was there, their expressions shifting from wariness to surprise as they saw us enter. Rylan stepped forward. He was one of the men I had seen with Eamon earlier—one of the hooded figures. He enveloped Eamon in a bear hug.

"What happened? We heard shouting outside—"

"The rebels found us," Eamon cut in, his voice strained. "We had to fight our way out."

Rylan's eyes widened, and he exchanged a glance with the others in the room. "Did you find what you seek?"

Eamon nodded, his expression grim. "We did. It's worse than we thought. The Astari are involved. They're working with the rebels, planning to overthrow Wintmore and use its forces to destroy Centralia once the war is over."

The room fell into a heavy silence, Eamon's words settling over us like a dark shroud. Rylan let out a slow breath, his eyes narrowing in anger. "We need to get this news back to Centralia."

"We will," Eamon replied. "From this point, we must be careful. They know we're onto them, and they are looking for us. We must be careful but must also move quickly."

The men murmured their approval of what we had done. They looked older, but they seemed to have accepted Eamon's leadership and quiet strength. I saw how they looked at him for guidance, and pride brewed in my stomach. We quietly settled down for the night. The others gathered the maps, documents, and weapons, and carefully placed them in their proper places. Eamon unfurled a mat near the door and we lay down together. Rylan claimed the bed, while the two men I didn't know well moved toward the hearth to sleep. Suddenly, a sharp knock echoed through the room and we all jerked up in one swift movement. Eamon and I locked eyes and my hand hovered over my sword. Then the knock came again followed by the splintering of wood as the door was kicked in. Before we could think, a group of rebels charged in, their weapons gleaming in the dim candlelight.

"Get out!" Eamon shouted, his voice cutting through the chaos. "Now."

# CHAPTER
# 30

The room erupted into chaos—steel clashed, men screamed, and blood spattered the stone walls. I lunged forward, my sword finding its place in the ribs of one of the rebels.

Beside me, Rylan fought with wild swings, his focus faltering. Suddenly, he screamed, "Eamon, go to—"

His words ended in a strangled gasp, his eyes widening as a rebel's blade pierced his side. Blood blossomed across his tunic, and he crumpled to the ground in a heap. His body lay on the blood-soaked ground, his lifeless eyes fixed on nothing. Eamon screamed as if his world had narrowed to the unmoving form of his friend.

"Rylan!" Eamon fell to his knees beside his friend, his body trembling. For a heartbeat, the battle noise faded into a muted hum, and all I could remember was the stubborn grin Rylan had flashed just hours ago. Eamon held Rylan and sobbed as if he had forgotten where he was. But the clash of steel dragged him back. The enemy pressed closer, their shadows stretching like claws over Rylan's lifeless body. Each step back felt like a race against death. Eamon clenched his jaw and forced himself to his feet. There was no time to grieve—I knew the suffocating feeling too well.

"Kaelan, let's go!" His face was blank. I looked around. The room was in disarray—Our comrades fought for their lives as the rebels poured through the shattered door. The sounds of clashing steel echoed off the stone walls. One by one, our men fell—their bodies crumpling to the ground.

Eamon grabbed my arm, yanking me toward the door. "Come on!" There was nothing else we could do for the others. He led the way, cutting a path through the attackers, his movements swift and precise. I followed, slashing at the rebels as we fought our way to the exit. The air was thick with the smell of blood and smoke, the flickering candlelight casting wild, dancing shadows across the stone walls.

\*\*\*

The cold night air slammed into us as we ran into the streets. The sounds of the fight faded as we ran farther away from the violence. Eamon pulled me down a narrow alley, our footsteps echoing in the darkness, the shadows of the city hiding us as we fled.

We ducked into a narrow side street, pressing ourselves into the shadows. The alley reeked of damp stone and rot, but even the stench couldn't smother the iron tang of blood still clinging to my senses. Eamon's eyes darted across the darkness, his body coiled like a spring, every muscle ready to snap into action at the faintest sound.

"We have to leave for Centralia at once," he whispered fiercely. "The Emperor needs to know."

"Lilah!" The thought of her slammed into me, hard and insistent, drowning out everything else.

I grabbed Eamon by the shoulders. "I must get Lilah! Please, Eamon! I made a promise!"

Eamon's brow furrowed, but his eyes softened as if he already knew there would be no convincing me otherwise. He opened his mouth to protest, but I cut him off, my voice shaking. "Stay here. Wait for me. I'll get her, and then we'll—"

"No." His voice was firm, a blade of resolve. "We go together."

"Eamon—"

"We're marked men, Kaelan," he said, gripping my arm tightly. "If we split up, we won't make it out of this city alive. But together, we might stand a chance."

I hesitated, torn between fear and urgency, the weight of my promise to Lilah clashing with the grim reality of our situation. The shadows of the alley seemed to close around us, heavy and suffocating. I clenched my jaw, my chest tight with unspoken thoughts. Could I risk her safety for our lives? Could I bear the thought of leaving her behind in this cursed city?

"Where is she?" Eamon's voice cut through my haze.

I swallowed hard. "The temple of Oerhzn."

His lips pressed into a thin line as he nodded. "Come. I know a shortcut."

Without another word, we slipped into the labyrinth of narrow paths. The city had become a ghost of itself, every corner laden with danger. Shadows loomed like silent sentinels, their edges flickering with the distant glow of torchlight. Every creak, every shuffle of rats in the gutters, set my nerves alight.

The cold was unrelenting, the wind slicing through my cloak and seeping into my bones. But I welcomed it. The bite kept me awake, kept me moving. Each step forward was a battle against the weight in my chest, the questions that gnawed at me: Would she even agree to leave with me? Would she trust me enough to follow me into the unknown?

As we turned a corner, the broader streets came into view, and there it stood—the temple. Its spires stretched into the night like the fingers of some long-forgotten god, silhouetted against the faint blush of dawn creeping over the rooftops.

"Kaelan…" Eamon murmured, but I was already moving, my legs carrying me forward before I could think. The air was alive with the distant sounds of the waking city—the clatter of merchants readying their carts, the bark of dogs, idle chatter—but all I could hear was the thunderous beat of my heart.

Inside, Lilah waited—but would she follow me home?

# CHAPTER
# 31

I knocked softly on the priest's door, the sound dull against the thick, weathered wood. It creaked open, and his kind, lined face emerged, framed by the flickering glow of a single candle. His faded eyes scanned me, then shifted to Eamon, before returning to mine with a faint frown.

"So, the wayward returns," he muttered, his voice a low rasp, his usual gregariousness gone. "And what kind of husband, may I ask, leaves his young wife alone for so long?"

His words hit harder than I cared to admit. "I've been a fool, priest," I said simply. I had no more to add.

He grumbled under his breath, words lost to the creak of the door as he stepped aside. The room smelled of parchment and incense, a familiar, almost comforting scent. Without waiting for further words, I strode past him toward the far end of the modest dwelling.

Candlelight spilled through the crack of an open door, and I hesitated my pulse quickening. When she appeared, her breath hitched as if she'd seen a ghost.

"Your alive, thank the gods," she breathed, her voice trembling, as she flew to me. Her arms wrapped around me tightly, as though afraid I might vanish again. For a moment, the world fell away. Her scent, her warmth, the rhythm of her breath against mine—everything felt like home.

I closed my eyes, my lips brushing her temple. "I'm here now, Lilah," I murmured.

She pulled back slightly, studying me with wide eyes. "Kaelan, you… you look different. Are you all right?"

A sharp laugh escaped me, unbidden and too loud for the quiet room. "I'm well," I said, though even I could hear the tremor in my voice.

Her fingers brushed my cheek. "You look like you've been fighting monsters."

I wanted to tell her everything. How the journey had stripped me bare, how the war loomed over us like a noose tightening around us. Instead, I forced a smile. "It's over now. I've found him."

Her gaze shifted past me to Eamon, her brow furrowing as she studied him. "This is your brother?"

"Yes," I said, a real smile breaking through for the first time. "Eamon, meet Lilah."

She tilted her head, scrutinizing him with an almost child-like curiosity. "He looks so much like you, Kaelan... It's almost uncanny."

"I'll take that as a compliment," Eamon replied dryly, his lips twitching with the faintest hint of a smile.

Before more could be said, I took her hands in mine. "Lilah, we must leave at once. Centralia awaits, and you must come with us."

The light in her eyes dimmed, hesitation flickering like a candle struggling against the wind. "Kaelan… this is my home. My whole life is here."

Eamon stepped forward, his presence suddenly commanding. "You don't understand the danger," he said, his voice low but urgent. "This war is a web of lies and manipulation. To stay here would be more perilous."

She looked between us. "What are you talking about?"

I sat her on the cot and knelt before her, my grip tightening on her hands. "The Wintmorians aren't the enemy, Lilah. Neither are the Centralians. There's more at stake than we ever imagined. If we don't warn our Emperor, this war will consume us all."

Her shoulders sagged as the enormity of it all weighed down on her. "And if I go?" she asked, her voice barely above a whisper.

"Then we fight together," I said. "And you and I will have a chance at something beyond survival. Something real." My voice faltered. "But if you stay… I can't leave you behind. I won't leave you behind…"

Silence stretched between us, heavy and suffocating. Her gaze dropped to the floor, hands clasped tightly before her. For a moment, I feared she would refuse. But then she looked up, and something had shifted. Her jaw was set, and her eyes shone with quiet determination.

"Fine. Let's go," she said, as if I'd just asked her to take a leisurely stroll instead of embark on a journey that could get us both killed.

I let out a breath I hadn't realized I was holding and pulled her into a brief embrace.

Eamon stepped closer, his expression stern. "You must understand, Lilah—this journey will be perilous. Ambushes, treachery—perhaps worse."

"And no soft beds," I added with a small smile, hoping to lighten the moment.

She gave me a slow, unimpressed look. "Oh no, whatever will I do without my daily fluff of the pillows?" Then she arched a brow at Eamon. "Ambushes, treachery, possible death—got it. But I assume none of that is worse than spending weeks trapped with you two? Because I have real concerns about that."

I shook my head, biting back a laugh. "We could leave you behind, you know."

She smirked. "And deprive you of my charming company? You wouldn't last a day."

Eamon raised an eyebrow, making a sound that might have been a chuckle. "Fair enough," he said.

We gathered our belongings swiftly and slipped out into the city under the pale light of dawn. Around us, the streets began to stir—the clatter of carts, the distant bark of a dog. It all felt too normal, a fragile façade masking the peril we carried with us.

As we moved through the alleys, I glanced at Lilah. Her gaze was fixed ahead, her steps steady. She didn't look back. And though fear twisted in my gut, I drew strength from her resolve.

"Dangerous journey," I murmured under my breath.

"Questionable company," Eamon shot back, a ghost of a grin on his face.

And so, we walked on, toward a future shrouded in uncertainty but lit by the fragile hope that together, we might endure.

***

Eamon kept his hood pulled low, and we followed his lead, keeping our eyes down, my right hand resting on the hilt of my sword while the other, gripped Lilah's hand. We moved swiftly through the winding lanes, sticking to the shadows whenever we could, making our way steadily toward the market square. Eamon took us down a narrow passage.

The market square's chaos roared just ahead as it bustled with activity. Vendors were busy setting up their stalls with animated chatter as they prepared for the day ahead. Brightly colored awnings flapped in the breeze and the air was filled with the scents of fresh bread and roasted meats. The market was already alive with movement, a growing throng of people weaving through the bustling scene, oblivious to the danger hidden within the shadows.

Eamon turned to me, his voice low. "We must make it to the gate, so we must blend in. Keep your hood up, and don't look anyone in the eye."

I stepped behind him and held Lilah close as we wove through the noisy crowd. Now and then, I caught sight of a figure that made my heart leap—a flash of a cloak, the glint of steel—but it was always just a merchant or a city guard.

A fruit vendor eyed us suspiciously as we passed. I forced myself to walk casually, but my mind raced. Too many eyes. Too much noise. The gate was just ahead, looming over the city—a massive structure of stone and iron, guarded by a handful of soldiers. Their armor glinted in the early morning light, and their eyes roamed the market.

I could see the line of people waiting to leave the city— merchants, travelers, wagons filled with goods—each one being checked by the guards before being allowed through. A few guards entered the far end of the marketplace, their eyes scanning the crowd. One of them paused, tilting his head slightly in our direction. I was a moment late, and our eyes met. I panicked and broke into a run, clutching Lilah by the hands.

"Oi!" the soldier yelled, weaving past the crowds to chase us.

Eamon saw the commotion and blended into the crowd, hurrying toward the gate where the guards checked each wagon as he waited for us. Lilah stumbled, and I grabbed her arm again, yanking her toward a narrow path between two stalls. Ahead, a cluster of children darted between the stalls, laughing and shouting as they played. I steered Lilah toward the children, using their chaos as a screen.

"Careful," Lilah muttered as I nearly tripped over a boy chasing a wooden hoop.

Suddenly, a commotion erupted to their left—a man shouting about a stolen purse. It was our chance. The guards at the gates were drawn to the disruption, and that was exactly what we needed. I pulled back my hood and ruffled my hair. Holding Lilah tight, I ran towards the gates.

Eamon glanced at me, a subtle nod passing between us. We edged closer, waiting for the right moment. The guards at the gate were focused on the robbery, their attention momentarily divided. Eamon moved, slipping around the side of a cart, using it as cover as we approached the gate.

Lilah and I followed. We could see the open road beyond the gate, the horizon stretching out, and freedom just within reach. In the chaos, Eamon was the first to slip through the gate, and Lilah and I followed right behind him, keeping our pace neutral until we were out of sight. Then we broke into a run, our footsteps muffled by the dirt road as we passed through the massive stone walls of Edmundshire.

We kept moving, the city fading behind us, the sounds of the market and the shouting guards replaced by the quiet rustle of the wind through the fields, the distant calls of birds greeting the new day. I took a deep breath, the cool, crisp air filling my lungs, the tension slowly easing from my body. We were out. We were free.

Eamon glanced back at me, a small, tired smile tugging at the corners of his mouth. "We did it," he said, his voice filled with relief.

Yes, indeed. But we needed to put as much distance as possible between ourselves and Edmundshire before the sun rose.

# CHAPTER
## 32

We moved through the night, the sky slowly changing from a deep indigo to a dull gray as the first light of dawn broke over the horizon. The road was empty, the landscape around us quiet and still, the fields stretching out like a vast ocean beneath the early morning sky.

We walked in silence, our footsteps the only sound as we pressed on. My eyes were heavy, my body weighed down with the burden of everything we had been through, pressing down on me like a physical weight. I glanced at Lilah, her eyes were focused on the road ahead, but her brow showed her weariness, as if sheer willpower alone could carry us through the miles still left to travel.

After hours of walking, we reached a river—a narrow, winding body of water that cut through the landscape like a silver ribbon. I knelt to drink, the cool water refreshing against my exhaustion. The chill helped to clear my mind, washing away the fatigue.

Lilah immediately jumped in, splashing away with pure childlike joy. "We'll camp here for the day," Eamon said over the ruckus Lilah was making. "We need to rest, and regain our strength." Eamon moved a few feet away, gathering some dry branches and twigs, his movements quick and efficient as he set up a small fire.

The wind had picked up, carrying a chill that cut through my cloak. I pulled it tighter around me and watched as Eamon worked, his face a mask of concentration. I sat on the river bank watching Eamon and keeping an eye on Lilah who was drifting further down the stream.

The small spark of the fire caught, growing into flickering flames, and a flicker of warmth spread through me—not just from the fire, but from the knowledge that we had a moment to breathe. Once the fire was crackling, Eamon and I sat beside it, his shoulders slumping slightly as the tension of the day eased.

Lilah joined us, dripping wet, her curls clinging to her face, and a wide grin lighting up her features. She threw her arms out dramatically. "That river's colder than it looks, and it's perfect!" she said cheerfully, plopping down near the fire. "And I think I scared off every fish in there. You're welcome." Eamon smirked faintly, shaking his head as he poked at the fire. I chuckled, leaning back on my hands.

"I'm not sure whether to thank you or apologize to the fish." Lilah laughed, wringing out her cloak. "At least now we know I've got more energy than the fish. That's something, right?"

Her lightheartedness was infectious, and for a moment, the weight of the journey lifted just enough for me to breathe easier.

***

We lay down near the fire, and I watched Lilah as she slept. Silently, we listened to the crackling of the fire and the sounds of the night.

Eamon broke the silence. "It's going to be a long journey, but we'll make it..."

I looked at him. "We will," I answered. He smiled and reached into his pack, pulled out a small piece of bread, and handed it to me. "Here," he said. "Eat something. We need our strength."

I took the bread, nodding in gratitude. The simple meal tasted like a feast after everything we had been through. I ate slowly, savoring each bite, my eyes fixed on the flickering flames.

As the night wore on, Eamon and I took turns resting, one of us always keeping watch while the other slept. When it was my turn to rest, I lay down on the hard ground, exhaustion making it easy to drift off despite the discomfort. My dreams were restless, filled with fragments of the past few days—flashes of battles fought, screams of dying men, and red flowing cloaks. I woke with a start, the remnants of the dream fading as I sat up, the fire still crackling beside me. Eamon was sitting by the river, his eyes fixed on the horizon. The sun was now peeking out from the clouds, casting long shadows across the landscape. I walked over to my brother, and we stood side by side, looking out at the road ahead as the day awoke.

With renewed focus, we packed up our camp, carefully stowing away what little we had—blankets, some dried food, our weapons. The fire had long since burned down to embers, and the cold wind of the afternoon reminded us that we couldn't linger. We set off along the riverbank, our eyes scanning the distant horizon. We knew we needed to move quickly. Edmundshire's forces would soon be scouring the roads, searching for the fugitives who had vanished into the night. As Eamon said, the road back to Centralia was a long one.

# CHAPTER
## 33

We walked for hours, following the winding path through the countryside. The distant hills rose and fell like waves, the fields stretching out in every direction, broken only by the occasional cluster of trees. The isolation was both comforting and unsettling—fewer eyes meant less chance of being seen, but it also meant fewer places to hide. As the sun began to sink lower in the sky, we spotted a farmhouse in the distance, its thatched roof barely visible over the rise of a hill. Smoke curled from the chimney; a sign of life, warmth, and shelter. Eamon pointed toward it, a thoughtful look crossing his face.

"If we can find horses," he said, his voice low, "we could cut our journey down by days. We might be able to make it before they even realize we're gone."

We glanced at the farmhouse, and Lilah asked, "You think they have any?"

"And what if they do?" I asked, my brow furrowing in a frown. "We can't just take them."

Eamon's expression hardened, his jaw set. "We have to, Kaelan. If we're caught, everything we've done will be for nothing. And we don't have time to spare."

A knot formed in my stomach. I knew Eamon was right. We couldn't afford to move too slowly, not when so much was at stake. I took a deep breath, nodding slowly. "All right," I said. "Let's go."

We rode through the night, the landscape blurring around us, and moonlight casting long shadows across the fields. I kept my eyes on the horizon as my thoughts drifted to Centralia, to those I had left behind, the fields of Elsenburg, the warmth of our family hearth, and the laughter of friends and neighbors. It felt like a lifetime ago—the world before the war, before everything had changed. I wondered if we would ever see those days again. I thought of arriving at Central and facing the emperor with the news we had, and finally seeing the war end. I imagined the emperor placing Eamon and me on a pedestal and rewarding us for the part we played in ending the war and bringing peace with Wintmtore. I imagined riding into Elsenburg; seeing Ma and Pa again; telling them, 'See, I promised you I would bring Eamon back. Your son has returned to you,' I would say beaming with pride. And perhaps, if the gods were kind, I would marry Lilah on our farm, with the breeze on our faces and the smell of pines and apples in the air.

Everything would be perfect.

But first, we had to get to Centralia.

Eamon gestured for Lilah to stay low as we made our way toward the farmhouse, keeping to the shadows. She shot him a look. "Oh, of course. Let the two of you handle this while I sit here twiddling my thumbs. Brilliant plan."

Before he could argue, she was already moving beside us, her footsteps just as silent as ours. The sun had nearly vanished, leaving the sky a deep shade of blue.

As we crested the hill, a small stable came into view beside the house, the faint outlines of two horses visible in the fading light. A pang of guilt hit me at the thought of taking something that wasn't ours, but I shoved it aside. We had no other choice.

Eamon slipped into the stable with practiced ease, and Lilah followed right behind him, her movements careful but quick. I brought up the rear, eyes locked on the farmhouse, scanning for any sign of movement. The stable was dark, the scent of hay and animals thick in the air. The horses snorted nervously as we entered, their ears flicking back at the disturbance.

"Easy, girl," Eamon murmured, running a steady hand along the neck of one of the horses.

Lilah moved to the other, already working to loosen the reins. "Let's move fast, boys. Preferably before we get an entire pitchfork-wielding family after us."

I grabbed a bridle, slipping it into place with trembling fingers. Every creak of wood, every shift in the air made my pulse hammer, half-expecting the farmhouse door to swing open at any moment.

We worked in tense silence, securing the tack as efficiently as possible. When the last strap was in place, I exchanged a glance with Eamon. "Ready?"

"Go."

With one swift motion, we led the horses out of the stable. As soon as we were clear, we swung into the saddles, urging them forward. The farmhouse remained still behind us, but I didn't trust our luck to hold.

Lilah mounted behind me with practiced ease, her arms wrapping around my waist as the wind whipped past us. "Stealing horses in the dead of night," she mused. "Truly, we are the pinnacle of morality."

I smirked, the rush of the escape making my blood sing. "I'll be sure to carve that on our gravestones."

"Please do. And make mine extra dramatic."

The stable faded into the distance as we rode, the thrill of the moment mixing with a strange sense of freedom.

\*\*\*

Gradually, the landscape shifted—wide fields gave way to rolling hills, the road winding through groves of trees that offered a brief respite from the relentless sun overhead. The horses were healthy and fast, and their hooves kicked up dust as we made our way through the countryside. The air was thick with dust and the scent of earth, and sweat trickled down my back. Our throats were parched and aching with fatigue. But we couldn't slow down. We only stopped to feed the horses and eat our meager meal. And Lilah flopped on the bark of a tree. Sweat had soaked into her hair. But she didn't complain, though her usual chatter had finally slowed.

"We're making good time," Eamon said, his voice low, almost as if he were trying not to disturb the peace of the moment. "If we keep this pace, we might make it to the border in a few days."

We mounted our horses again, urging them forward, the steady rhythm of hooves against the dirt resuming as we continued our journey south. The day wore on; the sun dipped lower in the sky, casting a warm glow over the landscape. Shadows grew long, stretching across the fields, and the air cooled as the day gave way to night.

We rode into the evening, the sky darkening above us, stars beginning to appear one by one, scattered across the vast expanse of the night sky. The moon hung low, casting a gentle light over the landscape, and the world around us seemed so quiet, almost peaceful. For a brief moment, it felt as if we could forget the danger we were in, the mission we carried.

Centralia was almost within reach. Hope began to flutter in my heart. We were finally leaving Wintmore behind. Every mile brought us closer to the Centralian border, to home.

# CHAPTER
# 34

We were about to take a break when something caught my eye in the distance—dark shapes against the horizon, moving swiftly as a cloud of dust rose into the air. My heart sank, and Eamon pulled his horse up short, his eyes narrowing as he followed my gaze.

"Do you see that?" Eamon asked, his voice tense.

Dread settled in my stomach, and I instinctively wrapped my arms around Lilah. The figures were clearer now—men on horseback, the glint of steel in the sunlight, banners waving in the air. My breath caught in my throat as the realization hit me: this was no ordinary group of travelers. It was an army—a Centralian regiment, and they were engaged in battle with Wintmorian soldiers!

Eamon's jaw clenched, his eyes scanning the scene. The sounds of battle grew louder—the clash of swords, the cries of men, the pounding of hooves. The wind carried the faint smell of smoke, and my heart pounded with panic. Lilah was tense, her fists clenching and unclenching. My amulet hung reassuringly around my neck, its warmth familiar, almost sentient.

"We need to go around," Eamon said urgently. "We can't risk getting caught in the middle of this."

But it was already too late. The battle was already upon us. Soldiers surged forward, a chaotic mass of bodies and weapons, and the banners of Centralia and Wintmore flying high as the two sides clashed. There was no escape!

The clang of steel and the cries of dying men filled the air, thick as smoke. It was chaos—bodies, banners, and broken weapons littered the ground, and the coppery stench of blood clung to my throat.

I scrambled down from the horse and lifted Lilah with me. I was deadened with fear. I shouldn't have brought her. I should have left her in Edmundshire. This was not a place for Lilah. Her pulse fluttered at her throat, but her eyes betrayed nothing.

She grabbed my arm.

"Kaelan, please, don't…"

There was no time to listen. I steered her towards a hill, behind a jagged boulder jutting from the hillside.

"Stay here, Lilah. Don't come out until…."

"Kaelan…" She wrested her hands from mine.

"Please, Lilah! Stay here!"`

"No!"

"What!"

"You can't…"

No!"

I turned to search for Eamon, but a blur of movement caught my eye—Lilah was already gripping a fallen soldier's sword. I barely had time to react before she lifted it like it was an extension of her hand, the steel gleaming under the pale light. Before I could argue, there was a flash of steel to my right—too fast. I pivoted, just in time, meeting the strike with a jarring clash. My arm burned from the impact, but there was no time to register the pain. Another soldier charged. I twisted and shoved him back, turning toward Lilah—only to find she was no longer behind the boulder. She had vanished.

"Lilah!" I cursed under my breath, and frantically cast my eyes around.

Ten paces away, she stood firm, gripping the reins of a terrified horse—one that had belonged to a fallen soldier now crumpled at her feet. The animal reared, eyes wild, hooves lashing the air, but Lilah held fast, whispering something to it. The animal trembled, then gradually calmed. And with one swift motion, she swung into the saddle, gripping tight, sword steady in her hand. Then she smirked at me, breathless but fearless.

I mounted my horse and fought my way to her. "Are you mad?"

"I need a horse, Kaelan!" With a kick, she urged the beast forward, her blade flashing as she plunged into the chaos.

There was no arguing now. I rode after her.

A soldier lunged toward me, blade flashing. I barely parried in time, the force rattling my bones. I slashed, my blade jerking suddenly, and the soldier tumbled off his horse. I saw Lilah in the distance. She was fast, weaving through the chaos, quick and precise. A man twice her size swung at her, and my heart lurched. But she ducked and drove her sword through the man's side with terrifying accuracy.

By gods!

"Kaelan!" she shouted over the clash of steel. "Stop gawking and try not to get yourself skewered!"

I gritted my teeth. "I'm not—"

She ducked another swing and snorted. "Eyes forward, soldier boy!"

I got out of my reverie, and with a growl, I shoved back the soldier in front of me and pushed forward, cutting through the melee toward the other side. Lilah was right there across from me, her blade dancing, her movements controlled, deadly.

We rode, with me a few paces behind her, hacking our way through the madness. Lilah fought with startling precision, her blade flashing under the storm-gray sky. A soldier reached for her horse's bridle trying to pull it down. She cut him down before he could come close.

"Stay close!" Eamon shouted from up ahead, his voice barely audible over the roar of the battle. He yanked on the reins, urging his horse to the left, trying to steer clear of the fighting. Lilah and I followed and we veered off the main path, towards the brush of woods. But the chance was gone. Soldiers on foot ran past us, their faces twisted in battle rage and their weapons flashing in the sunlight. Horses charged across the plain, their riders shouting orders. It was a blur of movement, a confusion of sounds—the clash of steel, the cries of pain, the smell of death.

Soon, a Centralian soldier stumbled in front of me, his face bloodied, his sword raised as he fought off a Wintmorian attacker. I pulled hard on the reins, my horse rearing slightly, barely avoiding trampling the man. My heart lurched as I caught a glimpse of the Wintmorian attacker's face—He was young and terrified, his eyes wide as he swung his weapon.

"Move, now!" Eamon shouted, his voice desperate, barely carrying over the noise. He swerved to avoid a Wintorian with a dagger and an arrow whistled through the air, striking his horse in its flank. The animal reared up, a high-pitched whinny of pain cutting through the clamor, its eyes wide with terror. My stomach dropped as I watched Eamon fight to stay on, his hands tight on the reins. But the horse's pain was too much—it buckled, collapsing to the ground, throwing Eamon violently from the saddle.

"Eamon!" I screamed as I saw my brother hit the ground, his body rolling through the dirt. I yanked on my reins, bringing my horse to an abrupt stop, and leaped off to rush to his side.

Eamon groaned, struggling to push himself up, pain etched across his face as he tried to regain his footing. "I'm fine," he managed, his voice strained. "But the horse..."

I glanced at the fallen horse. The arrow was embedded deep in its flesh and it heaved painfully, its agony clear. There was no saving it. Eamon lay helplessly on the ground, panting. I grabbed him immediately and pulled him to his feet.

I darted my face around.

"We need...we need another horse!" I yelled.

"Let's go on foot."

I cast a desperate look around. I didn't see Lilah. Not even a wayward strand of hair.

By gods! She has fallen.

Has she fallen?

Eamon was balanced against me; his arm swung across my shoulder. A Wintmorian soldier charged at us, his sword raised, his eyes blazing. Eamon and I came apart and I drew my sword. The soldier lunged, his blade arcing toward my head. I ducked, and brought my sword up, catching his blade with a resounding clash. The force of the blow sent a jolt through my arm, but I gritted my teeth and held firm, twisting my wrist to push his blade aside. I moved quickly. I stepped inside his guard and slammed my shoulder into his chest sending him stumbling backward. I didn't hesitate—I followed through, my sword cutting through the air and finding its mark.

I looked around for Eamon. He had found his footing. He stood with his sword drawn, and his frame crouched, ready for an attack. Another soldier rushed at us, and Eamon sliced through him with one powerful strike.

"We must leave now! Eamon yelled. He grabbed my arm and pulled me away from the fallen soldiers, our eyes searching for a way out of the chaos. But there was no clear path—only more soldiers, more confusion.

I cast my eyes around again for Lilah. Then, I saw her. She fought tirelessly, her eyes blazing like the mid-afternoon sun. Our eyes met. And her eyes furrowed in fury. "Don't get yourself killed, Kaelan. Focus!"

I heaved a sigh of relief. And turned to Eamon.

***

Eamon and I stood back-to-back, our eyes darting around, taking in the commotion around us. The battle was a blur of movement. The ground beneath us was slick with mud and the bodies of fallen men. Our swords flashed, our hearts pounded, and we moved, as one.

A Wintmorian archer spotted us, his bow drawn, his eyes narrowing as he aimed. My heart lurched, but before he could release the arrow, a Centralian soldier charged at him. The two men fell to the ground, their bodies a tangled mass of limbs and weapons.

But there was no time for words. I turned to tackle another soldier, a hefty Wintmorian wielding an axe. Suddenly, I heard a strangled gasp. My heart froze as I spun around, my eyes widening in horror. Eamon was on his knees and a Wintmorian soldier stood over him, his sword raised. Blood streamed from Eamon's chest and upper arm, forming a frighteningly red puddle on the ground.

# CHAPTER
## 35

"**E**amon!"

I screamed, my voice tearing through the clamor of the battlefield. I didn't think; I ran. The Wintmorian soldier standing over my brother didn't know what hit him. He'd barely turned before I barreled into him. My shoulder drove into his side, and he staggered back, the clang of his armor blending with the symphony of chaos around us. I wasted no time—my sword swept up and down, finding the vulnerable seam in his neck. A hot, thick spray spurted out from his wound, and he dropped like a sack. I fell to my knees beside Eamon, my breath ragged.

His face was pale, his trembling hands pressing against the gash in his side.

"Stay with me, Eamon." I pleaded, my hands trembling as I pressed them against his wounds. Warm, slick blood welled beneath my fingers. He groaned, his eyes half-closed, and his chest rose and fell in shallow gasps, each one fainter than the last.

"Don't you dare do this to me, Eamon!"

Eamon's lips twitched, his voice a ghost of itself. "Kaelan... Go."

"No!" I snapped.

I heard a rustle behind me. I swiftly turned, my sword raised. But it was Lilah. She leaped from the horse and ran to us, skirts torn, eyes blazing. She didn't hesitate. She ripped a strip from her ruined frock and pressed it against Eamon's wounds.

"Kaelan, move!" she snapped.

I sat rigid. My limbs refused to work.

"Kaelan!" she shouted again, her voice sharp as steel. "For the love of the gods, get the blasted horse!"

That snapped me out of it. I stumbled up and darted my eyes around the battlefield, desperately searching for anything—any hope. Nothing made sense. My gaze fell on my horse, its reins trailing in the dirt, its eyes wild with fear as it moved through the chaos. It skittered nervously, ears flicking back at the cacophony around it. "Easy," I murmured as I reached for the reins, the leather warm and slick in my grip.

Lilah had bound Eamon up as best as she could but his body sagged against her.

"Lilah," I held her face with my blood-soaked hands. "Listen to me. Head south, to the Centralian camp, right now." She hesitated, her gaze flittering between Eamon and me, worry flickering in her eyes.

"You'll be safe, I promise." She gave me a curt nod and swung onto her horse. She spurred it forward and I watched as she disappeared into the chaos, her hair flowing in the wind. Then, with a grunt, I hoisted Eamon onto the saddle. He slumped forward, his head lolling, and his breaths faint. I climbed up behind him and wrapped my arms around his body, holding him steady. His frame trembled beneath my grip, his chest's labored rise and fall rattling against me.

"Hold on, Eamon," I whispered. My voice choked with emotion. Tears stung at my eyes, but I blinked them away.

"We're getting out of here," I muttered, more to myself than him.

Then, I kicked my heels into my horse's sides, urging it forward. It leaped forward and the noise of the battlefield slowly faded behind us. I leaned low, shielding Eamon with my body from the arrows that still whistled through the air. "We're almost there, Eamon," I whispered, my voice breaking. "Just hold on, please."

I urged my horse faster, faster. But as we left the chaos behind, a crippling thought enshrouded me: I would not reach the Centralian camp before it was too late.

***

Ahead, the Centralian banners snapped in the wind, a beacon of hope amid the carnage. Lilah stood there in the front beside her horse, her face pale. She and other chirurgeons ran to meet us as I pulled the horse to a halt, their eyes wide as they took in Eamon's condition. Sliding from the saddle, I caught him as he slumped and helped him down. "Help him," I choked, my voice raw. "Please, help him." The chirurgeons worked quickly, their hands moving with practiced precision as they lifted Eamon onto a litter. Dark streaks of blood smeared their clothes, but they didn't flinch.

I followed as they carried him toward a makeshift triage area, my eyes never leaving his pale face. They moved quickly, their hands gentle but firm as they lay him on a slab of wood. They examined his injuries, their voices calm and steady as they began to work. I stood there, my heart pounding and my eyes fixed on my brother. Seeing Eamon like that—pale, bloodied—filled me with a cold dread, the kind that seeped into the bones and made it hard to breathe.

Beside me, Lilah stood, more terrified than I had ever seen her.

# CHAPTER
# 36

Healers scurried around Eamon, daubing his wounds with oils, and tying the gaping wounds with fresh pieces of fabric. The battle still raged, but the lines were beginning to break. The Centralian forces were pushing back. The chaos was dying down, replaced by a different kind of urgency—the urgency of the wounded, the urgency of survival.

I took a deep breath and turned away from my brother. I needed to find the commander of this regiment. We couldn't stay here. I had to get Eamon back to Centralia, to safety, before it was too late. A voice cut through the haze in my mind. I turned, and standing amid a cluster of officers was a tall, broad-shouldered man. His voice had an almost casual authority. His sharp eyes took in my bloodied appearance with an expression akin to surprise before recognition flickered in his eyes.

"Kaelan, isn't it?"

"Yes, Sire."

"I remember you. Sir Gareth's regiment, wasn't it? Centralian recruits with more guts than sense. You made quite the impression during drills."

I nodded, though I wasn't sure if his tone was praise or teasing. "General, I need your help. My brother—he's been gravely injured. I must get him to Centralia immediately. And we have a message for the Emperor. It's urgent."

Even as I spoke, I wondered if I was making any sense. His expression shifted, the faint humor fading into something more thoughtful. He studied me for a moment and glanced toward the tent where the chirurgeons tended to the wounded, his lips pressed into a thin line.

"You've been through hell, haven't you?" He said, his eyes shifting back to mine—sharp and probing. "It speaks of your loyalty. Or your recklessness. You've got the heart of a true Centralian soldier, lad."

"Please, Sire." I urged. "We need to get word to the Emperor. It's about the Astari."

The mention of the Astari caught his attention, his eyes sharpening. He glanced back at the officers around him, and they stepped back from us. He nodded at me and I told him everything.

"We can't fail, sire. This news—it could stop the war."

The General studied me for a moment, his face impassive. Then, he nodded. "Very well. I'll send a small contingent with you, led by one of my best. They will get you to Centralia safely. But you'll be on your own once you leave here."

Relief washed over me. "Thank you, sire. You have no idea what this means."

He clapped a hand on my shoulder, his grip firm. "If you truly have news about the Astari, we've all got more to lose than a few soldiers. You're doing something important, Kaelan. Central needs men like you. Get your brother home—and make sure the Emperor hears what you have to say."

I nodded, my resolve hardening. I turned back and glanced at Eamon on the wooden slab. His chest still rose and fell rhythmically.

"We'll make it," I whispered. "We have to."

For Eamon. For Centralia.

***

A soldier came to me as I waited by the tent. I caught sight of him from the corners of my eyes and turned. He looked strangely familiar. His armor was battered, streaked with mud and blood, and he moved with the weary ease of a man who had seen battle many times and was no more scared by it. His hair was damp with sweat, his face fuller than I remembered.

"Silas!"

He grinned and clasped his hand on my arm as he pulled me into a firm embrace. "By the stars above, Kaelan! I'm so glad to see you. I am the leader of the contingent to escort you to Centralia."

Gone was the nervous, pimply lad who had left Elsenburg with me that cold morning. In his place stood a hardened soldier—lean, sharp-eyed, and sure of his footing. I returned his embrace, gripping him like a brother.

"Silas. Of all the places to meet again! How do you fare?"

"I'm well, my friend." He regarded me with a smile. "When the horror of Brackenridge happened, word spread that you had fallen."

"I nearly did," I whispered.

"That battle claimed a lot of great men. I'm happy you made it out."

I patted his shoulder. "What happened to you? We were training in the camp before central, and you vanished without a word."

Silas exhaled sharply. "I deserted." His voice was steady as he looked me in the eye. "General Thomas found me tumbling around in the cold and took me. He could've had me executed, but he didn't. Instead, he ensured I wasn't punished, pulled strings at Central, and put me in his regiment." He glanced away for a moment. "We were trained in stealth—real stealth. And let's just say—I've never been happier being a soldier."

I studied him. The timid son of a miller who once fumbled with his leather strap was gone. In his place stood a soldier, sure-footed, at ease in his skin.

"He called you one of his best," I said in wonder.

Silas flushed, rubbing the back of his neck, a flicker of the boy he'd once been shining through the hardened exterior. But his smile was quiet, sure. "I'm glad he thinks so." His eyes found mine, steady and determined. "And I won't disappoint him. Or you. We'll get your brother home."

As the soldiers gathered supplies for our departure, I found Eamon by the tent surrounded by healers. I knelt beside him and ran my hand through his red hair. "Did you hear that, Eamon? We're getting out of here. We're going home."

Eamon's eyes met mine, a flicker of a smile crossing his face. "Home."

"Yes. Home, Eamon, " I replied and squeezed his hand.

A soldier from our escort came forward. "Healer! We need one of you to come with us! The wounded man needs constant care!" he yelled, his voice cutting through the clamor.

"There are very few healers for so many wounded soldiers." A chirurgeon muttered and darted into the other tent.

"I'm a healer!"

I turned. And Lilah stood there, clutching Eamon's bloody cloak —cut from his body by the chirurgeons—like something fragile. Her face was pale, and her eyes glassy with unshed tears. She had washed the blood and grime off her face, but it had done little to erase the battle. I'd watched her wield a sword— fierce, unrelenting, steel flashing and eyes raging like an angry goddess. She had cut men down and rode through the chaos with a steady hand. But now, in the quiet aftermath, she looked smaller somehow. Younger. Like a girl who had seen too much too soon. And yet—she was still standing. I stepped toward her. She heaved a sigh and reached for my hand; steadying herself— steadying me. And gods help me, I marveled at her.

In that moment, I knew. If anyone could heal Eamon, it was her. She had nursed me from the brink of death and Eamon couldn't have a better healer.

Eight soldiers accompanied us. Four carried Eamon on the litter, while four stood guard with swords. Lilah walked beside Eamon and I fell into step with them, my eyes focused on my brother.

Then we left the camp and got on our way to Centralia.

# CHAPTER
## 37

The clamor of battle faded into the eerie quiet of the open plains as we pushed forward. My legs burned, my lungs ached, and every step across the uneven, blood-soaked ground was a struggle. Sweat trickled down my back, mingling with the dirt and grime clinging to my skin. Yet, I kept my eyes on Eamon. His face was pale and slick with sweat, his chest rising and falling in shallow, fragile breaths. The soldiers carrying Eamon on the litter moved with care, navigating around fallen men and shattered weapons.

"Steady," one muttered under his breath as the ground shifted beneath them. Lilah walked beside the litter, her fingers constantly checking his bandages, her face a mask of quiet urgency.

"His pulse is fading," she told me softly. "We need to get him to safety soon."

A muscle tightened in my jaw. "We are close," I muttered, patting her arm. Her brows remained furrowed.

As we reached the edge of the battlefield, the sun dipped low, casting the land in hues of orange and purple. The dense forest loomed ahead, its shadows deepening under the twilight. The leader of our group, Silas, spoke firmly. "We press on through the forest. It's our best chance to stay hidden. No stopping until dawn."

Lilah shot me a glance, worry flickering in her eyes. The air beneath the trees was cold and still, the earthy scent of damp moss and pine filling my senses. Each crunch of leaves underfoot seemed deafening in the silence. The forest felt alive yet oppressive, its twisted branches clawing at the fading daylight.

The soldiers moved cautiously, their eyes darting to every shadow, weapons at the ready. More than once, we had to lift the litter over fallen logs or push through tangled undergrowth. All the while, Eamon's labored breaths were a constant reminder of the stakes.

I hated feeling so helpless. My whole life, I'd been the one to protect him, to keep him safe. But now, all I could do was stand here, useless, while others worked to save him. Frustration gnawed at me, twisting in my gut, so I turned to help the others, gathering branches, and stacking them around the fire to form a makeshift barrier against the chill of the night. We moved in silence. Our exhaustion hung heavy in the air, but there was no choice.

Lilah's voice broke the silence. "He's getting colder."

"I know," I replied, my jaw tightening. "We'll find a clearing soon."

Suddenly, a low growl shattered the stillness. The soldiers froze, their hands on their swords. A shadow moved in the underbrush—a wolf, its eyes gleaming with hunger.

"Form a circle!" I commanded, stationing others in Eamon's tent.

The wolves attacked in a flurry of snarls and flashing teeth. The night erupted with the clash of steel and the guttural cries of men and beasts alike. The soldiers fought bravely, blades cutting through the dim light as I swung my sword at the lunging shadows. Lilah was beside me, quick and relentless, her sword flashing as she slashed at a wolf snapping at her heels. She moved with a hunter's grace, her breath sharp and controlled, her arms steady even as the chaos surged around us. It was a blur of blood and fur, and when the last wolf fell, we stood panting, the silence pressing in again.

"We can't stay here," I panted, wiping blood from my blade.

Lilah protested, angry lines furrowed on her brow. Eamon needed to rest. And the men were weary. I shook my head. "No, Lilah. We'll camp soon."

She opened her mouth to argue, then stopped herself, her lips pressing together in a thin, frustrated line. Her gaze dropped to Eamon, softening as she looked at him, her hands trembling slightly before she balled them into fists. Finally, she nodded, her shoulders slumping in resignation.

Finally, after half a mile, I felt we could stop. "Rest while you can," I told the soldiers. "We move at first light."

The soldiers murmured as they prepared for a watch, their voices a faint hum against the vast, oppressive quiet of the forest. I sat apart from the men while I brooded. The fire crackled before me, its flames dancing wildly, casting restless shadows across my face.

Suddenly another sharp crack shattered the quiet, drawing every eye to the shadows beyond the firelight. My hand gripped my sword as I motioned for silence. Something moved—low, quick—slipping between the trees. I darted forward, blade ready while the soldiers forming a line behind me. The forest held its breath as I scanned the darkness, every muscle tense. But after a moment, all was still. The only sound was my own labored breathing.

# CHAPTER
# 38

I was lulled to sleep by the warmth of the fire and the sound of Eamon's breathing. Lilah remained close to him. She refused to sleep. She sat beside him crushing some strange red leaves and rubbing them into his ribs to ward off the fever. The words between us were few these days. I was numb. I had changed. I prayed furiously that the gore she had seen would not change her too. I wanted her to be happy. As I watched her silently spread the herbal paste across Eamon's chest with her herbs, I realized I needed to speak to her, to say something unconnected to Eamon. But my tongue felt like dry grass and tasted like ashes and I couldn't say anything.

Daybreak came slowly, the first light of dawn piercing through the dense canopy of the forest. The fire had long since died down, leaving only smoldering embers, their warmth fading into the cold morning air. The chill was biting, and I shivered as I slowly blinked awake. The chorus of birds began to fill the forest, breaking the stillness that had settled over us during the night. I rubbed my eyes, blinking against the pale light filtering through the trees.

We sat in silence watching Eamon. Lilah glanced at me, her eyes filled with a quiet understanding. "You love fiercely, Kaelan," she said softly. "He's lucky to have you."

I shook my head, feeling a lump form in my throat. "No," I said, my voice thick with emotion. "I'm the lucky one. He's always been the strong one, the one who kept us going. I can't lose him. I won't."

"I won't let that happen," she said, her voice thick with emotion. "I shall do my best, I promise."

I wished she would say that she was sure he would live. I willed her to say it. But she didn't, and I felt bereft.

I reached out, gently brushing a strand of hair away from his forehead. Eamon stirred slightly at the touch, his head shifting on the pillow. His eyes fluttered open, unfocused and glassy. "Centralia…" he muttered, his voice so soft I had to strain to hear. "Yes. We'll soon be in Centralia."

I clutched his hand in mine and my heart ached. Eamon had always been the brave one, tearing into danger without hesitation. Seeing him like this broke my heart.

I looked away, and my gaze shifted to the forest around us, the trees standing tall and silent, the light of dawn slowly spreading across the clearing. The world felt as if it was holding its breath, waiting for what would come next, and I knew I had to be ready. I had to be strong—for Eamon, for Centralia, for everyone who was counting on us.

\*\*\*

We packed up our makeshift camp with quiet efficiency, each of us moving with a sense of urgency and purpose. Lilah hovered over Eamon as the soldiers carefully lifted him onto the litter, her hands steady as she ensured his bandages were secure and his blankets were tucked tightly around him.

I took my place beside my brother as we began our trek. The air was cold, a biting wind weaving through the trees, and the ground beneath our feet was uneven, littered with fallen branches and the remnants of last night's frost. Lilah walked beside me, her expression tense as she kept her gaze on Eamon,

"Kaelan," she stopped and I was forced to stop too. "I think we need to consider another option. Eamon's condition is worsening, and every delay is making it harder for him to hold on. We might need to think about finding a closer settlement, somewhere we can get him real help, even if it's not Central."

I exhaled sharply, shaking my head. "No. We're getting him to Central. That's where he wants to be."

Lilah let out a frustrated sigh. "What if we don't make it? What if he doesn't make it because we keep pushing him too hard?" She stepped closer, softer now, but no less fierce. "I love you, Kaelan. And I love your brother. But I can't work magic. If we keep pushing forward like this, I'm afraid..."

Before I could respond, Silas stepped forward, his lips in a thin line. "Look, we all want to help your brother, but we're running out of time and options," Silas said, his voice low but tense. "We're in the middle of enemy territory, and we're not equipped to handle this kind of situation. We need to think about what's best for everyone."

I felt a flare of anger, my hands clenching into fists at my sides. I knew they were right—knew that they were only trying to help—but the thought of giving up, of stopping now, felt like a betrayal. I couldn't let go of the hope that we could make it to Central, that we could save my brother.

"Do you think I don't know that?" I snapped, my voice breaking. "Do you think I don't see how bad this is? But Eamon's my brother, and I'm not giving up on him. I can't."

Lilah stepped back, her gaze softening, her voice gentler now. "We're not asking you to give up, Kaelan. We're just asking you to consider what's best for him, for all of us."

Silas sighed, rubbing a hand over his face, the exhaustion clear in his expression. "We're all tired, and we're all doing our best. But if we keep pushing like this, we could end up getting caught, or worse. We need to make wise choices."

I felt the fight leave me, the tension draining from my shoulders as I looked at my brother, Eamon's face pale, his breathing shallow. I knew they were right.

I took a deep breath, my gaze shifting to Lilah, then to Silas. "I hear you," I said finally. "But I need to get him to Central. He'd only said one thing to me since this happened, and that is to get him to Centralia."

Lilah slipped her fingers through mine. "We'll get him to Centralia, Kaelan. But we need to move carefully, and we need to be ready for whatever comes our way."

Silas moved up beside me. "There," he said, pointing to the shadowy outline of a building in the distance—a house, abandoned and overgrown, half-hidden by the forest. "Looks like it's empty. We can try to take refuge there for the night."

I glanced at the others, seeing their weary faces, the exhaustion that had settled into every line of their expressions settled my doubts. I nodded and my gaze moved to Lilah. She gave me a quick, understanding nod in return. "It's worth a try," she said.

We moved slowly. The old house loomed closer, its dark silhouette becoming clearer as we approached. The roof sagged, ivy clung to the stone walls, and the windows were shattered and gaping like hollow eyes in the moonlit night. The place hadn't been lived in for years, but it would serve our purpose well enough.

We carefully lifted Eamon's litter and carried him up the crumbling steps to the door, which hung slightly ajar. The inside was as abandoned as we had expected—dusty and dim, with broken furniture scattered about and cobwebs hanging in every corner. I felt a pang of sadness at the sight—it could have been a home once filled with warmth, a place that had seen laughter and life, now reduced to little more than crumbling ruins.

"Over here," Silas said, pointing to a corner where the remnants of an old hearth still stood.

We set Eamon down on a pile of blankets we had brought and Lilah immediately tended to him, her hands moving deftly as she checked his wounds and his breathing. I moved to the hearth.  My hands shook as I fumbled to start a fire. Silas came up beside me and helped to gather wood from what remained of chairs and bed frames, breaking the planks into smaller pieces. Soon, a spark caught, the dry wood crackling as a flame began to grow, slowly at first, then brighter, casting a warm glow across the darkened room. The fire crackled, the flames casting flickering shadows across the walls, the warmth battling against the biting cold of the night. I held my hands out to the fire, feeling the warmth seep into my frozen fingers. I stayed there while the men ate and rested. I could do neither. My legs were as heavy as stone.

I don't know how long I stayed there. But suddenly, Lilah's voice tore through the quiet, sharp, and urgent, freezing my blood. I spun, my heart lurching. She was crouched over the wooden slab that had been Eamon's bed for the past four days, her hands pressed against his chest. The firelight danced on her pale, stricken face. I closed the space between us in a few frantic strides. Eamon lay so still. His face was ashen, his breaths shallow and fleeting. His half-lidded eyes seemed to gaze somewhere far beyond.

I dropped to my knees beside him. "Eamon?" My hand trembled as I reached out to touch his face, willing some warmth back into his cold skin. His eyelids flickered, and, for a moment, his gaze found mine. A faint smile ghosted across his lips.

"You made it," he murmured, his voice faint.

Tears welled in my eyes, blurring the edges of his face. "I'm here," I choked on my sobs. "We're almost there, Eamon. Centralia is only a mile away."

His head moved weakly, and he raised his trembling hand. I grabbed it with two of mine. It felt so light as if his strength had already slipped away.

"It's…too late," he whispered.

"No!" The word burst from me. "No, Eamon." My voice broke into loud sobs. "Don't say that. You're going home with me; to Ma and Pa!"

His grip tightened, just for a moment. His eyes, clearer now, pierced through the fog of pain. "Kaelan," he said softly, firmly. "Listen to me."

My hands clutched at his, desperate, helpless.

"It has to be you," he said, his voice trembling but resolute. "You have to finish this. You have to get back to Centralia. You have to tell them."

The war and everything it entailed were the last thing on my mind. Nothing mattered anymore. Nothing made any sense if my brother was not part of it.

I shook my head and glanced around desperately. The men stood around us mournfully. Lilah sat crouched beside me sobbing. I turned my gaze to my brother.

"That was why I gave you the Heartguard. I needed to make sure you made it back to Centralia."

There was silence as I tried to comprehend.

"I don't understand." But I did understand. It only dawned on me at that moment. My amulet had spent its powers, and Eamon had given me his to protect me as it had protected him all those months. He knew the danger, yet, he had done this. He had made the ultimate sacrifice to save my life; to ensure I returned to Centralia. My brother sacrificed his life for me.

"Why?" I whispered. "Why, Eamon---?"

He smiled again, but it was different this time—sadder, knowing. "You've always been the strong one, Kaelan," he said. "Stronger than you think. Stronger than I ever was. "

My throat tightened as tears slipped free, hot against my cheeks. "Don't say that. Don't... don't let go. Please, Eamon. Please."

He took a shuddering breath, his hand trembling as it cupped mine. His eyes softened, filled with a love so fierce it broke me. "I'm proud...of you, little brother," he whispered. "So proud."

I pressed his hand to my forehead and sobbed.

"Do it for Centralia," he continued, his voice fading, each word fainter than the last. "For all of us. Remember that."

His chest rose once more, then stilled. And his hand slipped from mine.

"Eamon?"

The word fell from my lips, a plea to the empty air.

I leaned over him, my hands clutching his shoulders, shaking him gently, then harder. His head lulled to one side, his eyes closed. He looked peaceful now.

"No!"

The stillness of the moment echoed louder than all the battles I had fought. Then, a broken sound clawed its way from my throat, raw and jagged, echoing into the silent night.

Eamon was gone.

He was gone.

# CHAPTER
# 39

I didn't know how long I sat there. The world around me blurred as grief consumed me.

It was as if time itself stopped, the world around me fading away until all that remained was Eamon's still form and the whirring sound in my head. The brother who had been my guide, my friend and my compass was now gone. My heart ached with a pain so profound that it seemed to echo through every part of me.

I reached out, my trembling fingers brushing a lock of hair away from Eamon's forehead. My vision blurred as the tears fell, each drop feeling as heavy as a stone. Memories flashed through my mind—Eamon's laughter as we raced across the fields of Elsenburg, the intensity in his eyes when he spoke of the things that mattered to him, his fierce protection when we were children. Every smile, every embrace, every moment we had shared came rushing back, a wave of memories that crashed over me, pulling me deeper into unrelenting anguish. He had freely given his life for me.

I sat there long after the men had cleaned him up and wrapped him in quilts and sheets. I remained there long after the sun had gone below the horizon, and the night birds had come out of their hiding places. I felt crippled. My tears dried but my heart ached with a loss that I could hardly comprehend. My hand rested on Eamon's chest and my shoulders shook as I knelt there. The soldiers watched in respectful silence. Lilah knelt beside me weeping, her hand still resting on my shoulder, her presence a small but steady comfort in the overwhelming darkness that had settled around me.

As I looked down at Eamon's face, my heart swelled with a fierce resolve. I had made my brother a promise. I had sworn to get him to Centralian lands, and I would keep that promise. Eamon would be buried in our homeland, beneath the sky we had both grown up under, surrounded by the people we had both fought to protect Lilah wrapped her arms around me and rested her head on my shoulder, her expression filled with sorrow.

"He gave his life for me, Lilah", I said clasping the amulet in my palm.

"I am glad for the chance to have known him," she whispered. "He was a man of great heart, and he loved you with an unwavering heart. You were blessed to have had such a brother in your life."

I turned and looked at her and I felt as if a cold spring had been poured upon my scorched soul. I was lucky to have had Eamon for all the years he was my brother, for all the years we lived together in Elsenburg, reveling in our boyish tricks. I was lucky to have had the grace to fight alongside him. I was lucky that he gave me the opportunity to save our empire with him. I leaned into her and allowed her embrace to calm my aching heart.

\*\*\*

"We're not leaving him here. We're taking him home. To Centralian lands."

Silas stepped forward, his face filled with sympathy, his eyes meeting mine. "We're with you," he said. "We'll help you get him home. Whatever it takes."

I turned back to Eamon, my eyes filling with tears.

"You hear that, brother?" I whispered, the tears shining in my eyes. "We're going home. You're going to rest in the land you fought to protect."

The landscape slowly shifted as we drew closer to Centralian lands. The air grew warmer, the wind sharper, and the trees that surrounded us became too thin, giving way to wide stretches of open land. I kept my eyes forward, my heart heavy with the grief that weighed down every step. Eamon's body rested on the litter which had been used to carry him in his weakened state.

The sun was beginning to set when we finally neared the border of Centralia. The land before us stretched out into the distance, rolling hills and fields leading toward the homeland we had fought so hard for. The sight of it filled me with a bittersweet sense of longing—a longing to bring my brother home, to honor his memory in the land we loved.

Silas glanced at me, his eyes filled with sympathy as he spoke quietly. "We're almost there. We need to find a spot—a place where we can give him the rest he deserves."

"I know the exact spot for my brother. He will rest in Elsenburg."

*** 

We made the rest of the journey in silence.

The air grew colder as the day wore on, the path before us winding and seemingly endless. As night began to fall, the wind picked up, cutting through our cloaks like a blade. Every night, we made camp in a small clearing and the trees provided some shelter from the biting wind. The soldiers took turns standing watch, and I spent the nights weeping into my quilt. Exhaustion pressed upon my mind. But I couldn't rest—not yet.

And then, as the light began to fade and the sun dipped lower in the sky, we saw it—the fields of Elsenburg. The sight filled me with a sense of relief. The massive fields in the distance, the village sprawling out behind it, the banner of Centralia flying proudly above.

Silas let out a sigh, his hand coming to rest on my shoulder. "There it is," he said, a smile crossing his lips. "We made it."

I nodded, my gaze fixed on the walls, the familiar sight bringing warmth to my chest, a feeling of belonging I hadn't felt since we had left for Wintmore. The small village was bustling, even from a distance I could see the movement, the life that filled the streets, the people carrying on their lives, unaware of the truth I carried with me.

The weight of the journey finally easing from my shoulders as we stepped into the village square. The home I remember was unchanged. Children still played in the square and the market was still rowdy. We passed the green hill and heard the gurgling of the stream as we went by the old stone wall. It was achingly familiar, but the air was stiff. We walked in somber silence till we reached the narrow path that led to our cottage.

We were home, I was home.

# CHAPTER
# 40

The first person I saw when we arrived was Ma. She stood by the door, watering her potted flowers, in the same spot where she had stood the day I left home in search of Eamon.

*Promise me you'll bring him back, Kaelan. Promise me.*

Ma's graying hair was pulled back, but the wind had loosened strands that framed her face. The lines around her eyes deepened as she squinted, her posture straightening when she caught sight of us. Her eyes darted around peering into our faces. Then her eyes met mine, and her expression shifted—first relief, then joy, and finally something akin to disbelief.

"Kaelan!" she called, her voice thin, and before I knew it, she was running toward me, her arms open wide. I dismounted quickly and met her halfway. She enveloped me in her arms, her embrace fierce, her tears soaking into my tunic. "You're home," she whispered, her voice trembling. "You're home, my boy."

"Yes, Ma. I'm home." She felt as soft as a feather and smelt like freshly baked gingerbread.

Behind her, Pa stepped out from the cottage, his weathered face breaking into a wide smile. He called out my name and ran toward me. Lilah dismounted beside me, offering him a shy smile. The soldiers hung back respectfully, their presence quiet and unassuming.

Ma pulled back just enough to cup my face in her hands and looked me over for any signs of injury. "You're all right?" she asked, her voice urgent. "And Eamon? Is he—"

Her question trailed off as she looked past me, scanning the group.

"Where's Eamon?" she asked, her voice catching on his name.

My throat tightened as the joy drained from the air. Pa had reached us now. He had a hat on, and his hands were stained with soil. He threw his arms around me.

"By the gods, you came back!"

"Yes, Pa." He peered into my face and his gaze flickered between Ma, me, and the soldiers. His brow furrowed. "Kaelan," he said cautiously. "Where's your brother?"

Lilah stepped closer to me, her hand brushing my arm, grounding me. I swallowed hard, glancing at her, then back at my parents. "Ma, Pa…" My voice broke, and I had to look away. "Something happened…"

The light in Ma's eyes went out, and in its place, a dawning horror that made my stomach churn. "No," she whispered, shaking her head. "No, Kaelan, don't—"

"Eamon…" I began, but my voice cracked. "Eamon's gone, Ma. He… he died bravely. Fighting for Centralia. For all of us."

Ma's legs buckled, and Pa caught her just in time. "No!" she screamed, clutching at his arm, his face pale and stricken. "No! Eamon!" Her voice was taut and guttural, like an animal in pain.

Pa stood frozen, his jaw working but no sound came out. His hand gripped Ma's shoulder as though holding her steady was the only thing tethering him to the earth.

"He was a hero," I said softly, my voice shaking. "He saved lives. He—he saved mine."

But the words felt hollow against their grief.

Ma broke from Pa's hold and stumbled forward, her hands clutching at my cloak as tears streamed down her face. "Where is he? Where's my son?"

The soldiers, silent and solemn, stepped aside, revealing the makeshift litter we had carried from the battlefield. Eamon's body lay wrapped in a clean shroud, his features serene, as if he were merely sleeping.

"No," Ma whispered over and over, falling to her knees beside him. She reached out, her trembling hands brushing over the shroud to reveal his face. Her sobs took a haunting tone, raw and unrelenting,

Pa knelt beside her, his broad shoulders shaking as he pressed a hand to Eamon's chest, his calloused fingers trembling. "My boy," he murmured, his voice hoarse. "My brave boy."

I stood there as if my legs were made of lead, unable to speak, as my parents grieved. Lilah's hand found mine, her grip tight, while her tears fell silently.

***

As the sun dipped low on the horizon, we gathered before the oak tree at the edge of the farm—the one he used to climb as a child, the one whose shade we always sought on hot summer days. I knelt beside my brother, my eyes glistening as I gazed at Eamon's still face, taking in every detail—the familiar curve of his jaw, the lines etched into his brow from a lifetime of determination, the faint scar that ran along his forehead, a mark from one of our childhood adventures. His face, was now still and serene. I reached out and brushed a lock of hair from his forehead, my heart breaking all over again.

"You're home, brother," I whispered, my voice breaking. "You're finally home."

I watched as the soldiers moved, their hands swift but reverent as they began to dig the grave. Each shovelful of earth seemed to carry the weight of our shared grief, the knowledge that we were saying goodbye to someone who had fought beside us, laughed with us, and believed in us. Slowly, I leaned forward, my forehead resting gently against Eamon's. "I'm sorry, brother," I whispered, my voice thick with emotion. "I'm sorry I couldn't save you. I'm sorry I wasn't there when you needed me most."

My tears fell freely and my body trembled as the grief washed over me. Every ounce of pain, every regret, and every memory I had of my brother poured out of me. I took a deep, shaky breath, my hand resting on Eamon's, and squeezed it gently.

"But I promise you, Eamon," I continued, "I will finish what we started. I will see this through. For you, for Centralia, for everything you believed in."

I pulled back, my gaze lingering on Eamon's face, my heart aching with the weight of the goodbye. I reached into my cloak and pulled out the amulet that had protected him, and protected me. It was proof of the ultimate sacrifice my brother made to keep me alive. With a steady hand, I placed it on Eamon's chest, the small emerald glinting in the fading light.

"Keep it with you, brother," I whispered. "May it guard you, as you've always guarded me."

Slowly, I stood, my legs unsteady, and I watched the soldiers step forward once more, their hands careful as they began to lower Eamon into the grave.

The sun sank lower in the sky, the golden light softening into deep hues of orange and pink. It painted the meadow in a gentle glow, the light reflecting off the tall grasses that swayed in the breeze. I watched as the shadows lengthened, the land around us growing quieter, the only sounds, the rhythmic scraping of shovels, and the distant rustling of leaves.

He was buried beneath his beloved tree, and that was a relief. The grave was simple, marked with a smooth stone that Pa had chosen. We stood in a small circle, Ma clutching a sprig of lavender she'd picked from the garden. Her tears had slowed, but her grief was etched into every line of her face. Pa's hand rested on her shoulder, his expression carved from stone.

I stepped forward, my voice steady though my chest ached. "Eamon was the bravest man I've ever known," I said. "He gave everything for us, for what he believed in. And I swear I'll carry his memory with me, always."

The wind whispered through the leaves of the oak, and for a moment, it felt as though Eamon was there, watching, smiling.

As we stood in silence, the first stars appeared in the sky, their faint light glimmering like a promise. And though my heart was heavy, I felt a flicker of hope. We had lost Eamon, but his courage, his love, and his sacrifice would guide us forward. Always.

# CHAPTER
# 41

I turned to Silas and the others and offered my thanks. "You're released from your duties. Thank you, truly. Go rest and tend to yourselves."

Silas stepped forward, clapping me on the shoulder. "Take care, Kaelan. You know where to find us if you need anything," he said, a tired smile crossing his lips. They all turned to depart, but Silas paused, a frown creasing his brow, and returned.

"Kaelan, I hate to be the one to speak of it, but I trust you understand—having the Wintmorian lass here in Centralia brings with it many dangers, both for her and for you. She's done no wrong, and truth be told, she's a fair maiden, even if I do say so myself. And aye, I see now that Centralia and Wintmore have no cause for war. But many do not yet know this. My advice is this, Kaelan: keep her hidden from sight, out of the public's eye. For if you don't, you may well lose her too."

The truth of his words jarred me perhaps because I never gave it a thought until he said it. And for a moment I was at a loss for words.

"I have a relative—my father's sister, a widow—who lives in Central. If it pleases you, I can make arrangements for her before I take my leave." He turned to leave.

"Silas."

"Aye?"

"Thank you for everything. I am truly thankful."

He gave a curt nod and was gone.

***

The following two days passed in a haze of sorrow and unease. The air in the house was heavy, weighted by a silence that neither the creaking floorboards nor the faint rustle of the wind outside could fill. Ma had taken to sitting by the hearth, her hands folded tightly in her lap, staring at the flickering flames as if they held the answers to the questions she couldn't bear to voice.

I sat across from her on the second night, the words already forming on my tongue, but dread held them back. She cast me sharp glances from time to time, her lips curled as if she was about to burst into tears. Her eyes were rimmed with red and almost swollen shut.

"You're leaving, aren't you?" she said, her voice brittle, as though the sentence itself might shatter her.

I nodded. "I have to."

Her hand flew to her chest, clutching at the fabric of her dress. "Kaelan, no! I've lost a son. I cannot—" Her voice broke, trembling as she whispered, "I cannot lose another. My heart cannot endure it."

The lump in my throat grew heavier. I wanted to promise her I'd stay, that I'd abandon my duty, but the weight of Eamon's sacrifice and the urgency of the truth I carried wouldn't let me.

"Ma," I said gently, leaning forward. "This is what Eamon wanted. What he died for. If I don't go to Central to give the emperor news of what I know, everything he gave his life for would be in vain."

Her eyes filled with tears as she shook her head, unable to speak.

From the corner of the room, Pa stirred, his face lined deeper than I had ever seen it, his shoulders stooped under the invisible burden he carried. He rose slowly, his movements deliberate as he shuffled to Ma and placed a hand on her shoulder.

"Let him go, Amelia," he said, his voice low and steady. "This isn't for us to decide. The boy has his path, and it's not here."

Ma turned to him, disbelief and heartbreak etched into her face. "How can you—"

"I grieve too," Pa interrupted gently, his voice cracking slightly. "But this is what must be done. Eamon would have wanted it. Let's not keep Kaelan from doing what is right."

Ma covered her face with her hands and wept. I wanted to speak, to thank Pa, but guilt and sorrow choked the words.

Lilah's presence was the only light in those suffocating days, a flame flickering stubbornly against the shadow of loss that enveloped us all. Though her grief was palpable, her hazel eyes had begun to regain their spark, and her sharp tongue danced with defiance. She had been there the evening I told Ma and Pa about my plans to go to Central. Now, as I spoke of my journey to the emperor and hers to Silas' aunt in Central, she was quiet; her silence uncharacteristic, her watchful gaze fixed on me as I spoke.

"You'll like her," I said, trying to mask my apprehension. "Aunt Rhoda is stern but fair. She'll take good care of you until I return."

Lilah tilted her head, folding her arms across her chest with mock solemnity. "Stern and fair? You mean like Ma, but with less shouting?"

Her quip caught me off guard, pulling the corner of my mouth into a reluctant smile. Across the room, Ma let out a sound that might have been a stifled laugh. It was fleeting, but in that moment, Lilah's irreverence chipped away at the sorrow encasing us, even if for a moment.

The following morning, Ma's defiance reared its head one last time. She stood by the door, hands trembling as she wrung the hem of her apron. The light filtering through the window highlighted the furrows etched deep into her face, lines carved by sleepless nights and silent tears.

"You can't take her to Central, Kaelan," she said, her voice thin.

"She'll be safer there," I said, my tone firm.

"It's safe here too," Ma muttered, a stubborn curl forming on her lips.

"She is a Wintorian girl, Ma. Everybody here knows that and people are angry. I don't want her to get hurt. Please, Ma." Ma bent her head, as she considered what I said. I continued quickly. "Nobody knows who she is in Central. Not even the woman she would live with. I intentionally did that so that she'd be safe."

Ma's lips pressed into a thin line, her resolve crumbling as she turned her gaze to Lilah, who stood quietly, her expression subdued. After a long pause, Ma's shoulders sagged. "Fine," she whispered, her voice so soft it almost disappeared into the room. "But you bring her back to me, Kaelan. Promise me that."

"I will," I said, though the lump in my throat made the words feel fragile.

***

Central bore the unmistakable scars of war, its once-vibrant streets now shrouded in exhaustion and despair. The market square was almost empty, a place once vibrant and filled with the shouts of merchants and the chatter of shoppers. The market, once bursting with bright fabrics and fresh produce, was now half-empty, its wares dwindled to a few bruised fruits and threadbare textiles. Children sat hunched in doorways, their faces smudged with dirt, their laughter a distant memory. A horse-drawn cart rolled by, its wheels creaking under the weight of firewood, the driver's expression as weathered as the cobblestones beneath his wagon. Supplies had grown scarce—flour, vegetables, and even simple fabrics were harder to come by. The merchants who remained called out half-heartedly, their tables displaying what little they had managed to acquire. But Lilah, as if to defy the somber backdrop, filled the silence with words.

"That man," she said, pointing to the passing farmer driving a cart laden with firewood, "possesses the most wondrous nose I have ever laid eyes upon. He could scent trouble before it arrives—think what usefulness such gift would be."

I chuckled and shook my head.

"And that boy there," she added later, gesturing toward a child looking longingly at a bread cart pushed by a thin man with a hat, "he's probably planning an elaborate heist of that bread cart. Mark my words, Kaelan— a deviser of criminal plots in the making."

Her voice was the thread that pulled me from my dark thoughts. Each observation, each teasing remark, reminded me of what I was fighting for—a world where her laughter could ring free of grief.

Silas's aunt lived in a sturdy stone house with ivy crawling stubbornly up the walls as if trying to claim it for the wild. Lilah stood beside me, her hands planted on her hips, her head tilted as she assessed the structure like a master craftsman judging inferior work.

"It's stern enough," she murmured. "Solid walls, no-nonsense roof. I imagine the chairs inside are just as unforgiving."

Before I could respond, Silas's aunt emerged from the house. Middle-aged and brisk, her sharp eyes swept over Lilah in a way that reminded me of a general appraising new recruits.

"She's stern enough too," Lilah whispered, her words earning her a warning look from me.

"What?" she said, feigning innocence. "If I'm to live here, I must know what I'm up against. Does she allow jokes? Or is this a strictly somber household?"

"Just behave, please," I muttered.

When the time came to leave, Lilah stood in the doorway with a hint of vulnerability that tugged at something deep within me.

"Don't go and jump right into trouble, Kaelan," she called out as I mounted my horse. "Or I'll come after you myself!"

Her words brought a smile to Aunt Rhoda's face, though she quickly disguised it with a shake of her head. But for me, it was the sound of Lilah's laughter—light and unrestrained, as if daring the world to darken it again—that lingered. It carried me down the road, a fragile shield against the uncertainty ahead. And as the house faded from view, I gripped the reins tighter, the weight of the journey settling over me like the chill of the morning air. The wind tugged at my cloak, but I leaned forward, spurring my horse on.

# CHAPTER
# 42

The grand halls of Centralia rose ahead, their stone facades casting long shadows across the street. Even here, the signs of strain were evident—the guards at the entrance stood with tired eyes, their armor dulled from a lack of proper maintenance, their expressions stiff. I could hear snippets of conversation as I passed—talk of rationing, of men forcefully dragged into the war, of the front lines moving ever closer.

The life that had once filled Central, the laughter, the music, the joy was now overshadowed. A group of soldiers was gathered near the side of the street, their shoulders slumped, their armor bearing the marks of wear and tear. They stood in clusters, their voices low as they spoke, their expressions lined with exhaustion. I slowed my pace to catch snippets of the gossip they traded,

"... They say the front lines have entered Centralian territory now," one of the soldiers muttered, running his hand over his tunic. "The Wintmorians are pushing hard, and we don't have enough men to hold them back."

Another soldier furrowed his brow. "And I heard that one of our regiments is nearing Edmundshire, but it's a mess out there. We're stretched too thin, and we can't keep this up forever."

A third soldier let out a bitter laugh. "It is a lost cause, isn't it? We're losing ground, losing men... and for what? The Crown Prince is dead, and now we're all paying the price."

My heart clenched at their words, the despair etched in their voices. I could see it in their eyes—the doubt, the fear, the sense of loss. The hope that had once driven us had begun to wither, replaced by the harsh reality of a conflict that had claimed so much and given so little in return.

I couldn't let myself fall into that same despair. I had seen what was happening beyond the borders, the forces conspiring to tear apart everything we had built. I had seen the truth behind the war, the manipulation, the deceit. And I knew that we had to act, to fight, not just against the enemy we could see, but against the hidden forces driving this conflict.

The towering silhouette of the Imperial Palace rose in the distance, its spires reaching toward the sky like sentinels watching over the city. The palace, which had once been a symbol of Centralian strength, a beacon of hope and grandeur, now seemed like a mockery of what it used to be.

Even the air around it had changed— the vibrant, bustling activity that used to surround the palace had dwindled to an eerie silence.

The grand avenue leading to the gates was largely deserted. It was a far cry from the days when merchants, emissaries, and nobles traveled this path, their carriages rolling over the cobblestones, banners fluttering in the breeze. Now, only a handful of guards remained at their posts, their eyes scanning the street with a mix of vigilance and exhaustion. Our people had grown wary, fearful of what the future held, and that uncertainty had reached even the palace, wrapping itself around the walls like an unseen force.

The courtyard was empty, the vast space echoing with a sense of stillness that made the hairs on the back of my neck stand on end. It was as if the palace had twisted inward, pulling itself away from the city, from the people it was meant to protect.

The palace gates once open to the people of Central—welcoming petitioners, visitors, and those seeking an audience—were now tightly shut, the heavy iron bars a testament to the isolation the palace had adopted as the war closed in.

I slowed my pace, my eyes narrowing as I took in the scene before me. I stepped forward, my gaze meeting the eyes of the guard closest to me. His posture stiffened, his hand tightening around the spear as I approached.

"Halt," the taller guard barked, his voice echoing through the empty courtyard. "State your name and purpose."

I took a deep breath. "Kaelan of Elsenburg," I said. "I must speak with His Majesty at once. It concerns the safety of all Centralia." The guard's eyes narrowed as he appraised me, his eyes lingering on the dust caked onto my boots. He cast a glance at the other guard, then turned back to me with a look of practiced aversion. The shorter guard raised an eyebrow, his stance rigid. "Urgent, is it?" His voice was laden with skepticism. "And what makes you think we are fools?"

My jaw tightened. "I do not," I admitted, stepping closer. "But you must listen—what I carry cannot wait. The war, the Wintmorians... there is more happening than you know. I bear grave tidings for the Emperor. Lives hang in the balance!"

The guard shook his head, holding his ground. "No writ, no audience," he said curtly. "Palace orders are absolute."

Desperation surged within me. I stepped forward unbidden, my voice rising. "I don't have time for this!" My voice rose, my desperation slipping through. "You're standing there, guarding an empty gate, while Centralia teeters on the brink of ruin. Let me pass, or all of this—" I gestured toward the palace, the city beyond, "—will fall!" The guard's spear came up, the gleaming tip leveled at my chest. "Enough!" he snapped, his eyes cold. "Another step, and you'll find yourself in chains." He looked at me with an upturned nose. "You think you're the first to beg for an audience? Every man with a sob story comes here claiming to save the Empire." I stared at the guard, my heart pounding, and my mind racing. I wanted to push forward, force my way inside and demand to be heard. But I saw the resolve in the guard's stance, the unyielding obedience etched into his face. No words, no pleas would move him. A vein throbbed in my temple as I stepped back.

"Wise choice," he said, though his voice held no kindness. He lowered the spear but kept a wary eye on me. "Be gone from here. Return without proper clearance, and it will be the dungeons you'll find, not an audience with the Emperor."

I turned away slowly, my pulse hammering in my ears. A few steps in retreat, and I spun back, locking eyes with the taller guard. "You're making a mistake," I said quietly, my anger simmering beneath the surface. "When the fires reach these gates, remember that I tried to stop it."

The guard's expression flickered, just for a moment—uncertainty, or perhaps regret—but he said nothing. The gates remained shut behind me, an impassable barrier between me and the answers Centralia desperately needed.

# CHAPTER
# 43

I turned away from the gates, my shoulders slumped, my heart aching with frustration and defeat. I moved through the city streets my mind in turmoil. Central was hollowing out. Its pulse was still there, but weaker, quieter, as if the city was holding its breath. Eamon's pale face haunted me, his stillness a constant weight in my chest. I had made him a promise—and I intended to keep it. For that, I needed help, the kind only someone inside the city's inner leadership could give.

That's when Darius's name surfaced in my mind. Darius. I hadn't seen him in years. We'd endured the same drills, the same harsh marches, and the same exhaustion together. The last time we spoke, he was chasing ambition like a man possessed. Rumors said he'd made it, climbing the ranks faster than most. I had heard whispers over the past few months that Darius had been promoted, now serving as an officer with certain privileges in Central, and he might have access to the palace grounds. If anyone could pull strings, it was him. The question was whether he'd care enough to try. I made my way to the old Grand Hall.

The Grand War Hall loomed before me—with banners bearing the Centralian crest fluttering wearily in the cold wind.

The sight of it brought a rush of memories back—memories of long days of training, of laughter shared with my comrades, and of the blood and sweat spilled for a greater purpose. I took a deep breath, gathering my courage. If Darius was still stationed here, I would find him.

At the gate, two guards eyed me warily, their grips tightening on their spears.

"What's your business here?" one of them demanded.

I adjusted my cloak, my insignia catching the torchlight. "Kaelan of Elsenburg. I'm here to see Darius."

The guard exchanged a glance with his companion. "Darius?" he repeated, drawing out the name like he was testing its weight. "What do you want with him?"

"Old friend."

"Aye, he's still stationed here. Last I heard, he was in the officers' quarters. Head straight down that way. You'll see his quarters beyond the training yard."

I murmured my thanks and slipped through the gate. The yard was alive with soldiers—sparring, shouting, their swords flashing under the torchlight. Memories came rushing back—memories of my training, and for a moment, I felt the ache of belonging. I found the chambers, a modest stone building with light spilling through its small windows. The door creaked as I knocked, and when it opened, there he was—Darius. He looked older, his face lined with the weight of responsibility, but his eyes were the same—sharp, intelligent, and filled with the familiar spark. For a moment, there was silence as we both stared at each other and slowly, recognition dawned in his eyes.

"Kaelan?" He said, his voice uncertain. Recognition dawned slowly, and then his face split into a wide grin as he enveloped me in a bear hug. "By the gods, it's been months. What brings you here?"

I smiled, though it didn't quite reach my eyes. "I must talk to you, Darius. Can I come in?"

"Of course!"

The room was sparse with a small desk covered in rolls of parchment, a cot shoved against the wall, and a map of Centralia pinned above it like a silent judge.

"I need your help," I said, skipping the pleasantries. "It's urgent."

Darius crossed his arms, leaning back against the desk. "Urgent, is it? Let me guess. You need access to the palace."

I blinked. "How did you—?"

"You're not the first desperate man to knock on my door," he cut in. "What makes you think I'd risk my position for you?"

The coldness in his tone wasn't unexpected, but it still stung. "Because you know me, Darius," I said, my voice low. "And you know I wouldn't ask unless it mattered."

He studied me, his gaze sharp enough to slice through armor. "Why the palace?"

I hesitated, the weight of what I carried pressing down on me. "I have news," I said finally. "About the war. About a danger greater than the Wintmorians—one that looms over us all, darker than any storm we've faced."

Darius's expression didn't change, but something shifted in his eyes—a flicker of curiosity, or maybe caution. "You think you can simply stride in and tell the Emperor how to govern his realm?"

"No," I said. "But I think I can stop him from losing it."

For a moment, silence filled the room. Then Darius sighed, rubbing a hand over his face. "You're serious about this."

"I am."

He let out a bitter laugh, shaking his head. "You always did know how to put me in trouble."

Reluctantly, he moved to the map on the wall. "The palace is a fortress," he said, tracing a finger along the lines of walls and gates. "If you seek to gain entry, you'll need far more than mere luck and noble intent."

"What about the servants' entrance?" I asked, stepping closer.

Darius's finger hovered over a mark near the southern wall. "It's a possibility. Not heavily guarded, true, but hardly an open invitation. You would need a guise—and a plan sharp enough to cut through their vigilance."

I nodded, hope flickering to life. "We shall find a way. Together."

Darius snorted. "You've ever had a knack for drawing folk into the most impossible of schemes, Kaelan."

# CHAPTER
# 44

We worked late into the night, our voices hushed as we discussed our plan, our eyes constantly flicking to the door. The map lay between us, covered in hastily scrawled notes, with lines and arrows pointing to potential routes and escape points. It was risky—far riskier than anything I had done before—but it was our only option.

The next day, I set out into the city, my hood pulled low over my face as I moved through the bustling streets. I asked questions in hushed tones, approaching merchants who delivered goods to the palace and laborers who had worked on the grounds. The city felt different—an undercurrent of fear and uncertainty ran through it, with people wary of strangers, their eyes darting nervously as they spoke. I learned about the layout of the servants' corridors, the narrow staircases that led up to the higher levels, the doors that were always locked, and the ones that sometimes stood ajar.

It was not much, but it was enough to give us a morsel of hope. When I returned to the cramped chamber where we had taken refuge, Darius was waiting with a bundle of tattered, grimy tunics clutched in his hands. He looked exhausted, with dark circles under his eyes, but there was a triumphant glint in his gaze.

"I got them," Darius said, holding up the uniforms. "It wasn't easy, but I convinced one of the workers to let me have these. They think I'm doing a favor for a friend."

I took one of the uniforms, the rough fabric scratchy against my fingers. We had a way in!

"Good work," I said, clapping Darius on the shoulder. The following night, we set out under the cover of darkness, my heart pounding as we approached the palace. The uniforms were a poor disguise, the fabric hanging loosely from our shoulders and the sleeves too long. We moved quietly, keeping to the shadows, the weight of what we were about to do pressing down on us with every step.

We reached the servants' door, the small entrance barely visible in the darkness. I glanced at Darius, his expression tense, and he nodded, his hand tightening on the handle of the door. Slowly, I pushed it open, the hinges creaking softly in the stillness of the night. We slipped inside, the door closing behind us, plunging us into darkness.

We moved cautiously, our footsteps muffled against the stone floor. I could hear the faint sounds of the palace above us— the distant clatter of dishes, the muffled voices of servants. We were inside, but the hard part was still ahead of us. We made our way through the servant corridors, the narrow passages winding and twisting, the walls closing in around us. Every creak of the floorboards above us, every shadow that moved in the flickering torchlight, made my breath catch in my throat.

Finally, we reached the staircase that led up to the higher levels. Darius paused, his hand resting on the banister, his eyes meeting mine. There was a hesitation in his steps, but I gave him a reassuring smile as I began to climb. Darius followed, the narrow steps creaking beneath our weight, the air growing colder as we ascended. The staircase seemed to stretch on forever, the darkness pressing in around us, the weight of what we were doing heavy on my shoulders.

At the top of the stairs, we paused, listening for any sound of approaching footsteps. The hallway was empty, the faint glow of torchlight casting long shadows across the stone floor. We moved quickly, keeping close to the wall, our eyes darting from door to door, searching for the one that would lead us to the Emperor.

But as we turned a corner, I heard it—a voice, low and commanding, coming from just ahead. I froze, my heart leaping into my throat. My eyes met Darius's and we nodded at each other. We were close—too close. If we were caught now, everything would be over.

Darius motioned for me to follow, his movements slow and deliberate as we backed away from the corner, our footsteps silent on the stone floor. We needed to find another way, a way that would lead us to the Emperor without being seen.

But before we could move, the door at the end of the hallway opened, and a rotund man with a bald head stepped out, his eyes locking onto us. He squinted and peered into our faces, his voice sharp and accusing. "You there! What business have you here?"

My heart skipped a beat, my mind racing as I searched for an answer, an excuse, anything that would get us out of this. But before I could speak, Darius stepped forward, his voice calm and steady.

"We're new," he said, his eyes meeting the man's. "We were bid to bring these supplies to the kitchens. Mayhap, we have taken a wrong turn." The man frowned, his eyes narrowing as he studied the two of us. I held my breath, my heart pounding in my chest as the silence stretched on.

Finally, he nodded, his expression softening slightly. "The kitchens are two floors down," he said, voice impatient. "Be quick about it."

I let out a sigh of relief, my eyes meeting Darius's. We nodded our thanks and turned, making our way back down the hallway. When we were out of sight, I turned to Darius, my voice a whisper. "We need to find another way."

We moved quietly through the halls of the palace, our senses heightened, every creak of the floorboards, every distant footfall making our hearts race. I was relieved that Darius was willing to take the gamble. Our goal was the Emperor's inner chambers, a place where Darius believed we could find someone willing to listen. We passed doors that loomed tall, each guarded by soldiers who were, fortunately, either absent or preoccupied in other parts of the palace. The farther we ventured, the more oppressive the atmosphere became. The corridors seemed to close in around us, each turn leading us deeper into the heart of power.

"This way," Darius whispered, his eyes darting around. His voice was barely audible above the sound of our own footsteps. He led me down a narrower hallway, one that branched off from the more frequented main corridors. This part of the palace was quieter, more secluded, and as a result, more intimidating. I could feel my heartbeat quicken, the pressure in my chest building as each step brought us closer to our goal.

"We are close," Darius continued, glancing over his shoulder. His expression was grim, his eyes focused but tinged with worry. Suddenly, we heard voices. Darius held up a hand, signaling me to stop. We both froze, pressing against the cold stone wall, our ears straining to pick up the conversation. It was a pair of guards, their voices approaching from the hallway ahead, echoing off the marble walls. My heart hammered in my chest. I exchanged a glance with Darius, my eyes wide.

"They're getting closer," Darius hissed. He gestured to a nearby alcove. We pressed ourselves into it, the heavy fabric brushing against our faces. It smelled faintly of dust and old parchment, its intricate weave depicting a battle long past. I tried not to think about how little it concealed us, how easily a stray glance could betray our presence. The guards' boots clattered closer, the cadence a steady drumbeat of dread. Without wasting a moment, we ducked into it, the thick fabric offering a flimsy shield from the guards' sight. We waited, hardly daring to breathe.

***

The guards walked by, their footsteps reverberating in the narrow space. "Have you heard the rumors about the Wintmorian front?" one of them said, his voice muffled but distinct enough for me to make out.

"Aye," the other replied. "Doesn't sound good. They're saying the enemy's moved deeper into our territory. The front lines are struggling."

Their voices faded as they walked past, the tension slowly dissipating as their footsteps grew more distant. I let out a sigh and glanced at Darius. He nodded, signaling it was time to move again.

We continued down the corridor, my senses still on high alert. Darius led the way to a door, one that was different from the others—more ornate, with intricate carvings etched into its dark wood.

"This is it," Darius whispered, his eyes meeting mine. He swallowed hard. I reached out to push the door open when he reached out and grabbed my arm.

"Kaelan."

I turned. His grip lingered on my arm, tighter than before. His face was pale, his gaze darting to the shadows like a man expecting ghosts.

"What is it?" I asked, lowering my hand from the door. The unease threading through my chest tightened.

For a moment, he didn't answer. His mouth opened, then shut, and the silence between us grew heavy, thick with words left unspoken. Finally, he sighed, the sound heavy with something I couldn't place.

"The Emperor isn't there," he said. His voice was like the scratching of metal.

I froze. "What are you talking about? You said—"

"I know what I said." His tone hardened, but his gaze didn't meet mine. "I never thought we'd get this far."

"Darius." My voice dropped, edged with suspicion. "What are you trying to say?"

He looked up, and something cold flickered in his eyes. Something sinister. My stomach twisted. Slowly, his hand drifted to the pommel of his sword.

"I'm saying this is where it ends—for you."

The words hit me like a blow, knocking air from my lungs. "What?"

Darius stepped back, his movements slow and deliberate. His hand rested on the pommel of his sword now, his knuckles white. "You don't understand, Kaelan."

My heart sank. Darius was one of us —a fellow soldier, a comrade who had stood beside me in battle. We'd shared laughter and bloodshed in equal measure. He used to be one of the best. He was not in my circle like Jaric and Cedric were, but we had shared a table and he was my comrade. Darius wasn't just a fellow soldier—he was my brother in all but blood. But now, his expression was cold, as if I meant nothing. As if I was nothing. This wasn't just betrayal. It was the shattering of something I thought was unbreakable.

I took a step forward, my hand instinctively hovering over my sword. "Darius, why are you doing this?"

"I could ask you the same," Darius said smoothly, his eyes flicking between my face and my sword. "But I already know. You think you can just stride into the palace and have the Emperor's ear?" His tone dripped with mockery, but beneath it, there was something darker.

"You're with them, aren't you?" I said, my voice low, the realization dawning like a storm cloud.

Darius shrugged, his hand resting casually on the pommel of his sword. "I want the best for this empire, Kaelan. My vision is for a better Centralia. "

I stiffened. "You're betraying your people for power!"

"For survival," he shot back, his voice sharp. "You think the Emperor knows us? Remembers our faces? While we bury our brothers, he drinks wine from golden goblets." Darius's voice was low, trembling with anger. "I've seen men like him my whole life—safe behind their walls, sending others to die for their ideals. Tell me, Kaelan, how many more have to fall before you see it?" His voice wavered, his grip on his sword tightening like a lifeline. "You don't see it, do you? We're not saving Centralia. We're bleeding for it, day after day."

"Darius—"

"The Astari… they offer something different. And gods forgive me, Kaelan, but I believe in them."

I felt my fists clench at my sides. I wanted to understand his motivations. I wanted to believe he was simply unguided, but rage boiled in my chest.

"And what about Eamon? He believed in this kingdom. He died for it."

Darius flinched at the mention of my brother's name, but his resolve didn't falter. "Eamon was a good man," he said quietly. "But he was blind—just like you. Clinging to these beliefs of yours is unwise."

The words hit me like a blade to the gut. I took a step forward, my voice trembling with controlled fury. "You have no right to utter Eamon's name!"

He was unbothered by my fury. "I was right. There's no room for your kind in the world we're building."

His hand tightened on the hilt of his sword as two men emerged from the shadows, their cloaks blending into the dim light, their daggers catching the faintest gleam. They moved with a deliberate calm, their gazes sharp, their intent unmistakable.

The silence pressed in, heavier than the walls themselves. Darius hadn't moved. He was unnervingly still, like a coiled snake ready to strike.

I took a step back, then another. My breath felt thin, every beat of my heart a cruel countdown to the moment he'd strike.

"Don't make this harder than it has to be," he said finally, his voice softer, almost pleading.

I shook my head. "You'll regret it, Darius! I swear it!"

Darius sighed, a weary sound, and drew his sword. The steel glinted in the torchlight. "I hoped you'd say that."

Before any of us could move, a few guards wandered in, unsuspecting. I seized my chance and bolted.

"Oi!" I heard one of the palace guards call, the unmistakable glint of a blade flashing before my eyes. I rounded a corner and saw another armed guard. Surprise flashed across his face as he immediately gave chase. The air grew heavy as the hallway exploded into chaos.

When I had put enough distance between us, I slowed my steps, gasping for breath as I pressed myself into the shadows of a narrow alcove. I heard Darius's voice carrying through the stone corridors behind me.

"Stop him! He's an intruder!"

My heart clenched at the words. His tone was filled with righteous indignation, loud enough to be heard by anyone nearby. The echoes carried the weight of conviction, a performance meant to disguise his guilt. "Intruder!" he shouted again, pointing in my direction. Panic surged through me as my eyes darted around for any route of escape. Behind me, I could hear the guards yelling, and the clang of armor as they gave chase.

I raced down the hallway, turning sharply into another hallway, my eyes scanning for any way out. Their shouts rang in my ears, their footsteps pounding against the stone. I rounded a corner and made for the backdoor. But it was no use.

# CHAPTER
# 45

A hand wrenched me backward, and a fist followed, striking hard and fast. My back slammed into the wall, my vision spinning as pain erupted across my face. I struggled, my hands pushing against the guard, but there were too many. Another guard grabbed my arm, twisting it behind my back, forcing me down to my belly.

"Stop struggling," one of them growled, his voice filled with authority. "You're under arrest."

My heart pounded in my ears, my eyes darting around desperately, searching for any sign of Darius. He was gone, vanished into the maze of palace corridors. I felt a sinking feeling in my stomach as the guards roughly pulled my hands behind my back, binding them with a thick rope. As their rough hands seized me and dragged me forward, a strange sense of relief washed over me. Darius had sought my death—cold and swift—and would have had his way were it not for the timely arrival of the guards.

"Get him up," one of the guards ordered. I was hauled to my feet and my shoulders twisted backward from the force of their grip.

"Move," the guard barked, shoving me forward, my feet nearly stumbling over themselves as they pushed me down the hallway. The reality of my situation sank in with every step we took, the distant hope I had carried with me growing dimmer.

\*\*\*

The dungeon reeked of mildew and decay, the damp air clinging to my skin. Water dripped somewhere in the distance, the steady sound blending with the distant clank of armor and murmurs of guards moving through the winding corridors above. I was in a small, dark cell—the iron bars rusted, but strong enough to keep me in. A narrow slit near the ceiling allowed the faintest trickle of light to enter, barely illuminating the grimy stone floor beneath my feet. I sank onto the cold ground and clenched my jaw as a creeping sense of defeat threatened to overwhelm me.

It was eerily quiet, with only the faint rustle of chains and the occasional cough or groan from other prisoners breaking the silence. The walls felt as if they were closing in, the dark corners of the cell seeming to breathe with shadows that stretched and twisted, shifting with the light. Moments passed, or perhaps days—time was difficult to gauge and everything blurred together in an endless stretch of darkness and uncertainty. The rations they brought were meager—a piece of stale bread and thin, tasteless gruel, delivered with little ceremony by guards who hardly spared us a glance. I took what I was given without complaint, focusing only on surviving. Every bite, every drop of water, every breath was an act of defiance.

From time to time, I heard the shuffle of boots—the guards changing shifts, their conversations echoing down the dim stone halls. I strained to listen whenever they passed by, hoping for any scrap of news. It was during one such moment, as I lay awake upon the cold stone floor that I began to catch fragments of a conversation between two guards stationed at the far end of the corridor."

"You hear what they're saying about the council meeting?" one of the guards asked, his voice low and conspiratorial.

I could barely make out the other guard's response. "Aye... more trouble brewing, that's for sure. With the Emperor holed up like he is..."

"And those assassination rumors," the first guard continued, his voice lowering further until I had to strain to hear. "They say it's Centralians planning it. Some group of them, trying to put an end to all of this."

My breath caught in my throat, and I felt my pulse quicken. Assassination rumors? Centralians? I pressed myself closer to the bars, hoping to hear more of the conversation. The guards' voices waxed and waned, the words sometimes muffled by the thick stone walls and the clank of distant chains.

"It's all falling apart, if you ask me," the second guard said, his tone heavy with resignation. "No one knows who to trust anymore. The Emperor doesn't even trust his own council, they say. And now with our own people sneaking about... if they manage to pull it off, gods know what'll happen next."

My mind reeled. Assassins? The Centralians plotting their own emperor's death? It was madness. Yet, a part of me couldn't ignore the weight of the words. If even the Emperor's people couldn't be trusted, then this war was far more precarious than I'd ever imagined. Could it be Darius? Could it be another group of Centralians? Who were these assassins, and how did they even get this close to the palace? And what did it mean for Centralia?

I leaned back against the wall crippled by my impotence. The Astari plot—the conspiracy to turn Wintmore and Centralia against each other, to weaken them both for their own gain— was still unfolding, and every moment I spent in this cell was a moment lost in stopping it.

The rumors of assassination had given me something to pursue—a glimmer of hope amidst the darkness. If there were others, others who sought to change things, then perhaps—just perhaps—I might find an ally.

As the guards' voices faded into silence, I let my gaze linger on the darkness beyond my cell, a resolve hardening within my chest. I was not yet undone. Not by a wide measure.

Days passed, blurring into one another as my body grew accustomed to the cold, damp air of the dungeon. In the cell adjacent to mine, I began to notice movement—a flicker in the shadows that, over time, grew more distinct. At first, I paid it little mind, too consumed by my own turmoil. But the voice… the voice was harder to ignore. It muttered things at first—half- heard phrases about "the folly of men" and "how power devours reason." There was a rawness to it, a weariness that came from years of battles fought, and a long time spent in captivity, but there was also a sharpness, a keen edge that made me curious. And beneath the rasp, there was an edge, a clarity of thought that struck a chord. It crept in like a distant memory, stubborn and unshakable.

"General Aldric?" I finally ventured one evening, leaning toward the bars. My voice was low, almost disbelieving. "Is that you?"

The shadows shifted. A dry chuckle rose from the other cell, laced with bitterness. "So, the boy remembers," came the reply.

"Gods above, Kaelan! Of all the men who might have crossed my path again, I'd not have wagered a Emerul on you."

His words stung slightly, though I couldn't tell if he meant them as an insult. "You fell in battle in the courtyard... I saw it happen," I whispered, grasping at the improbability of it all. "You were... supposed to be dead."

He chuckled again, an unfamiliar sound. "I'm made of tougher skin," he muttered. "Before I learned how easily empires devour their champions. What brings you here, Kaelan? Did you dare question too much, as I once did?"

Over the next few days, we spoke in whispered snatches, careful not to draw the attention of the guards patrolling the damp halls. General Aldric was discovered, unconscious and half dead, by the battalion that cleaned the battleground. He was taken to Central to recover, and none of us were told.

"I heard whispers, Kaealan, of people meeting in the shadows and perpetuating mischief. I spoke out and they said, 'the great General Aldric had gone raving mad.'

I looked at him. Even in captivity, he carried himself with the air of a man used to commanding. His voice, though weathered, still had its authority, his words deliberate and sharp.

"I stood before the council," Aldric said one night, his voice low and bitter. "I stood before the council, Kaelan, thinking reason could sway them. But power doesn't listen to reason—it listens to ambition." He let out a bitter laugh, dry as the air around us. "Reason. What a fool I was. You see, Kaelan, power fears reason. I was cast aside for my insolence and tossed into this pit to rot."

"You deserved better," I said, suddenly saddened that such would happen to Aldric.

"Better?" He scoffed. "I deserved what I got. I failed to see that my words alone could never shift the tide. Power requires force, not whispers." He fell silent for a moment, the weight of his words filling the space between us. "But enough of my failures. Tell me, why are you here? A voice like yours does not belong in these shadows."

I hesitated. But there was something in Aldric's tone. I leaned closer to the bars, lowering my voice. "General," I began, "I know why the war began… why the Crown Prince was killed."

His head snapped toward me, his dark eyes gleaming in the dim light that trickled through the narrow window above. "Go on," he said, his tone sharp as a blade.

"It wasn't just the Wintmorian extremist," I whispered. "There's a shadow force—a group of Astari assassins. They orchestrated the assassination to pit Centralia and Wintmore against each other. Their goal is to weaken both empires until neither can stand. And they have loyalists here in Centralia."

Aldric's expression darkened, his jaw tightening. For a moment, he said nothing, the silence stretching between us. When he spoke, his voice was low, measured, yet brimming with fury. "The Astari, "The vipers slithering in the dark. I should have known."

"You believe me?" I asked, unable to mask my eagerness.

"I've seen their handiwork before," Aldric replied, his gaze distant. "Years ago, they tried to kidnap the emperor. Whispers of betrayals orchestrated from the shadows, alliances undone by unseen hands. I heard stories. I thought them mere rumors. But if what you say is true, Kaelan, then you carry knowledge that could change the course of this war."

"I need to get out of here," I said, my voice trembling with urgency. "We need to warn someone—anyone who will listen."

Aldric leaned closer, his expression sharpening into something resolute. "There is one who might aid us," he said, his voice dropping to a conspiratorial whisper. "Sergeant Roderic. He was once a loyal man, true to his conscience. He served under me before I was cast down. If he still walks these halls, he may yet be convinced to help."

"Why hasn't he helped you already?" I asked, suspicion creeping into my tone.

Aldric's lips twitched into a bitter smile. "Fear binds men as tightly as chains, Kaelan. But the right spark—truth, desperation—can ignite even the most reluctant soul. If we can get a message to him, I believe he will act."

My mind raced. "And if he doesn't?"

"Then we find another way," he said firmly. "But first, we try. He knows the cost of war—he's lost friends, and family. You say you carry a burden of knowledge. Then let us put it to use. Together, we will find our way out of this pit."

The quiet intensity in his voice kindled a spark of hope within me. "How do we reach him?"

Aldric glanced toward the iron door, his eyes narrowing in calculation. "The guards change shifts thrice daily. Roderic has a pattern—he often lingers near the western wing after the evening change. When the time is right, I will call out to him. If he still remembers me, he will listen."

"And if he turns us away?" I asked again, my voice quieter this time.

Aldric's lips pressed into a thin line. "Then we make him listen."

# CHAPTER
# 46

The plan sounded straightforward, almost too much so, but it was our only chance. As the evening shift neared, we rehearsed what Aldric would say, how he would appeal to Roderic's better nature. My chest tightened as the sound of boots echoed down the hall, heralding the arrival of the new guards.

A few minutes passed in tense silence before Aldric called out, his voice almost as loud as it used to be when he led us in battle. "Roderic! Roderic, it's Aldric. I need a moment of your time, son."

A shadow moved at the end of the corridor. A tall figure approached, his armor clinking softly with each step. The torchlight caught the sharp lines of his face—stern, weathered, and etched with fatigue. It was Roderic. But instead of slowing, Roderic's steps quickened, his eyes narrowing as he reached Aldric's cell. His voice, when it came, was a low growl. "You have no right to call my name."

Aldric didn't flinch, his hands gripping the bars of his cell. "Roderic, listen to me. This war is a lie—"

"Quiet," Roderic hissed, his gaze darting to the other guards stationed further down the hall. "Do you think I don't know the risks I take, standing here? Do you think I haven't heard enough of your madness? You've ruined your life, Aldric. Don't drag me into the pit with you."

Aldric's expression faltered, but only for a moment. "I speak the truth, Roderic. You know this war is tearing us apart, that it benefits no one. If you won't listen for my sake, then do it for your own. For your family. For Centralia."

Roderic's jaw clenched. I could see the war waging behind his eyes—loyalty, fear, doubt. For a moment, it looked like Aldric's words might reach him. Then he leaned closer, his voice a harsh whisper. "Do you know how many have died for speaking less than you just did? You think I don't want to help? I have a wife, Aldric. And young children. The only reason I am standing here is because you were once kind to me. But I can't risk my family for your cause."

"Roderic," I interjected before I could stop myself. "If you don't act now, there won't be a Centralia left to protect them."

His gaze snapped to me, as sharp as a blade. "And who are you? Another fool following Aldric's doomed cause? Do you think the people who are behind this will pardon you if you expose the truth? They'll bury you so deep no one will remember your name."

His words stung more than I wanted to admit, but Aldric didn't give me time to falter. "And what will you tell your children, Roderic? That you watched the empire crumble while you stood idly by? That you could have made a difference yet chose fear instead? I know you, Roderic. You are better than that."

The silence that followed was thick. Roderic stared at Aldric for what seemed like an eternity, his chest rising and falling with uneven breaths. For a moment, I thought he would walk away. But then, with a low curse, he turned back to us, his face a mask of resignation

"I can't," he whispered. "They're watching me, Aldric. I've seen the spies lurking in the shadows. If I'm caught—" He broke off, shaking his head. "But… there might be a way."

Hope flickered weakly in my chest. "What do you mean?"

Roderic hesitated before glancing over his shoulder. "There's a tunnel—an old passage beneath the dungeon, used during the reign of Emperor Alland. It's not guarded anymore. If you can create a distraction, I can guide you. It's all I can offer."

Aldric's face softened and a rare smile appeared at the corners of his mouth. "That's more than enough, old friend."

But Roderic didn't return the smile. "This is madness. If you're caught…" He shook his head again. "Just be ready. I'll do what I can. But after this, you're on your own."

The days passed in the dim, cold dungeon, each one blurring into the next. Aldric and I waited in uneasy silence, our only company the rattling of chains and the distant footsteps of the guards. Each time I heard footsteps drawing near to our cell, a flicker of hope stirred within me, only to wither when it proved to be but another faceless guard passing by. By the third day, I had started to wonder if Roderic would return at all—or if fear had finally won.

One night, as Aldric and I sat in the corner of the cell, the clanking of keys echoed down the hallway. I looked up, my heart pounding. A figure emerged from the shadows, illuminated by the flickering torchlight. It was Roderic. I scrambled to my feet, Aldric following close behind, our eyes locking onto the guard's face.

Roderic approached the cell slowly, the keys jangling in his hand. His face was a mask, giving nothing away as he stopped before the cell door. The torchlight cast jagged shadows across his features, making him look as worn as the stone walls around us. His eyes flicked between Aldric and me. He remained silent for a moment, and my heart hammered. Then, he shuffled closer.

He didn't waste words on pleasantries. "I'm not promising anything beyond getting you an audience. It won't be the Emperor himself, but someone close. Someone with enough influence to make a difference, to take this information to the Emperor's ear."

I swallowed hard, my throat dry. "Thank you, Roderic, Truly."

He raised a hand to cut me off. "Don't thank me yet. If anyone finds out what I'm doing, it won't just be your head on the block." He stared at me for a moment longer, as if he was weighing me on a scale. Then he stepped back and reached into his pockets. It was a small, folded piece of parchment. He slid it to me through the bars. "Tomorrow night."

Without another word, he vanished back into the shadows.

# CHAPTER
# 47

The next day dawned heavy with expectation. The parchment's lines and symbols were seared into my mind; I had studied it until my eyes blurred. In the far corner of the cell, beneath a film of dust and neglect, lay a stone slab. Its faint grooves hinted at something hidden— something that might change everything. But all I could do now was wait. Roderic's signal was my cue, and until then, I was trapped in my thoughts. My pacing wore tracks on the cold stone floor as I replayed his instructions, trying to steady my nerves. Aldric sat in the corner, watching me silently. He hadn't spoken much since last night, and it made me uneasy. Finally, the sound of heavy boots echoed down the corridor. My head snapped up, my heart pounding as I turned toward the barred door. Roderic appeared, brows furrowed in a frown, and his lips pressed into a grim line.

"Leave immediately. Meet me at the end of the tunnel. Don't waste any time."

"Of course. We will leave at once."

Roderick narrowed his eyes, and his voice dropped to a near whisper as if his words were carefully chosen. "I can only get one of you an audience with the chancellor. No more."

My stomach churned with anxiety. I longed to be the one to meet the Chancellor, yet I knew I wasn't ready for it. What could I, a soldier and a second-born, possibly say to the Chancellor that Aldric couldn't? He held greater clout, and I held him in the highest regard. "Very well, Aldric, you must—"

Aldric raised a hand, silencing me. "No, Kaelan," he said, his tone steady but firm, "Listen. You must go—"

"No, General," I interrupted, shaking my head, my voice rising in desperation. "You should be the one to go. You know the palace, the council, the people who might still have influence. I—I'm just a soldier."

Aldric's gaze softened, and for a moment, a faint, wistful smile curved his lips. "And what do you think I am? I'm also just a soldier—like you. But the world doesn't need people like me anymore. I'm a relic of battles long lost, a shadow of the choices that ruined this empire." He pressed his hand to the rusted bars, his fingers wrapping around the cold iron. "You, though… you're different. You carry something I cannot anymore: hope. The kind of hope that can light a fire in dark places."

I stepped closer to the bars, my heart pounding. "But you—" My voice cracked. "You're a leader. I'm just a messenger."

"Exactly," Aldric replied, his voice steady, the weight of his words deliberate. "Messengers move unseen, unnoticed. A man like me? I wouldn't make it past the first checkpoint. I'd be stopped, silenced, long before the message reached its mark."

Roderic shifted uncomfortably, his hand gripping the hilt of his sword. "I've done what I can. Don't waste time arguing over it."

I looked at Aldric, searching his face for a crack in his resolve. But his face was set, and his jaw tightened as though he had already braced himself for this decision. "If he listens," I said quietly, "If everything goes as planned, we'll not leave you here. We'll find a way to get you out—later. When it's safe." I realized I was doing it again. I was making grand promises when I didn't know what the future held for me.

Aldric smiled faintly, but his voice remained even. "When the time comes, Kaelan, you'll do what is right. Your duty is all that matters. Whatever you've seen, whatever truth you carry— it must reach the right ears. And you must do it alone."

My throat tightened, the words catching as I tried to find something to say. But his hand left the bars and clasped my shoulder firmly. "Do not waste this chance, lad. It comes at great cost."

Roderic cleared his throat, his eyes shifting toward the corridor behind him. "If we're going to do this, it has to be now. The night watch won't last forever."

Aldric stepped back, his hand slipping from my arm as if releasing a burden. "Go," he said. I nodded and looked again at the parchment Roderick had given me.

Roderic regarded us for a moment and turned, left the same way he had come darting furtive glances into shadows to make sure no one was watching us. I glanced at Aldric. He stood there, his hand resting on the bars, his gaze resolute as he watched me leave.

***

I crawled out of the old crusty tunnel, and Roderic grabbed my arm, guiding me quickly down a cold stone hall. The air was damp, the dim torchlight flickering, casting long shadows that danced on the walls. My pulse raced, and a sense of disquiet thrummed through my entire body.

Roderic moved with purpose, his demeanor stern. We navigated the palace's narrow corridors until we reached a staircase leading up. As we ascended, the air grew warmer, and the oppressive stone gave way to opulent furniture and polished wood, the change in atmosphere almost disorienting. At the top of the staircase, two guards stood watch, their expressions unreadable, their hands resting on the pommels of their swords, and their faces blank beneath the sharp angles of their helmets. I tried not to glance at them, but their silent presence grated on my nerves. I couldn't tell if they were escorting me or ensuring I didn't bolt.

"Let's move," Roderic said, his voice low and commanding. The air grew warmer as we approached, but it did little to ease the knot tightening in my chest. The torches lining the walls burned brighter here, their golden glow throwing long, flickering shadows that danced like ghosts across the intricate carvings on the walls. Every step forward felt heavier as if the air itself resisted my passage. He led the way through a labyrinth of halls, each more elaborate than the last. I caught glimpses of the palace's grandeur as we moved—a flash of a high vaulted ceiling adorned with golden filigree, the shimmering silks draped across the walls, richly woven rugs, ornate vases, and the flickering light of chandeliers hanging from intricately carved ceilings. It was beautiful, but also cold, almost suffocating in its majesty. This wasn't the palace of stories or songs; this was a fortress of power, and authority.

As we approached a massive set of double doors at the end of the corridor, my pulse quickened. The doors loomed ahead, carved with intricate scenes of Centralia's history—victories, coronations, treaties. They were beautiful, but the stories they told seemed far away, detached from the struggles I had seen firsthand. I wondered if the Chancellor lived in that same detachment, surrounded by beauty and power but blind to the chaos outside these walls. The doors were guarded by two more soldiers. Roderic exchanged a few words with them before one of the guards pushed the doors open with a low groan, revealing the room beyond. The air inside was cooler, almost unnervingly so, and the high ceilings seemed to stretch endlessly upward, making the room feel vast and hollow. Tall windows lined one side, their heavy curtains drawn back to let in the pale morning light, which spilled across the polished floors like liquid gold. A long table dominated the center of the room, its surface scattered with maps, scrolls, and quills.

And there, seated at the head of the table, was the Chancellor.

He was not what I had imagined. His frame was lean, his robe of deep blue trimmed with gold catching the light. His neatly combed hair was streaked with silver, and his face, though marked with age, was sharp and focused. His eyes, dark and piercing, fixed on me the moment I entered.

"Step forward," he said, his voice was unusually gentle, and yet laced with a quiet authority that unsettled my nerves.

I hesitated for a moment and then stepped forward. The guards stayed close as I moved toward the center of the room, each step echoing loudly in the cavernous space. The Chancellor's gaze didn't waver, his expression unreadable as he studied me like a strange rodent he'd just discovered under his bed.

Roderick stepped forward, his tone formal. "This is the man who requested an audience, Chancellor. He claims to have urgent news regarding the security of Centralia."

The Chancellor leaned back slightly, steepling his fingers as his eyes narrowed. "And what, pray tell, makes these tidings so urgent that they warrant disturbing me at this hour of the night?"

The weight of his gaze pinned me in place, and for a moment, I felt like a child being reprimanded. My mind scrambled for the right words as the air thickened, every breath a conscious effort while the silence stretched.

"Thank you, Chancellor, for granting me this audience," I began, trying to keep my voice steady despite the nerves gnawing at me. "My name is Kaelan, a soldier of this empire. I have recently returned from Wintmore. What I bring is not rumor or speculation—it is the truth about a conspiracy that threatens not only Centralia but also the future of our entire realm."

His expression didn't change, but something in his posture shifted, a faint flicker of interest breaking through his mask of indifference. "Go on," he said, his tone clipped.

"The war we are fighting—this endless bloodshed—isn't what it seems. The Wintmorian rebels who assassinated the Crown Prince did not act alone. They had covert support from the Astari. "

I paused, trying to gauge his reaction. His eyes narrowed further, and I pressed on, the words tumbling out now in a desperate rush. "I witnessed their meeting myself. The Astari are manipulating both Centralia and Wintmore, driving us into chaos so they can strike when we're at our weakest. They aim to see both empires fall."

For the first time, a flicker of something—shock, maybe disbelief—crossed his face. It was fleeting, quickly replaced by his usual guarded expression. He leaned forward, his hands resting on the table as he fixed me with a penetrating stare.

"You realize the gravity of what you are saying," he said, his voice low and deliberate. "And the danger of lying to me."

"I do," I said, my voice firm. "But I swear to you, Chancellor, on the honor of my brother who gave his life for this knowledge, that every word I speak is true. I saw Astari assassins meeting with Wintmorian rebels in Edmundshire. They are planning to seize control of Wintmore, and once they do, Chancellor, they will turn their sights on us. Their goal is to ensure that when they come for Centralia, we will be too divided, too broken to resist."

He studied me for a long, agonizing moment. The unease in the room was suffocating, the silence heavy with unspoken doubts and unvoiced decisions. My heart hammered within my chest, my hands slick with sweat. Finally, he spoke.

"You claim the Astaris conspire against us. You claim your brother died for this truth. But truth is a slippery thing, soldier. Without proof, it's a mere tale."

I swallowed hard, my throat dry. I had anticipated this response, but it didn't make it any easier to hear. "I saw them," I said finally, my voice cracking under the weight of the moment. "In Edmundshire, in the dead of night. They spoke of our borders as if they were already theirs. They wore no banners and carried no sigils, but their tongues were sharp, their plans sharper still. They mean to destroy us, Chancellor."

His gaze flickered—doubt, curiosity, or something darker, I couldn't tell. He tapped his fingers against the table, the sound unnervingly rhythmic. "And yet, here you stand, without a shred of evidence. Honor is a fine thing, soldier, but it is not enough to sway the Emperor. If what you say is true, this is a matter of utmost importance. But without proof, without something tangible, there is little I can do. Do you expect me to present your story to the Emperor based on your word alone?"

My breath hitched. "No, Chancellor. But if you give me the chance—"

"Chance?" The Chancellor's voice cut through mine like a blade. "A chance is not what I need, soldier. I need proof. And if you cannot deliver it, then you are wasting my time—and yours."

I felt a sinking feeling in my chest. "Yes, Chancellor," I said, trying to keep the strain from my voice.

"Very well. Roderic will return you to your cell. "

He gestured to Roderic, who stepped forward, placing a firm hand on my arm. As we turned to leave, the Chancellor's voice stopped us.

"One more thing, soldier," he said, his tone softer. "I hope, for all our sakes, that you are wrong. But if you are not—may the gods be with you."

A lump formed in my throat, and I nodded. Roderic guided me out of the chambers, his grip firm as we moved through the grand hall. As we walked, Roderic gave me a sideways glance, his voice low. "You've got guts, I'll give you that—"

I clenched my jaw as we continued through the halls. The grandeur of the palace quickly gave way to the damp chill of stone corridors and the stale scent of the underground. By the time we finally reached the entrance to the dungeon, an idea had formed in my mind.

"Wait," I said, in a whisper.

Roderic stopped, his brow furrowing as he glanced at me. "What is it?"

I took a deep breath, steeling myself. "The rumors—the ones about an assassination plot against the Emperor. What do you know about them?"

Roderic's eyes narrowed, his expression guarded. "Why do you ask?"

"Because if there's any truth to them, it might be the proof we need," I replied, my voice tight with urgency. "If I can find out more—if you can delay putting me in the dungeon for some time—it could be what convinces the Chancellor."

He stopped abruptly. "Surely, you are jesting?"

I stared at him.

He scoffed. "I shouldn't even be speaking to you like this," he said, his voice low but sharp. "Do you realize what I'm risking by doing this?"

"I do," I said, meeting his gaze. "And I wouldn't ask this of you if it weren't important—if it weren't for the future of Centralia."

He scoffed, running a hand through his cropped hair. "The future of Centralia." The words came out bitter, almost mocking. "Do you think you're the first to invoke those words? Every fool with a cause believes they're saving the realm."

"But I'm not just invoking words, Roderic," I pressed, "If we don't act, everything we know will fall apart. I'm not asking you to risk your life for me—I'm asking you to help save everyone we swore to protect."

His jaw clenched, and he looked away, staring at a crack in the wall as if it held the answer to his turmoil. The silence stretched, and I could almost hear the battle raging in his mind.

"Do you have any idea what it's like to work in this palace?" he asked suddenly, his voice quieter now, almost bitter. "To see the corruption seep into every corner, to hear whispers of betrayal and know there's nothing you can do? You think your war is out there, soldier. But in here—" He tapped his temple. "In here is where the real fight is."

I stepped closer, forcing him to look at me. "Then why keep fighting? Why not let the Astari win? If it's all hopeless, why not let it all fall apart?"

His eyes snapped to mine, anger flashing in them. "Don't mistake my frustration for surrender, Kaelan. I've given too much to this kingdom to watch it crumble."

"Then help me," I urged, my voice rising. "Let me prove what I've seen. Let me find the proof that can stop this war before it destroys everything."

Roderic hesitated, his hand dropping to his side. His fingers twitched as if he were weighing the chains of his duty against the spark of hope I was offering. For a long moment, he simply stared at me, his breathing shallow.

"If I let you out," he said finally, "and you're caught, there will be nothing I can do to save you. I'll deny everything. Do you understand me?"

"I do," I said, my heart hammering. "I don't need saving—I just need a chance."

His shoulders relaxed slightly. "You're truly willing to risk it all, aren't you?"

I nodded. "For this empire, yes."

He studied me for another heartbeat, then gave a small nod. "All right. But this is dangerous territory, Kaelan. If you're caught, there's nothing I can do."

"I understand."

Roderic glanced around and then leaned in closer. "Kaelan, I've heard whispers—nothing concrete, but enough to know that something's brewing.

"What kind of whispers?"

"There are those within the palace who are displeased with the Emperor's decisions, who believe the war has endured far too long. They are desperate, and desperate men are wont to act rashly. If there is a plot, it will be woven in the shadows—likely in places where few dare to look."

"Do you know who they are?"

He hesitated. "I've heard rumors in the western wing," he whispered and gestured towards a narrow side hallway, his eyes darting to ensure no one overheard. "I have heard men who speak too freely and act too boldly for their station. If there's anything to find, it'll be there. But mind yourself, Kaelan. These men wouldn't hesitate to slit a throat if they thought it necessary."

# CHAPTER
# 48

I didn't waste any time. The western wing was quieter than the rest of the palace. I moved cautiously, pressing myself against the cold stone walls, listening intently to every sound. The palace at night was full of creaks and distant echoes, but soon, I caught the unmistakable sound of hushed voices. I froze, focusing on the sound, and began to edge closer, moving slowly to keep my presence hidden.

A soft glow emanated from behind a half-closed door ahead and the murmurs of a conversation came from within. My heart clenched as I crept closer, carefully leaning forward to peek inside. Then I saw it—a faint light seeping from beneath a door slightly ajar. I stilled, straining my ears. Low voices. Urgent.

Creeping closer, I pressed myself to the wall, careful to avoid the creaking of loose stones.

Three men stood in a cramped chamber, their faces barely illuminated by a flickering lantern. They were dressed like palace staff, but something about them felt strange—the way they held themselves, their stance—it set my teeth on edge.

"It has to be tomorrow," one of the men hissed. He was an old man, with deep lines etched into his face and a head crowned with a full mane of white hair. "The council meeting shall leave him exposed."

Another, a wiry young man with an anxious stutter, shifted nervously beside him, his fingers twisting the edge of his cloak. "And the …the guards? If…if….they catch us—"

The older man snapped, his tone sharp and irritated. "Hold your tongue. I've told you before—everything is in place. We've come too far to falter now, and you know this as well as I. Centralia is lost to us if we do not act now. This is our only future."

I felt my blood run cold. This was the assassination plot the guards had whispered about. I fought to stay calm, to not make any sudden moves.

The third man, shrouded in the shadows, stepped forward. He was tall and lean, with cold, dead eyes. "Our allies in the north have given their word. They will back our efforts once the emperor falls. They know what must be done."

My eyes widened. The Astari. The words landed like a hammer blow, the truth of it stricking me to my core. This wasn't just a plot against the Emperor—it was part of a calculated, deliberate effort to weaken Centralia from within, to leave us exposed. My hands trembled as I fought to keep still. I needed to get this out. This was the proof we needed—

We'll meet at the western gate an hour before dawn," the older man said, his voice lowering. "From there, we move quickly. . ."

I slowly backed away, careful not to make a sound. My heart pounded as I turned, slipping back into the shadows, and retracing my steps down the hallway. The stone floor was unforgiving beneath my boots, and I fought the urge to glance over my shoulder. My heart felt like it would burst out of my chest, but

I didn't stop. Quickly, I navigated the darkened halls back to the entrance of the dungeon where I knew Roderic was stationed. I glanced around furtively, then stepped out of the shadows. I caught sight of him standing at the far end of the corridor. His back was turned and he was pacing nervously. When I finally reached the entrance to the dungeon, I allowed myself a single, shaky breath. I'd heard enough. My legs were unsteady, but I forced them to move faster as I spotted Roderic in the corridor ahead. Relief mixed with dread as I approached him, my voice low but urgent:

"You were right. They're planning to assassinate the Emperor tomorrow."

\*\*\*

Roderic hesitated, his eyes meeting mine. He could see the desperation in my gaze, the urgency I felt. Finally, he nodded again, his expression hardening. "Very well. Follow me."

We moved swiftly through the darkened passages of the dungeon, back to the Chancellor's hallowed chambers. I feared for what I would see with the chancellor whose gaze was as cold as the stone walls of this palace.

While I fought through the path from Wintmore to Centralia, I had thought it was the greatest battle I would ever face. But that…that was nothing! This was the true battle. If I failed, all would crumble. But if I succeeded… gods help me, I'd have made an enemy of every shadow in this palace. Yet, this was why Eamon had died. To ensure the empire stood. For that, I'd lay down my life without hesitation.

In his chambers, the Chancellor stood at the far end of the room, his gaze fixed on me as I approached. His sharp features were unreadable as I spoke to him again, my eyes almost pleading. When I was done, he did not speak. Silence stretched between us, uncomfortably thin. I shifted on my feet, my throat dry as I pushed on. "Chancellor, I have no reason to come here with lies. These men are already moving—the Astari, Wintmorians, and half the palace staff. If we hesitate even a moment, the Emperor will—"

The Chancellor raised a hand, cutting me off. His movements were deliberate, his expression giving away nothing. "I asked you before Kaelan, do you have proof? Words alone are not enough to accuse loyal servants of treason. The consequences, if you're wrong, could fracture the Empire."

I opened my mouth, then closed it, my pulse hammering in my ears. "I overheard them plotting in the western wing," I pressed, my voice rising. "They said tomorrow—during the council meeting. They mentioned the Astari and their support. What more do you need?"

The Chancellor's eyes narrowed, his sharp tone cutting through the space between us. "I need certainty, not the hearsay of a young soldier stumbling into something beyond his station."

The words hit me like a blow, and for a moment, the air seemed to leave the room. I even heard Roderick gasp beside me. He didn't look pleased. I clenched my fists and forced down the anger rising in my chest. "Do you need names? I know that Darius, an officer within the Grand Hall, is among them—he sought my life earlier but I escaped. Another is a man of this palace, an elder with hair as white as winter's frost. I know not his name, but his influence runs deep within these walls. They plan to strike His Majesty on the morrow. I've risked my life to bring you this," I said, my voice trembling. "If you don't act now,

Chancellor, the Empire will fall. The Emperor will die. And his blood will be on your hands."

The Chancellor's jaw tightened, his lips pressed into a thin line as something that looked like anger flashed through his eyes. I braced myself for his order to throw me back into the dungeon. Roderic, who had been silent until now, stepped forward, his voice low but resolute. "I know Kaelan. He is not one to exaggerate or act without cause. If he claims there is a threat, I trust his word." My face flushed at Roderic's unexpected show of faith, and I glanced at the Chancellor expectantly. But he didn't reply. Instead, he paced slowly across the chamber. The flickering candlelight threw his shadow against the walls, larger than life. I watched him, each step dragging out the unbearable tension.

Finally, he stopped and regarded me, his hands clasped behind him. "You have accused men of great stature. This can ignite the flames of war."

I stepped forward, the words spilling out before I could stop them. "War is already upon us, Chancellor. It's just hiding within the shadows of this palace. We can either face it now or let it consume us."

The room fell silent again, the weight of the moment pressing down on us like a suffocating fog. His gaze lingered on me, and suddenly he nodded sharply. "Very well."

Relief surged through me. The Chancellor strode toward the door, his movements brisk and purposeful. "This is a matter of utmost urgency. Roderic, take one of your men and bring me Halvar at once. Tell him His Majesty requires his counsel tonight." He turned to me, his eyes sharp. "Kaelan, you will accompany me."

My breath caught in my throat. "To the Emperor, Sire?"

The Chancellor paused at the door, glancing back at me. "Yes. We meet the Emperor tonight."

# CHAPTER
# 49

Emperor Valerius III had not changed much since I had last seen him during the parade before we left Central for the war several months earlier. He turned, his sharp gaze settling on me, and I stared back. His robes were deep crimson, lined with gold, and his crown glittered. His eyes, dark and intelligent, studied me with curiosity.

"Step forward," the Emperor said, his voice surprisingly calm. The Chancellor moved to stand beside the Emperor, his gaze flicking between us. "Your Majesty," the Chancellor began, "this is the young man who uncovered the plot. His name is Kaelan. He mentioned Darius. I did not believe him until he also mentioned Halvar as one of the conspirators. He didn't call Halvar's name, but he described him to the teeth."

The emperor seemed deep in thought. "You have always warned me about my advisor."

"Yes, but even I never imagined he could plan to have you murdered, Your Majesty. Or that anyone within these walls was making such plans."

Valerius nodded, his gaze never leaving mine. "So," he said, his tone thoughtful, "you are the one who has brought this to light. I have heard much about your journey, Kaelan—from the battles you fought to the risks you took to reach us here. I must say, I am intrigued."

I swallowed, my throat dry. I bowed my head respectfully. As we ascended the grand staircase, the opulent décor and the intricate carvings on the banisters leading to the Emperor's chambers, I had thought of how to present my case. Now, I stood before him, and the words tumbled out.

"Your Majesty," I said, my voice steady despite the tenseness coursing through me. "I have done what I could for Centralia. The plot against you, the alliance between the Astari and Wintmorian extremists—it is all true. I only wish to help protect our people."

The Emperor regarded me for a long moment, his expression unreadable. Then, slowly, he nodded. "Very well, Kaelan. I wish to hear everything you know—every detail. You may yet prove to be the key to turning the tide in our favor."

I took a deep breath, feeling the weight of the moment settle on my shoulders. I spoke of the battle at Brackenridge, the chaotic fight that had separated me from my comrades. I remembered the screams, the clang of steel, and the desperation that had gripped me as I fought to stay alive. I told him about my desperate march through Wintmore, the long days spent hiding from enemy patrols, surviving on scraps, and the kindness of strangers who had risked everything to help me along the way.

I described the smugglers who had helped me enter Edmundshire, my search for my brother Eamon, and the shocking discovery that he had been working as a spy for the Centralian Empire. My voice grew thick with emotion as I told the Emperor of Eamon's sacrifice—how he had fought to keep the information safe, even when it cost him his life. I described the brutal journey back to Centralia, carrying my dying brother, determined to bring the information to the Emperor no matter what.

The memories flooded back, raw and painful. I could still see Eamon's face, pale and drawn, his eyes filled with courage even in his final moments. I could feel the weight of his body as I carried him, the exhaustion that had threatened to break me. I spoke of the Astari plot, the Wintmorian rebels, and the alliance that sought to destroy everything that Centralia stood for.

The Emperor listened in silence, his eyes fixed on me, his expression unreadable. When I was done, there was a long moment of silence in the chamber, the air heavy with the weight of my words.

Suddenly, the heavy door swung open, breaking the tense silence, and Roderic strode in with Halvar in tow. I blinked. It was him—the man I had seen in the western wing, speaking in low whispers with the conspirators. The same man, wearing lavish purple robes that glimmered like they held a piece of the night sky, a gold sash draped proudly across his chest. His white hair shone with an almost ethereal light, catching the flicker of the torch flames that danced along the stone walls.

"Your Majesty," he greeted, his voice smooth as oil, unaware of the snare that had been set. A smile played on his lips, wide and too bright. "I was about to retire for the night, but I live to serve my Emperor."

I studied him carefully.

The Emperor regarded him, his face blank. "Yes, Halvar, as my Chief Advisor, I urgently need your counsel tonight." His words were measured and as deliberate as the steps I knew he was about to take.

Halvar approached, his smile only widening as he closed the distance between him and the Emperor. It was an expression that sent a shiver down my spine, too calculated, too certain of its own power. He looked like a snake weaving through the grass, ready to strike when least expected. My eyes never left his face, studying the way his features barely shifted, betraying nothing—nothing, except perhaps a flicker of something in his eyes. It was a subtle flicker, almost imperceptible.

The Emperor allowed a long silence to settle between us. Then, he spoke, almost casually. "Halvar, there's been much whispered around these halls, and I'm afraid it's time you answered for it."

Halvar's smile faltered, just for a fraction of a second, but it was enough to know the Emperor had struck a nerve. "What are you speaking of, Your Majesty? I—I know of no such whispers." His hands shifted nervously at his sides, the edges of his robe fluttering as if the slightest breeze had unsettled him.

The Chancellor stepped forward, anger brewing on his countenance. "The western wing. The plans to assassinate His Majesty tomorrow. The Astari." He let the words hang in the air, watching as Halvar's face shifted ever so slightly, like the first tremor before a storm. "You didn't think we would hear, did you? Or did you assume we wouldn't understand the significance of those names?"

Halvar's face hardened, his mouth pressing into a thin line, but his eyes betrayed him, flickering, shifting. He stepped back slightly, his posture straightening, but the air had shifted. It wasn't the confident, self-assured man who had walked into the room.

"I… I know not what you mean, Your Majesty." He turned towards the Emperor his eyes pleading, "You must have misunderstood. I have done nothing wrong. I am afraid the Chancellor has hated me since I became your advisor. He has taken it too far. I am but your loyal servant, Your Majesty." he stammered, his voice losing its usual silky quality.

"Time will tell," the Emperor said, his tone cold. "I have learned of the plot to take my life tomorrow during the council meeting. There's only one way to find out if Kaelan has lied to me."

His eyes darted to me and to Roderic, who stood silently at the door.

"I will not have a traitor advising me, Halvar. If I find out you are one, you will be executed for your treachery. For now, you will be kept in the red room downstairs until tomorrow when the truth is revealed."

Havar's face paled and his mouth curled in a snarl. For a moment, his eyes twisted into something darker, more venomous. "This empire does not want you anymore!" he spat, his voice rising in fury. "Your crown is false, your throne full of lies! And with you at the helm our kingdom will die!"

Silently, the guards stepped forward and gripped his arms tightly. They began to hustle him out of the chamber, his struggles feeble against their iron grasp. As they dragged him from the room, Halvar's voice echoed with a string of vile and angry expletives, until the heavy doors closed behind him.

The Emperor heaved a sigh and glanced around impassively.

"Summon Darius to my presence at once."

Two guards bowed before him and left the chambers.

# CHAPTER
# 50

By the time the events of the night had come to an end, the hour had long since passed midnight. Darkness stretched across the palace, cloaking everything in its shadow. Only the Emperor's chambers remained untouched by the night's black veil, where the flickering torchlights along the stone walls cast an eerie glow, bathing the room in a haunting half-light.

"Now, Kaelan. You uncovered this scheme, and you must be the one to see it through. We have little time. Tomorrow, during the council meeting, these traitors will attempt to take my life. We must be ready for them. I need you to make a plan—one that will allow us to catch them in the act and put an end to this plot once and for all."

I nodded, a sudden fire in my eyes. "I will do whatever it takes, Your Majesty."

"Then listen carefully", he continued, leaning forward. "The only way to prevent this assassination attempt and expose those who wish to bring down Centralia is to draw them out. We need a plan—one that ensures they reveal themselves while keeping me safe."

I listened attentively as the Emperor gestured for his other advisors to gather around. He outlined the details I had provided—the timing of the assassination, the expected Wintmorian distraction outside the palace, and the location of the planned entry point. As he spoke, a glimmer of something passed over his face—an almost imperceptible smile. The arrogance in the Astari's plan was clear; they believed the path was set, their victory certain. And that arrogance would be their downfall.

"The council meeting will take place as scheduled," the Emperor said, his voice measured and calm. "Only, I will not be there. Instead, we will have one of my trusted soldiers, dressed as me. We will use him as bait to lure the assassins into action."

"Very well, Your Majesty."

"The guards will be stationed discreetly," the Emperor continued, "but not in their usual posts. I want them out of sight but close enough to act the moment the assassins reveal themselves." He turned his gaze to me, his eyes sharp with focus. "You, Kaelan, will have a key role. You and Sergeant Roderic will position yourselves in one of the alcoves within the council chamber. You must remain hidden and strike when the time comes."

I exchanged a glance with Roderic and he gave me a nod.

"The sham must be prepared," one of the advisors said, looking at the Emperor. "And we must ensure that the real council members are informed of what is happening. We cannot risk a misinterpretation of our intent."

"Everything must proceed smoothly," the Chancellor added, "If we succeed, not only will we prevent an assassination, but we will also have the proof needed to unveil the truth about the Astari influence in this war."

I took a deep breath, the gravity of the situation settling on me like a mantle. "I understand, Your Majesty. I won't let you down."

"Then let us prepare," the Emperor said standing. "Tomorrow, we will face our enemies."

\*\*\*

Morning arrived slowly, the first rays of sunlight barely breaking through the heavy curtains of the council chamber. The grand space, usually illuminated by tall, arching windows, was transformed into something much darker today. Heavy, velvet curtains concealed the outside world, ensuring that nothing—neither light nor prying eyes—could breach the secrecy of the meeting that was about to take place.

There was unease in every corner of the chamber, in the whispered voices of advisors, in the quiet rustling of robes and armor. I could feel the unease in the air, settling over everyone gathered, wrapping us in a sense of foreboding. I was stationed in the shadows, hidden behind an intricately carved pillar, my eyes sharp and focused. Beside me, Roderic kept his stance relaxed, but I knew better—the slight tension in his jaw, the way his hand rested too near his sword hilt, spoke volumes about the state of his nerves. We had one chance, and one chance only, to catch the Astari loyalists before they succeeded in plunging Centralia into deeper chaos.

The false Emperor sat at the head of the long, polished table. He was convincing—dressed in the red and gold robes. He carried himself with a royal swagger, every gesture careful, every movement deliberate. Around him, trusted advisors sat, speaking in low voices, their faces tense but composed. The grand chamber, which had once felt imposing, now seemed to shrink in on itself, the walls pressing in as if in anticipation of some violence.

We waited, the anticipation almost unbearable. My eyes swept across the room, every motion amplified. The guards were carefully positioned, seemingly relaxed but ready to spring into action at the first sign of trouble. I had trained for combat and had fought my way through Wintmore, but this—waiting in silence, not knowing from which shadow the threat would emerge—was a different kind of battle.

Suddenly, I caught a flicker of movement near the side door. A shadow slipped through the narrow opening almost imperceptibly. My muscles tensed, and my eyes narrowed as I strained to listen, focusing beyond the hushed voices of the advisors. There it was again—a whisper of fabric against stone, the soft scuffle of feet. I glanced at Roderic. Our eyes met for a brief moment and a thin, wry smile appeared on the side of his lips.

I held my breath as I turned my attention back to the false Emperor. His face gave no hint, not a twitch, not the slightest flicker to betray his thoughts. Yet, beneath the folds of his fine apparel, I knew there lay a sharp dagger. The advisors continued their quiet discussions as if they were oblivious to the danger lurking just beyond their sight.

Then, there was a new sound. From the courtyard beyond the heavy curtains, I heard a distant clamor—yelling, the unmistakable clash of metal. The distraction had begun. My heart jumped, the pounding almost deafening in my ears. The assassins were creating their diversion just as the Astari loyalists had planned, drawing away guards, and drawing attention.

My eyes darted back to the side door. I saw it open, barely a crack, then widen as a figure emerged—a cloaked and hooded individual, his face obscured. The figure moved with careful, calculated grace, and behind him, more shadows slipped through the door—three, four, maybe more. Each moved with the same quiet efficiency, their eyes locked onto the false Emperor.

I felt my breath quicken, my hand inching towards the hilt of my sword. My eyes flicked to Roderic, whose gaze was fixed on the approaching figures, his jaw clenched in concentration. The assassins were here. The moment we had been waiting for was upon us.

The leader of the group paused for a heartbeat and lifted his hand to signal the others to stop. His gaze swept across the room; over the gathered council members, the false Emperor, and then beyond—to the shadows where Roderic and I waited. I pressed myself back, willing the shadows to conceal me. My heart pounded in my throat and my body was rigid with strain, every muscle pulled tight as though drawn by unseen strings. The leader lowered his hand, and the assassins began to fan out, their movements like a silent wave of darkness, closing in on the large table. I watched as one of them reached into his cloak, drawing forth a slender, glinting blade.

This was it.

Roderic met my eyes, and without a word, we moved. We burst from our hiding place, our footsteps echoing across the chamber. My sword was in my hand before I even realized it, the weight of it familiar, comforting. A shout rang out—Roderic's voice—a warning, a rallying cry.

The council members jerked back from their seats and drew their swords, while the false Emperor stood abruptly, his hand reaching for the hilt of his weapon. A melee erupted around them. The assassins, caught off guard but undeterred, reacted swiftly. Astonished by the readiness of their quarry, they moved with precision, blades raised and lunging forward. The guards who were hidden in the shadows burst from their positions in a surge of fury, their armor clinking, their boots pounding as they intercepted the attackers. Metal clashed against metal, the sharp, ringing sound echoing through the grand chamber, reverberating off the walls like a thousand bells. The table was upended, and chairs were knocked aside as council members scrambled for cover.

My focus narrowed to the figure before me—a hooded assassin with a blade glinting ominously in the flickering torchlight. I lunged forward, meeting the assassin's blade with my own. The clang of steel rang out, the force of the blow sending vibrations up my arm. Sparks flew from the impact, casting brief flashes of light that illuminated the masked face of my opponent.

The assassin before me was skilled, his movements fluid and seamless, like a shadow. But I matched him, my blade a blur as I parried, deflected, and countered. The assassin feinted to the left, then swung in from the right, his blade slicing through the air. I ducked, and the blade whistled just inches above my head. I twisted, my body moving like water, my sword arcing upward, clashing against the assassin's dagger with a deafening clang. I pushed forward, using my shoulder to drive the assassin back, our bodies colliding with a thud as I drove my blade into him.

From the corner of my eye, I saw the leader of the assassins glide across the chamber floor, his eyes locked onto the false Emperor. He moved with purpose, every stride precise, and his blade poised, ready to strike the fatal blow. I saw the intent, the cold determination in his eyes—a predator zeroing in on its prey. I knew I had only moments to act.

With a burst of speed, I rushed forward and threw my entire weight into him—slamming my shoulder into his side.

The impact was bone-jarring, and he stumbled, his blade thrusting wildly as he fought to regain his balance. The tip of the blade passed mere inches from the false Emperor's chest, the air humming with the force of the near miss. I could hear the false Emperor's sharp intake of breath, but there was no time to look back.

Roderic was suddenly there beside me, his sword drawn, his face a mask of steely resolve. He stepped in front of me, meeting the next assassin head-on. Their swords clashed, a whirlwind of flashing steel, each strike purposeful. His movements were fast and forceful, each swing of his blade precise, the strength behind his blows driving his opponent back.

I turned my focus back to the leader, who had regained his footing, his hood falling back to reveal a scarred face twisted in rage. His eyes were dark, filled with hatred and an unwavering resolve to complete his mission. He lunged at me, his blade aimed for my throat, the force behind the strike leaving no room for error.

I twisted to the side, narrowly avoiding the deadly arc of the blade. I brought my own sword up in a powerful, sweeping motion, feeling the steel slide into his side. His eyes widened, a flash of surprise and disbelief crossing his face. He fell to the floor, his weapon clattering away from his lifeless hand.

The air was thick with the smell of sweat, metal, and fear. The cries of the wounded mingled with the sounds of swords clashing, and the grunts of exertion as the guards fought fiercely, pushing back the assassins. The guards who had been stationed in the shadows were now fully engaged, their swords rising and falling, their movements calculated.

The assassins, despite their skill and training, were outnumbered, and their element of surprise was lost. Their formation broke under the relentless pressure of the guards. I saw one of them fall, one after another—their resolve breaking as they were pushed back, overwhelmed by the sheer force of the guards' defense.

Suddenly, my eyes locked on the last remaining assassin. Before I could react, a guard hurled him against the chamber wall, his head striking the stone with a sickening crack. He fell, eyes wide with shock, his body crumpling to the cold, stone floor.

Silence fell over the chamber, the echoes of the battle fading into nothingness, leaving only the heavy breathing of the survivors and the muffled groans of the wounded. The guards moved quickly, securing the fallen assassins, their faces set with grim determination, their movements swift and practiced.

I took a step back, my chest heaving. I turned my gaze to Roderick, and his eyes met mine. At that moment, a silent acknowledgment passed between us—a nod of gratitude, of respect. We had done it. We had protected what mattered most.

# CHAPTER
# 51

The Emperor stepped inside, his eyes sweeping across the room, taking in the scene—the fallen assassins, the overturned furniture, the guards standing victorious. He moved towards the head of the table, his presence commanding, his expression one of calm authority. The Emperor rose from his seat, his gaze never leaving mine. He stepped forward and placed a hand on my shoulder. "Centralia owes you a great debt, Kaelan of Elsenburg," he said, his voice filled with a rare warmth. "For your bravery, and for the sacrifice of your brother, I shall honor you."

My eyes widened in shock. The events of the day had taken their toll, and praise was never my intention. This honor—it belonged to Eamon. He was the one who had made the ultimate sacrifice. A lump rose in my throat, threatening to choke me.

The Emperor's voice thundered in the chambers. "Kneel."

I slowly knelt before the Emperor. He drew his sword, the blade glinting in the firelight, and gently rested it on my shoulder.

"In the name of Centralia, and in recognition of your service to this Empire, I hereby name you Sir Kaelan." His voice carried the weight of authority. "Rise, Sir Kaelan of Centralia."

I stood, my heart swell with pride. This was for Eamon—for everything we had fought for together.

The Emperor sheathed his sword and gave me a measured look. The Emperor turned to the gathered advisors, his voice carrying across the chamber. "We have seen today the lengths our enemies will go to destroy us. The Astari plot is real, and it threatens not just our kingdom, but the very future of our people. We must stand united, not divided. We must end this war—not for power or conquest, but for the survival of Centralia."

The council chamber fell into a tense silence, the words hanging in the air like a challenge to every man and woman present. I watched as Emperor Valerius III took a step forward, his commanding presence filling the room. His eyes moved from one advisor to the next, his expression hard and resolute, like steel forged in the fires of determination. Then, his eyes settled on me. "You have done well, Sir Kaelan. Your bravery and loyalty have not only saved my life but have given us a chance to change the course of this war."

I bowed my head. My heart swelled with pride. I had done it. I had fulfilled my mission and honored my brother's sacrifice. And now, we had a chance—a real chance—to save Centralia.

"The war with Wintmore must end," the Emperor declared, his voice ringing with authority, echoing off the high stone walls. "It is not the true battle. We have been blinded by our hatred, our grief, our anger. But the real enemy is not Wintmore. The true threat lies beyond, hiding in the shadows, seeking to divide us, to make us weak. The Astari Empire has sought to manipulate us, to plunge us into chaos. They wish to see Centralia and Wintmore destroyed, ripe for their conquest. This ends now."

His words reverberated through the room, each syllable a blow against the walls of fear and doubt that had built up in the hearts of his people. I could see it in their eyes—the advisors, the guards, even the servants who stood in the corners of the room, their faces pale and drawn. The years of war had taken their toll on all of us and had seeped into our bones and our hearts until it seemed there could be no other way. But the Emperor spoke with such clarity, such conviction, that a flicker of hope began to spread among those gathered.

A murmur swept through the council, hesitant at first, then growing louder as the reality of what the Emperor was proposing began to sink in. The weight of his words settled over them slowly, like a heavy snowfall. The advisors looked at one another, uncertainty etched into their faces. This was a drastic change—a sudden turn away from years of war and conflict. The hatred between Centralia and Wintmore was deep-rooted, and cultivated over generations. To propose an alliance was to ask them to challenge everything they had believed in, everything they had fought for.

But Emperor Valerius stood there, unyielding, his eyes blazing. "I call for an immediate ceasefire," he continued, his voice ringing through the chamber. "And I propose an alliance—an alliance with the Wintmorian people. Together, we must face the true threat of the Astari. We must come together as one. Only then can we hope to protect our lands, our families, our future."

He turned to one of his aides, who stood to the side of the chamber, stunned but attentive, his face a mix of disbelief and awe. "Send messengers to Wintmore," the Emperor commanded, his tone brooking no argument. "Inform them of the Astari plot, tell them of our discovery, and our intent to end this senseless war. The Astari wants us divided. We must show them that we are stronger than they believe."

The aide nodded quickly, snapping out of his stunned silence. He bowed, then rushed out of the chamber, his footsteps echoing in the silence that followed. The room seemed to hold its breath as if the walls themselves were waiting to see what would happen next.

I stood among the gathered guards, my heart pounding. This was the moment my brother and I had fought so hard for, the moment we had dreamed of when everything seemed lost. I wished, more than anything, that Eamon could be here to witness it. I could almost see his smile, and hear his laughter. We had finally taken a step toward the future we had dreamed of—a future without war, without pointless death. A future where we could stand against the true enemies together, not as fractured kingdoms but as united allies.

# CHAPTER
## 52

As the Emperor still spoke, the heavy wooden doors of the council chamber exploded open with a thunderous crack, the sound reverberating off the stone walls like a war drum. A rush of cold air swept into the room, carrying with it the acrid tang of sweat and dust from the frantic messengers who stumbled inside. Their boots struck the polished floor with uneven, hurried thuds, their breaths ragged and sharp as though they had run all the way from the Eastern Border itself.

The chamber seemed to hold its breath, the charged silence pierced only by the faint creak of the still-swaying doors. The air itself felt heavier now, tinged with the faint scent of fear as if the gravity of their news had seeped into the room before they even spoke. The Emperor's eyes narrowed, his face darkening with concern.

"Your Majesty," one of the messengers stepped forward and bowed deeply. His voice was strained, his chest heaving as he tried to catch his breath. He held a sealed scroll in his trembling hand, the wax emblem of the Centralian military still intact.

"Urgent news from the Eastern Border. The Astari Empire has launched an attack. Our defenses are under siege."

A heavy silence fell over the room, the words sinking in like stones in water. It felt as if the heat in the chamber had suddenly dropped, the gravity of the situation settling over us like a suffocating blanket. The Emperor stepped forward, his face hardening as he took the letter from the messenger. His jaw clenched, and a flicker of anger flashed in his eyes as he scanned the contents. His face, already lined with the weight of leadership, seemed to grow even graver, the lines deepening as he read.

He looked up, his eyes meeting those of his advisors, his expression filled with both determination and urgency. His gaze shifted to me, then to Roderic, who stood near the back of the chamber, our faces pale but resolved. Then, he stepped forward, clutching the scroll as if it weighed as heavily as the crown on his head.

"The enemy is at our gates," he said, his voice steady, but the underlying urgency unmistakable. "They think us weak. The Astari Empire has seen our struggles. They've seen our divisions, our wounds from within and without. And now, they strike— not just at our borders, but at the heart of who we are." His voice hardened, the raw edge of frustration breaking through. "They think this kingdom is crumbling. That I—your Emperor—am a man whose strength has long since faded with time and war.

He paused, letting the weight of his words settle. The tension in the room thickened as all eyes fixed on him. "They are wrong," he said, his voice rising with a conviction that burned through the air. "For I may carry the scars of years past, but those scars remind me of what we fight for. I have seen fathers bury their sons. I have heard the wails of mothers cradling what remains of their children. I have felt the cold breath of despair on my neck—and still, we stand."

His voice rose, reverberating on the stone walls. "We must act swiftly," he said at last, "Send word to all corners of Centralia. Mobilize our forces. We will defend our lands, and we will fight back. The Astari Empire seeks to tear us apart—but they will find that we are united."

He paused, letting his words hang in the air for a moment before continuing, his voice rising with passion. "For this empire! For our people, our homes, our families! We will not fall to the shadows. We will stand, and we will fight, side by side with Wintmore, against the true threat."

The council members, the guards, the advisors—all seemed to stand a little taller, their eyes hardening with hope. Hope that, perhaps, this time, we were on the right path. That we could finally bring an end to the senseless cycle of bloodshed and focus on what truly mattered—protecting our homes, our families, and our future.

I took a deep breath, my heart swelling with fierce pride. This was what Eamon had died for. This was what we had fought for. And now, standing here in the council chamber, hearing the Emperor speak of unity and hope, I knew that my brother's sacrifice had not been in vain.

The Emperor turned, his eyes locking onto mine. There was something in his gaze—something that spoke of respect, of understanding. "Sir Kaelan," he said, his voice carrying across the chamber, "you remind me of the strength we hold. Your bravery and determination have not only saved my life but have given us a chance to change the course of this war. Your brother Eamon... his sacrifice is a wound I carry with me, just as I know you do. His bravery is not forgotten, nor will it ever be. The courage he showed runs through your veins. And it is that courage that gives me hope that we can still rise." He paused and looked into my eyes. "You have proven yourself time and again, and now, I ask for your continued service. Centralia needs you."

I stepped forward, bowing deeply. "I'm at your service, Your Majesty," I said, my voice filled with emotion. I could feel the eyes of everyone in the room on me, could feel the weight of the moment pressing down on my shoulders. But I did not falter. I had a purpose, and I would see it through.

He straightened, peering into the faces of his people. "We cannot promise peace, not yet. But we can promise each other this: the Astari Empire will not tear us apart. They seek to find a kingdom fractured. Instead, they will face a people united—not for glory, not for conquest, but for our homes, our families, and the memory of those we have lost."

The Emperor gave a nod, then turned back to his advisors, his voice once again commanding. "Send our messengers to Wintmore. We have no time to waste. The Astari are here, and they are counting on our division. Let us show them that they have underestimated us."

The advisors moved quickly, their discussions turning urgent as they began to make arrangements. The room became a flurry of activity, but at its center stood Emperor Valerius III—a figure of strength, of hope. He was not a perfect man, but he was the leader we needed. And with the forces of Centralia and Wintmore united, perhaps, just perhaps, we stood a chance against the shadows that loomed over us.

I had hoped, even if only for a brief moment, that we had reached a turning point—an opportunity to turn our energies towards peace. And yet, it seemed that fate had other plans. The Astari Empire's attack on our eastern border had turned hope into an urgent call to action. There was no time to mourn or reflect, only time to prepare for the onslaught ahead.

As the Emperor's command rang through the council chamber, I felt a fire ignite within me. We were about to face a war unlike any we had ever known. I knew there would be no rest, no pause. And yet, for just a fleeting moment, my thoughts drifted back to a simpler time, before the shadows of war loomed over our lives. I allowed myself to remember—

Once, the sun hung low in the sky, casting long golden hues over the sprawling fields of grain that bordered my home of Elsenburg, the quiet country village in the heart of the Centralian Empire. The rhythmic sway of the tall wheat stalks moved in tune with the warm summer breeze, a comforting and nostalgic lullaby that whispered of hard work and simpler times, only months before all that had happened.

Standing at the edge of my family's farm, my hands rested on the rough wooden fence that my great-grandfather had built so long ago. It was still sturdy, still unbroken, weathered—but standing. Just like we were, Eamon and I. We used to sit on this very post, daring each other to climb higher, leap farther, race faster. He always won. I always jested it was because I let him win, but the truth was that he was simply better. He poured himself into everything he did.

My gaze wandered to the mesmerizing waves of the grain, each sway and dance bringing back cherished memories. I had once thought home would always be here, waiting. That I could step away and return unchanged. But now, I knew better. There was no coming back—not to what once was. Only to what remained.

The sun dipped lower, staining the horizon in bittersweet hues of pink and orange. In the distance, the dry rustle of leaves stirred and threaded through the fields, slipping between the wheat stalks like a secret half-spoken, a memory half-remembered. The sound lingered in the air, neither welcome nor unwelcome—just there, like all things that refused to be forgotten. An evening chorus of crickets and the occasional hoot of an owl filled the stillness, creating a natural symphony—a reminder of the life that had once been before the shadows took hold. Yonder, the silhouette of the village hall stood tall against the fading twilight sky, its ancient bell tolling in the gentle breeze. The sound reverberated across the fields, a poignant reminder of time's passage and the fleeting nature of moments that now seemed so distant. I could almost hear the laughter of the villagers, the chatter of families gathering for evening meals, and the sound of children playing in the open fields. Those memories felt like they belonged to another life.

The crisp evening air carried with it the scent of earth and growth, mingled with the subtle fragrance of wildflowers that bordered the fields. I took a deep breath as I let the smells fill my senses. As darkness descended, the first stars began to appear, twinkling in the vast night sky. I hadn't noticed the stars in what felt like a lifetime. Yet, they endured, shimmering against the abyss. I remained at the edge of the fields, leaning on the old fence. Memories of happier times mingled with the present—an odd blend of longing and sorrow. It enveloped me, wrapping around me in the embrace of the darkening night.

I closed my eyes, letting myself drift back to those days. For a fleeting moment, the world was as it should be—whole and untainted, Eamon was still by my side, the war never happened, and the only challenge was the labor of the field. The future was still bright and full of promise. I could almost feel the weight of the tools in my hands, the warmth of the sun on my skin, and hear Eamon's voice as we worked side by side, talking about dreams that now seemed impossibly far away.

But as I opened my eyes, the spell was broken. The present came rushing back—the weight of my journey, the sacrifices that had been made, and the urgency of what was to come. Something had changed. The shadows creeping at our borders had grown a darker red, their whispers carried on the wind. It threatened not just Centralia, but the entire realm. I would have to be ready. For Centralia. For Eamon. For everything we had dreamed of and fought for.

As the capital's bell tolled in the distance, a chill ran down my spine. I knew that my journey was far from over. The shadows of the Astari Empire were on our doorsteps, and the real battle had only just begun.

# Afterword

Dear Reader

If you've made it this far, thank you for walking beside Kaelan through the wreckage, the snow, the silence, and the shadows.

This book means a lot to me. It's a story born from a dream to finally write and put this world I've imaged for many many years onto paper, and questions of what it means to hold on to hope when the world around you is falling apart. Writing Cloak of Shadows wasn't easy. There were long nights where I second-guessed everything, where the weight of the book felt like too much. But I kept going, the same way Kaelan does one step at a time, even when the path ahead isn't clear.

I'm grateful you chose to read this. Truly. Whether you're new to the series or returning from Whispers of War, your time and attention mean more than I can say. You didn't just read a book you gave these characters life you the reader truly make these characters alive. You carried their story in your hands. That's no small thing.

Thank you for taking this journey with me. There's still more to come. The road ahead is uncertain but Kaelan isn't done yet.

And neither am I.

-C.L. Gill

# About the Author

C.L. Gill is an author in the realm of medieval fantasy. For over thirteen years, he has been building the world of Craylavros—piece by piece, place by place—long before a single word was ever put onto paper. What began as quiet daydreams, scattered maps, and deeply imagined roleplaying with friends as a child has grown into a sprawling, living world carried entirely in his mind and now on paper.

Hailing from Texas, Gill crafts stories filled with richly imagined landscapes, deeply human characters, and the slow-burning tension between duty and identity. His writing combines vivid imagery, emotional stakes, and the kind of quiet resilience found in those who endure.

Tales from Centralia: Whispers of War marked the beginning of that journey. Cloak of Shadows carries it forward—and there's still more to come.

He is deeply grateful to every reader who chooses to walk the roads of Craylavros with him and his characters inside it.

# Coming Soon

*A new tale in the Tales from Centralia Series*

## Tales from Centralia: Shadows of Wintmore
### A Lilah prequel novel

Before Kaelan crossed her path in the shadowy streets, Lilah had
already learned how to survive a war.
In a kingdom crumbling beneath the weight of civil unrest and foreign invasion, a sharp-tongued girl must navigate the brutal world of
Wintmore during and after the devistating civil war. Haunted by loss
and hardened by necessity, Lilah walks a path forged in shadow long
before fate ever brought a Centralian soldier to her door.

This is her story.
Before Brairwick. Before the rescue. Before this adventure there
was another.